EVERYTHING SPONTANEOUS IN THE LAND OF DOLL PARTS

J. S. NATHANIEL

Published in

DENVER, COLORADO

EVERYTHING SPONTANEOUS IN THE LAND OF DOLL PARTS

Library of Congress Control Number Available

ISBN: 978-1-967522-12-5 (Hardcover)
ISBN: 978-1-967522-13-2 (Paperback)
ISBN: 978-1-967522-15-6 (Audiobook)
ISBN: 978-1-967522-22-4 (E-book)

"Persons and images depicted are models and used for illustrative purposes only."

ALSO BY J. S. NATHANIEL

Stardust Angel

Juliet + Juliette = Love in Mafia Land

Primitive Beauty: Author's Sketchbook

Dominion of the Divine

Narrator of Lies

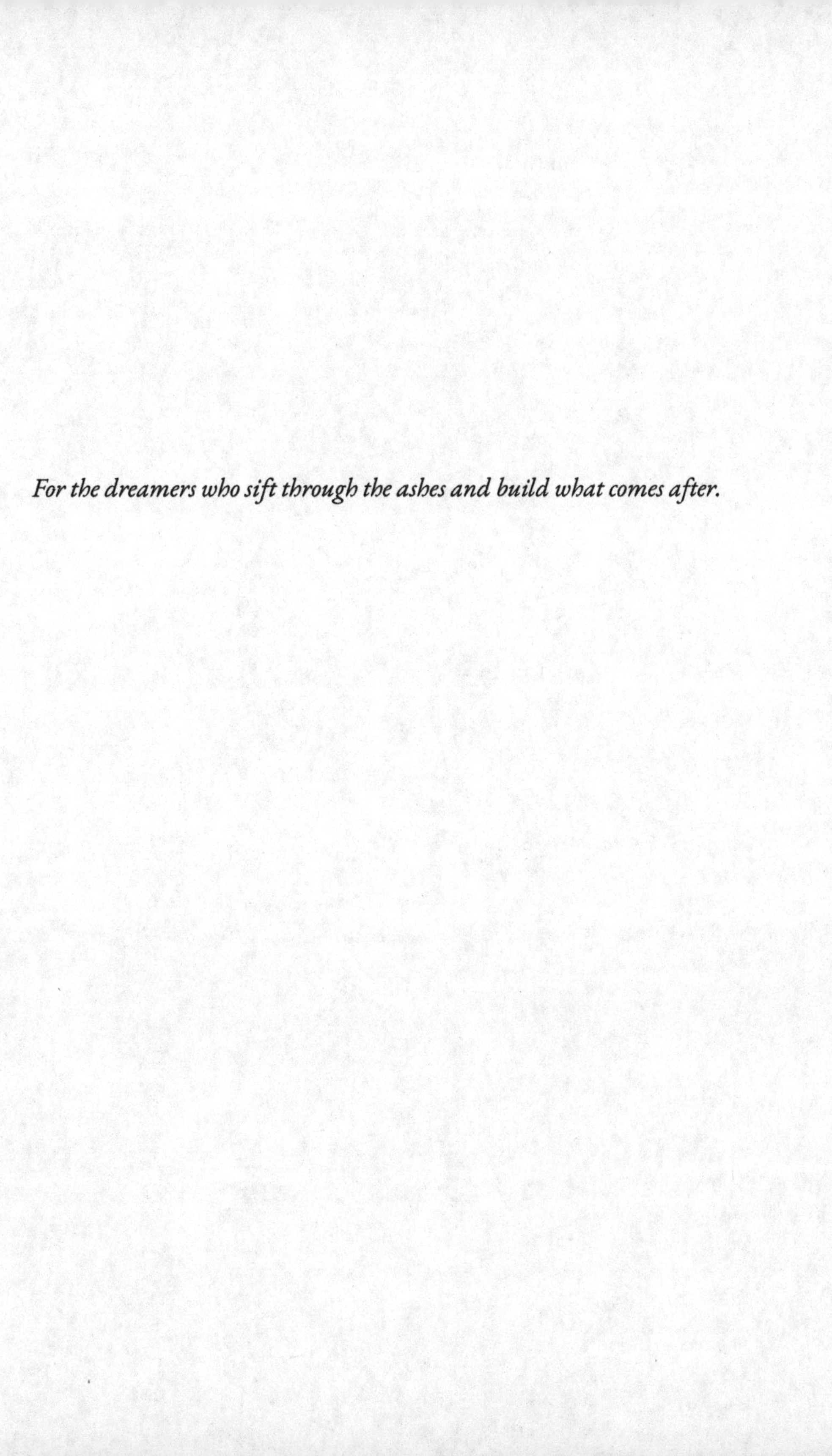

For the dreamers who sift through the ashes and build what comes after.

CONTENTS

RAVENOUS SQUIRREL

IT HAD BEEN four days since her last meal. Dante crawled from the woods on trembling limbs and reached for the glossy asphalt. Hot vapor distorted the air above it, and the road seared her fingertips. The wild had shaped her, teaching that survival required the heart of a wolf. In this unclean world, you ate what you found or faced death.

A bloated squirrel lay by the fog line. Its vacant eyes glaring as if she'd stolen its soul. The dry winter air had mummified its flesh, its fur. The stench made her gag, but at least the meat was maggot-free. Two days dead, by her guess. Better than her last meal.

She pulled a log from the rain-slicked pile and tossed it into the pit. The flames roared crimson while soot floated skyward in shimmering particles. This was how it had to be done now, heat hot enough to disintegrate bone, to purify what was left. Like the flame that had taken Jack, leaving only ash and tears.

The squirrel dissolved in her mouth like cinders. Everything turned to ash eventually, that's what SHC had taught her. She'd watched it happen, watched people burst into flames without warning, their bodies becoming human candles in seconds. Jack's eyes had found hers in that last moment, before the combustion took him too.

Dante tried swallowing the squirrel in one bite but failed. She nibbled the bones clean, her teeth collecting every bit, even the marrow. The tiny bones slid down her throat painfully and silenced the hunger. The hunger never wandered far these days. It sank its teeth into her with every passing moment, poisoning her brain, rattling her gut. Sometimes she wondered if madness would claim her before starvation.

Her hands had that purplish hue again. Not cancer, she'd pray for cancer, given the choice. These hands were combustible, like everything else now. "Devil's hands," she whispered, splaying her fingers toward the icy morning light.

The tremors started, right on schedule. She braced herself as vicious spasms racked her limbs. Her body crumbled under the weight of agony. She sank to her knees and choked out stringy foam and squirrel, the only substance left in her stomach. Without warning, she convulsed. Darkness scribbled in quick, as though God had smothered the sun. Her eyes rolled back. A black wave swept her away.

When consciousness returned, the pit smoldered from neglect, faint embers whispering against nightfall. Everything dipped in a spidery haze as though she'd eaten poisonous mushrooms. Nothing mattered anymore. Nothing except the memory of Rory, which haunted her like the wolves that howled toward that ghostly moon every night.

Death had guided her heart down this path, some ghostly, desolate wilderness that stretched endlessly, steeped in mist and skeletal remains. She hadn't known love until she met Rory. Now her world had rushed back to emptiness. Her heart scattered among the trees like ash molecules. From ash, more ash comes.

She rose from the frozen earth and tossed another piece of wood into the pit. Pine sap hissed and popped like microwaving popcorn. Oh, how she salivated for buttery popcorn, for any reminder of the world before. But those memories burned too, like everything else in this combustible nightmare.

Leaning against a boulder, she stared into the shadows, trying to decide what she missed more, Rory's beating heart or her eyes. Those eyes that had haunted her since the day everything went combustible. Time proved to be the cruelest punishment since SHC began. It took its time torturing those left behind, while everything else evaporated into fumes.

The hunger crept along, each needle prick distinct, nanosecond by nanosecond. Thirst accelerated with ridiculous speed, as it had in the old world. Except the new world's thirst lacked the convenience of same-day delivery. Days stretched like pine sap. Seventy-two hours became the new twenty-four, melting together in a dizzy kaleidoscope of sun and stars, stars and sun. Time ceased to exist in this land of doll parts. Yet love's presence still devoured those endless hours at the speed of a fiery pit.

She buried her face in the crook of her arm and sobbed. SHC had incinerated modern civilization right before her eyes, yet her thoughts circled only to Rory. She never felt hunger when Rory was at arm's length. Not that they'd eaten like royalty in this unforgiving land. Food was scant, life was scant, wildlife lethal and uncooperative. SHC had knocked humans to the bottom of the food pyramid, reduced them to mice stealing crumbs from an animal kingdom with no crumbs to spare.

Every night before bed, their stomachs ached with the same painful rhythm. Still, Rory's heartbeat had shone light against the cold black. When she'd laid her head on Rory's chest, a delicious symphony purred in her ear. Their shared warmth, their solace, had made the hunger disappear. Rory's heartbeat fed her spirit like chocolate once had, like crème brûlée melting on her tongue and traveling straight to her soul. The sun had constantly glinted off Rory's face, even in total darkness. Rory was the sun. Rory is the sun.

Dante dried her eyes with her sleeve and entered the shelter. They had built the hut with mud and evergreen and river rock—the way Jack taught her. Despite the countless pine boughs covering the roofline, rain still found its way in. She sat there for two more days, staring into the skeletal forest while torrential downpour beat the little hut to nothing. Her hair turned crunchy and helmet-like, tiny droplets freezing at the split ends to sparkle diamond-like in the dark.

On the first day, sunlight had broken through gray clouds to illuminate the tree line, alternating between blinding and warming the earth. But the temperature plummeted on day two when a thick overcast swallowed the fire in the sky. Water flowed from every direction, pooling at the structure's base and flooding the floor. She didn't move. She sat there wearing vacancy, staring into the stretch, and an oversized flannel clinging to her skin, feet and bottom soaking in icy water.

The harsh elements painted her skin bluish. She folded into herself for warmth and shuddered while her hemoglobin sought shelter elsewhere, branding her skin with an anemic glow. Frost billowed from her busted lips as she whispered into the dark: "Rory, Rory, Rory."

This image haunted her: Rory floating downstream, battling rapids while Dante ran along the riverbank screaming "Wake up, wake up!" until the waterfall blocked her path and swallowed Rory into the raging river below. A jagged cliff had made the traverse impossible. Death waited at the bottom. She had to stop pursuing, at that great height, at the point of no return, she collapsed screaming Rory's name. Failure wore her to a nub. She was so exhausted from failing those she loved.

She'd sat there for hours, expecting Rory's body to emerge from the angry, foamy river. It never did. Day turned to night, and Dante sobbed until her eyes melted into the black near the cliff. She refused to abandon Rory and promised to stay indefinitely. Not even death's fiery grip could sever their bond. In her mind, Rory would surface like a rubber duck. She'll float to the top. She must float to the top.

Three days of rain cast a veil of mist over the land. The sun's rays pierced the tree canopy like a thousand pinpricks, barely illuminating the tiny encampment. Branches and pine needles from the hut topped the fog line, the pointed roof ascending like a hobbit hole, a beacon to any watching eyes.

Marauders crept into camp while Dante woke from a dream. She shot up to find mud coating her face. Soil jammed inside her nose. Clay and pine coating her tongue and silt lodged between her teeth. She'd fallen asleep face-down in the earth that would eventually claim them all.

She cleared the mud from her nose by blowing into her sleeve. A whistle cut through the fog. Twigs cracked near the hut, as boots thudded against earth like a herd approaching. Her hand found the knife at her hip, but it was too late. A dark figure yanked her from the shelter. Brute strength and biting hands overpowered her petite frame until she dangled in their grip.

At first, the attacker's powerful grip bore male qualities. Workhorse hands, her father would have called them. They wrapped around her neck like a vise. The knife twirled from her grip, lost to the mud. The marauder pulled her close, inspecting her with menacing eyes. Dante drove her boot heel into their shin. A feminine howl barreled from behind their mask as the grip released.

She stumbled groundward, losing all sense of direction. The thick fog blinded her from the knife's location. Before she could catch her breath, another intruder tackled her. This one was male. She felt it in the violent threat of his body pressing against hers as they wrestled in the mud.

"I'll kill you!" Dante screamed.

He cackled and struck her face with something blunt. A fist, maybe. The rapid sequence blindsided her. He head-butted her straight in the nose. Blood exploded. The impact stunned her and sent her body limp. Twinkling stars scattered across her vision. Her head swelled as though ready to detonate. She clawed at his ski mask, but he head-butted her again. Another flash of light eclipsed everything. He pinned her hands and butted twice more for good measure. Stars. Light. Blur. Then darkness.

Dante woke to a burning sensation eating her face. She adjusted her eyes but saw only a sliver of firelight in the distance. Her fingers traced the swollen landscape of her face. Top half dry, lower half soaked. Instinctively, she reached for the knife at her waist and discovered someone had removed her jeans.

The invaders' laughter radiated through the dark. Their voices sharp but incomprehensible, celebratory, as though they were having the time of their lives. Those cackles chilled her blood. Her nearly-swollen-shut eyes throbbed as she squinted into the cold, suffocating darkness. Desperation clawed at her as she fumbled blindly for anything to use as a weapon. If only she could find her knife. If only she could see.

Her fingers found a baseball-sized river rock, not round but oblong, formed to a sharp edge. She found her jeans strewn in the mud and pulled them on, clutching the rock like a talisman. Every motion sent sharp pain through her stomach. The slightest shift made her gasp for breath.

Something toxic teased the air. A scent she hadn't found in a while. Her fingers bore the smell of turpentine. Her skin was now flammable.

In the reach, she heard them lying in wait like hyenas ready for another feast. Tears rolled down her cheeks as she whimpered. Dante had known girls who survived sexual assault, back when the world was full of people. It hadn't ended well for her best friend Katy. She doubted it would end well for her either, here in this dead forest, in these lawless end days.

But then she remembered Rory's words from that last day: "The fire inside us is stronger than anything the world can steal." She gripped the rock tighter, feeling its sharp edge against her palm. Maybe she was flammable now. Maybe that was exactly what they should fear.

IVORY ROAD

Dante kept her knife ready as she approached the figure curled on the road ahead. The sun cast a cobweb pattern across the woman's skin, highlighting every ravage of deprivation. Her wiry hair hung in greasy tangles, and moth-eaten gauze barely covered her lower half. Atrophy had claimed every inch.

"Water," the woman croaked through blackened teeth.

Dante maintained her distance. "Are you alone?"

"No one." The woman's voice carried smoke. "Just me."

Dante unclipped her knife, keeping it trained on the woman. "I don't want to kill you, but I will."

The woman's head slumped forward. "I escaped."

"Show me your hands."

"I can't." Creature-like fingers trembled as the woman raised her arms a few inches. "Water."

After scanning the empty road, Dante slipped off her pack, never lowering her blade. She retrieved a bottle with her free hand. "Drink."

The woman sat motionless, eyes glazed. Dante cursed under her breath and knelt beside her, knife still ready. She pressed the bottle to the woman's cracked lips. The sound of desperate swallowing filled the air with strange thuds as the water hit her stomach. Liquid dribbled down her chin.

"More."

Dante pulled out her last bottle, the plastic crinkling in the silence. "This is all I have." This time, the woman drank slower, as if savoring each precious drop.

"Who did this to you?" Dante studied the marks on the woman's exposed skin.

"Brother."

The word sent ice through Dante's veins. Her eyes swept the tree line, heart hammering against her ribs. "Which direction did you come from?"

The woman's head swayed as she tried to orient herself. "Somewhere over there."

"How long have you been here?"

"I don't know."

Dante clipped the knife back to her belt and pulled out a granola bar. She unwrapped it carefully, the foil crackling too loud in the open air. "Try to eat something."

The woman took small bites, but her stomach rebelled. She heaved, expelling water and partially digested food onto Dante's shirt. The vomit came thick and foul, followed by a belch that seemed to drain the last of her energy. Her eyes, filled with momentary hatred, rolled back as she slumped unconscious.

Dante stood frozen, weighing her options. She and Rory had sworn never to play hero alone, it was a death wish. But looking at the woman's scarred body, seeing the evidence of torture etched into her flesh, Dante couldn't walk away. Human decency had become as rare as clean water, but she refused to let it die completely.

She cleaned the woman as best she could, picking twigs from her matted hair and scraping dirt from beneath her fingernails. It wasn't much, but it was something. A small piece of dignity restored. As dusk approached, Dante lifted the woman, who weighed no more than a child, and carried her into the cover of the woods. The road wasn't safe at night. Nothing was safe at night anymore.

Dante steadied the woman into a sitting position, offering another drink. Death lingered on her breath. "Slower this time."

The woman grunted as she swallowed, her throat working like she'd swallowed acid. When she looked up, Dante saw her eyes clearly for the first time, solid ivory, no iris, no pupil. Just white, like polished bone. A chill ran through Dante's spine. How had this woman found her way to the road?

"You need to eat something."

"I'll try."

Dante shared the last of her granola. "Take it slow." After the woman finished, Dante surveyed their dwindling supplies. "I need to find more water."

The woman's hand shot out strongly. "Don't leave me."

"I won't be long."

"Wait."

"Trust me."

"Messenger of Light will get you."

Dante paused. The name didn't frighten her as much as 'Brother' had, it sounded almost holy, like Joan of Arc. But that made it worse somehow. "I'll be careful."

"She likes pretty girls like you."

Those sightless eyes seemed to see straight through her. Dante didn't want to know the horrors behind the woman's scars, the human bite marks, the lashes across her back, the brand on her chest like cattle. It was a common story now, but that didn't make it less horrifying.

"I'm lightning," Dante said, forcing confidence into her voice.

The woman's twisted fingers clutched Dante's leg. "I don't want to die." Desperation glinted in those ivory lenses.

"Rest now." Dante eased her back down.

She waited until the woman's breathing steadied before venturing deeper into the forest. Jack had taught her to read the land, deer scat meant water nearby. The earth was packed and dry, leaving no tracks, but Dante pressed on, searching for signs of wildlife.

Hours passed as she descended into a steep valley. The landscape changed, tall grass, wildflowers, the promising buzz of bees. A patch of wild strawberries caught her eye, white flowers dotting the ground beside them. Her father's voice echoed in her memory, teaching her which berries were safe, but she couldn't trust those memories anymore. The risk wasn't worth it. What would Rory do without her? What would become of the woman?

The stream revealed itself eventually, sunlight dancing on its surface. Time was running out, she'd taken too long, and darkness was coming. Dante pulled out her water bottles and saucepan, falling into the familiar routine. Collect. Sterilize. Leave no trace. But today was different. The sun was already setting as she filled each container.

The climb back proved treacherous. Water sloshed from the pan with every step, precious drops soaking into the thirsty earth. By the time she reached their hiding spot, barely a quarter remained.

The woman lay exactly as Dante had left her, but something was wrong. Her gaze was fixed on the canopy above, jaw clenched, lips drawn tight. Dante knelt beside her. "Hey."

No response. The woman's skin was cold to the touch. When Dante nudged her shoulder, a horrifying gurgle escaped, followed by an oddly sweet smell. Not decay, but something else, like tree sap. Those ivory eyes stared into nothing now, holding secrets Dante would never know.

She covered the body with the thermal tarp, hands shaking. Then she settled against a nearby tree, positioning herself to watch both the corpse and the surrounding forest. Her muscles screamed from the valley climb, but sleep wasn't an option. Not with death so close. Not with those eyes seeming to watch her through the tarp.

Her tongue took on the texture of gravel as thirst clawed at her throat. Two days without water—she'd given every drop to the frail woman. That's what Jack would have done. What Grace would have wanted.

Dante's chest heaved with dry sobs, her tear ducts as barren as the land around her. Grace and the frail woman—two ghosts now, two weights pressing against her ribcage. She didn't have the strength to build a fire and couldn't even think about searching for kindling. The forest seemed to breathe around her, waiting.

Darkness crept across the thermal tarp, not just shadowing the body but consuming it, as if night itself had developed an appetite for flesh. In this new world, even darkness fed on the living. Dante couldn't shake the image of Brother, of the Messenger of Light. One of them—maybe both—had killed the frail woman long before she'd collapsed on that road. She'd been walking dead, running on borrowed time and desperate hope.

What haunted Dante most was the woman's voice—childlike beneath the rasp, innocent despite everything. How old had she been? Her body suggested seventy, but torture aged people differently now. Forty? Thirty? Twenty? The truth would remain buried with her, and maybe that was mercy. Sometimes mystery was kinder than knowledge. Sometimes fantasy was the only thing strong enough to carry you through one more day.

PRIMITIVE THINGS

DANTE TRIED to fasten her jeans, but the marauders had destroyed both the button loop and zipper hem. They'd made sure of that. *Less chance of escape.* Without the ability to secure her jeans, she was vulnerable, forced to fight for her life half-naked.

She wrapped her flannel shirt around her hand, embedding that sharp rock into her palm, a makeshift weapon. Jack had taught her how to turn anything into a means of survival. "When the odds are against you, mijita, do whatever it takes to survive," he'd warned.

Dried blood crusted around her eyelids, turning her world crusty and blurred. Her skin burned everywhere, as if scraped with razors. When Dante struggled to her feet, a paralyzing jolt erupted in her uterus and shot through her stomach. The pain sent her crashing into the mud. Warm liquid trickled down her leg as that familiar tangy, turpentine scent wafted up again.

Slumped over, she focused on the men's voices. One name kept surfacing—Brother. They all called him that, over and over. The name sent ice through her veins as she remembered the frail woman.

Terror rose in her chest. She forced down the pain, disconnecting from her body as she stood. Every muscle quaked. She gulped cool air, mouth wide, struggling to breathe. Her swollen eyes darted through the pitch-black while her heart thundered, threatening to knock her unconscious. Within seconds, she collapsed again.

These men would overpower her easily. Fighting seemed impossible, escape even more so. Her pelvis exploded in agony with each tiny movement, the pain in her uterus crippling any hope of mobility.

Yet despite her broken state, mud-covered and defeated, Dante let loose a blood-curdling scream. Horror struck her instantly, and she clapped a hand over her mouth, listening as the world's cold blackness swallowed her cry. *What had she done?*

The world beyond the hut fell silent. Men hushed each other, their mutterings too low to understand. Dante shifted into survival mode, bracing for what would come. Time seemed to freeze. Gripping her primitive tomahawk, she forced herself upright. Lightning pain shot through her core as she stood, followed by a violent head rush that made the earth tilt beneath her feet.

She threw out her arms for balance as heavy footsteps approached. Her ninety-pound frame stood no chance against these marauders, but she had to swing harder, harder than she'd ever swung anything. The woman who'd strangled her had shown no mercy, nor had the man who'd beaten her face to pulp.

Despite her weakness, she held one advantage. Dante knew what awaited captured victims. Fight to the death now or live long enough to beg for it later. If they enslaved her, she'd age ten years for every year in captivity, just like the frail woman.

Her head spun wildly, scrambling her thoughts. The hut's interior was darker than night itself, broken only by a distant fire pit's faint glint. A marauder stumbled inside. "What's all the fuss?" he asked, as if soothing a crying infant.

Dante backpedaled, swinging her tomahawk wildly at the silhouette. She waited for the crack of impact, for any promising sound. But only the whoosh of her weapon cut through the air.

"Don't make me get Brother." His voice remained calm, almost nurturing.

"Go to hell, fuckface." Fear strangled her words.

The man, an SHC creation designed for this new world, moved

closer. "You got some fight in you. I'll enjoy this." She heard the sneer in his voice.

Dante cocked her makeshift weapon and swung upward with all her strength, praying for a nose strike. Jack's words echoed: "Hit square in the nose, mijita. That'll land even the biggest man on his ass." He'd been right. She knew from experience how a nose hit could paralyze.

The crack came instantly, rock meeting bone. The sharp point severed an artery, filling the hut with gurgling sounds. Something massive crashed into the mud.

The man dropped to his knees, but Dante couldn't see it. She swung again, the angle awkward and vertical. The rock skipped across his skull with a wet whack, tearing the scalp from bone. He pitched forward onto her feet. Dante scrambled backward, screaming, certain he was reaching for her.

Outside, a man mockingly echoed her scream. "Ahh, ahh." Laughter followed. Then more men joined in, twisting their voices into fake screams, mocking her terror.

Tomahawk ready, she waited for her attacker's next move. She stood in the cold blackness, prepared to swing as the man twitched in the mud, gurgling his final breath.

Soon he went still. The marauders continued their laughter in the distance, but Dante held her ground. She wouldn't abandon her safety bubble. Jack had drilled that into her: "Keep your safety bubble sound, mijita." For long minutes, she expected the man to rise, to attack again, but he remained motionless in the mud.

INSTALLATION BY FIRELIGHT

THE MARAUDERS SETTLED for the evening as their fire dwindled, popping and crackling in the frigid night air. Burned pine infected every morsel of the woods, its acrid smoke climbing toward distant starlight. Dante's feet, anchored in ice-cold mud, made her bones clatter. Her jaw ached from chattering teeth, her lower half both numb and searing with pain. Everything burned like Jack had burned. How could someone be numb and burn all at once? Then she thought, *Jack knew.*

The dead man lay face-down in the icy mud. Despite his stillness, she needed time to gather courage before examining him. Her feet shuffled forward, tomahawk ready if he needed putting down again.

He hadn't moved an inch. She sank to her knees in the mud and frisked him, noting the turpentine stench on his hands. The hunting knife strapped to his thigh took seconds to find. Those thighs were massive, thick as thirty-pound turkeys. He was easily six feet tall with a Hercules build, now face-down and motionless. When she checked for a pulse, her fingers slipped into the gaping hole in his neck. Dante pulled the knife from his sheath and set to work. The blade bewitched her. Cold steel slid through his existing wound until it hit bone. She cut white-deep, severing muscle, nerves, and cartilage in an upward slice, hacking her way to the occiput.

Decapitation hadn't been the initial plan, but rage had other ideas—ideas her mind hadn't fully processed. Once she started slicing, her bloody hands took over. The blade split human tissue like paper.

Sweat beaded on her brow as she worked. He was a bleeder, producing enough blood to fill a baby pool. The process proved easier than breaking down elk. Her father could process one in under thirty minutes, bowels and all. She was Jack's daughter, bearing the hands of a skilled hunter.

Blood saturated beyond the knife and hands. She bathed in its warmth. The ice-cold mud transformed beneath its flow, everything turning slick between her fingers with the consistency of motor oil. Removing an enemy's head drained what little energy she had left.

Despite the carnage, escape remained paramount. She needed to move fast and quiet before the others woke. Naked and blood-covered wouldn't work in the wilderness. Blood lured predators. Mountain lions prowled these woods. Still, she'd freeze to death before becoming prey, succumbing to hypothermia or blood loss before reaching safety.

Her boots close by, thankfully intact, would help. She ran fingers along his clothing like reading braille. A long-sleeve flannel topped with a stiff canvas jacket would be enough. His cargo pants yielded treasure in one pocket, something that crinkled. Food.

She touched the tip of her tongue to the bar. Salty. Chicken, maybe. Her battered nose made it hard to tell. She devoured it in two bites. Nothing had ever tasted so exquisite.

The morsel hit her stomach and ignited ravenous hunger. That little square barely touched her starvation, but time pressed hard. She needed distance between herself and the marauders. Especially Brother.

She peeled clothes from the corpse until his bare ass gleamed in the moonlight. Wrestling with dead weight felt like undressing a five-hundred-pound pig. The work inflamed her pelvis, pain radiating through her stomach and down her legs. A strange numbness settled in her feet. Something was ravaging her body. Something she had no time to diagnose.

Dante donned his clothes, rolling sleeves and folding pant cuffs, tucking where possible but leaving most unsecured. She looped his leather belt around her waist multiple times, tying it in an awkward knot. She looked like a child playing dress-up.

Survival demanded mobility. A full range of motion for kicking, clawing faces, hammer-punching Adam's apples. Whatever defense needed for eluding her captors. Jack's words echoed: "Remember mijita, eyes, nose, throat... then balls. Don't forget about the balls, that'll put them down." The clothes bound her like a straitjacket, but freezing to death wasn't an option.

Before leaving the hut, she noticed his anatomical oddities. Her experience with the male anatomy was limited, but even she recognized his parts were backward. Dennis at Humble Traveler would have destroyed this fuckface with a crude punchline. Guilt and shame washed over her for finding humor here. It wasn't funny. Yet laughter perched in her throat, threatening to escape.

Then a devious plan hatched. She'd send a message to the marauders, especially Brother. The knife made quick work. Dante gathered body parts and walked brazenly toward the fire pit. Her gut screamed to run, but she decorated the pit instead. She positioned his head and parts near the low fire, staging her message: This is what you get for hurting me. Jack would approve.

She suppressed a cry while admiring her handiwork, an art installation in carnage. The fire cast orange flickers across her swollen face, dancing in her eyes.

Evil smiled everywhere she looked. They'd trashed the camp. Food wrappers, empty tins, and used toilet paper littering the earth. A brighter plan emerged. All that rooted pain and anger boiled over. If I kill them here, there's no reason to run.

She tucked away the pain, not for survival now, but for vengeance. For the frail woman. For people who came before. For people who would fall victim after. Dante decided there would be no after. Not for the marauders. No glee. No thrill of the hunt. Only cold blackness.

Dante crept, paying each marauder a visit. Some stargazed in their sleep with silky jugulars exposed. Side-sleepers would die last. Their arrangement struck her as odd but beneficial. They didn't huddle together like Rory, and she had. They slept fearlessly, away from the fire, isolated from each other around camp.

Killing the first marauder inside the hut had been effortless. The rock cut deep and clean. Now she needed more than luck. She positioned herself carefully, preparing for the kills. Dante knelt before each one, locking their heads between her thighs.

The second kill was a young man, maybe still a teenager. Age was hard to gauge after the collapse. SHC had aged everyone badly, adding ten, sometimes twenty years to their appearance. This one was only bones devouring skin. His emaciated neck was delicate as glass.

Dante sliced downward, but the cut ran shallow. Instead of killing him, it only startled him awake. He lay there a moment, staring at the stars, adjusting his eyes while blood pooled in the hollows of his bony neck.

The delayed reaction vanished in an instant. When his eyes locked onto Dante, hell broke loose. He gripped her throat with impossible strength, lifting her inches off the ground and squeezing out every molecule of air. His grip spoke of decades spent snapping necks.

His supernatural power defied logic. Dante gasped and flailed as he increased pressure. She rammed the knife into his Adam's apple, blood fountaining from the wound. He didn't flinch. He kept squeezing. Time stretched like taffy. Her world melting at its edges. What felt like forever lasted only seconds before he bled out. When consciousness returned, everything moved wrong. Too fast or too slow. Her second kill had been disastrous, but she'd learned, prepare to fight to the death. Five more to go.

Each kill wrote its own story. Two marauders never woke, bleeding out peacefully as she plunged the knife deep into their throats, marking their passing with only occasional low-pitch gurgles. Some gasped, tried forming words as their life drained away. One refused to die, taking knife wound after knife wound until daybreak finally crept through the canopy to see his last breath. Seven fell to her blade.

Her mission succeeded, yet Brother taunted her from somewhere in the evil darkness, beyond her reach. The body count meant nothing if Brother still lived. One marauder stood apart, well-groomed, with manicured nails and tailored clothes. He bore a haunting resemblance to Tom Baker, that movie star who'd been named sexiest man alive. His ensemble screamed pre-collapse, like he'd stepped through time.

He fit the serial killer template perfectly—handsome, wholesome, innocent features. The classic recipe for charismatic cult leaders—the kind perverted enough to brainwash followers into hunting women and children during end times. She imagined he'd been born with the gift of gab, slick enough to navigate SHC's murky waters.

But she couldn't be certain this movie star lookalike was Brother. He wore no name tag. She'd given everything she had and made peace with that. Still, the thought of Brother walking free haunted her.

She sat surrounded by death while considering her next move. Psychotic laughter bubbled from her lips as she studied her installation slumped in the pit. Who knew body parts had such a short shelf life?

Nothing lasted in end days. The corpse turned carbonated within an hour. She'd expected his severed parts to decay similarly, but instead they shriveled pathetically within minutes. The headless man's eyes had sunken, cast downward, as if ashamed. Her installation hadn't achieved the impact she'd hoped. Her laughter transformed into a wail.

EMERALD HILL

SHE COULDN'T LIVE among the dead much longer, despite the compulsion to stay for Rory. Fresh meat's stench had already swallowed the frigid air. She had no intention of giving the marauders a proper burial. The only luxury they deserved was becoming food for this ungodly land's creatures. Wolves and mountain lions would soon feast on organs and flesh, leaving the rest for the crawling things and fungi beneath the soil.

More strange food bars and military rations lay scattered near the fire pit, along with aluminum canteens. She took those with shoulder straps, leaving the rest. Her backpack remained lost, but one marauder had carried a fine leather satchel. She hadn't seen hand-stitched leather since SHC. She took inventory and loaded what little she could carry.

Unknown to her, Brother never slept with his group. The Lord's spirit, he claimed, guided him to safer sleeping spots in the deep woods. Superstition and paranoia ruled him. He often dwelled on the disciples' betrayal and Jesus's crucifixion. He trusted no one.

The marauders' paltry loot puzzled her. They carried barely enough for an afternoon hike. How had they survived this far? The wild demanded foresight. Even experienced survivalists could die from a simple sprained ankle. You couldn't call "time out" anymore. Gone were the days of walking to 7-Eleven for water, Twizzlers, and gum. That world had died with everything else. No longer visible in life's rearview mirror.

Daylight revealed the discharge oozing down her leg, blood mixed with stretchy slime. Maybe her period approached, reliable as always.

A week ago, she'd found a boarded-up pharmacy. The brick building stood small, two large windows flanking the main entrance. No emergency exits, no back door, no side windows, a fatal trap. That entrance was a coffin lid. Getting caught alone in any building meant death, assault, or worse, capture.

Someone had winterized it. The nails, burrowed deep in plywood, showed pristine rust— a glorious sign in end days. No signs of tampering. Scavengers had passed it by, sharing her fear. She'd never enter alone, though she imagined it overflowed with supplies. She'd planned to tell Rory, and dreamed they'd raid it together someday soon.

Scavenging meant survival but invited death. After SHC, she'd watched gangs murder couples, assault survivors. Single mothers and children stood no chance. They faced two outcomes: captured or killed.

They'd spent nights dreaming of finding pads and toilet paper. God, how they missed toilet paper. Toothpaste. Lip balm. But Rory had drifted lifelessly downriver before hearing about the pharmacy.

The sun told her the pharmacy lay three days away. They'd adapted to dish sponges for periods. Not a new idea, but ancient, Rory had said. Women used sea sponges in ancient Greece. Rory had found a package in an abandoned trailer and tucked them in her backpack. The pack now lost.

Something was gravely wrong inside her. The pharmacy might have antibiotics, gauze, anything to stop the bleeding. Dizziness clouded her thoughts. Just keep moving became her mantra. Putting distance between herself and camp took longer than expected. Her battered condition hadn't factored into her timeline. Three days could stretch to six, even nine. She couldn't dwell on that, it would break her resolve.

Pain seared from stomach to legs. Arms and hands throbbed as if locked in downward dog for days. Murdering six people had consequences. Every muscle screamed, and hiking only taxed her thighs more.

Jack had taught her to bleed elk properly. Time and patience made meat less gamey. She'd never eaten meat then, but his technique served her well bleeding marauders like elk. Three fights had turned savage, their heads bucking between her legs until her thighs burned and quivered.

Sunlight sparkled through the trees, dappling the earth with a pink glow. She couldn't see water droplets glinting like diamonds on leaves but felt warmth radiating through the canopy. The forest smelled like a wet cat. She prayed that didn't mean mountain lions prowled nearby.

Her senses failed her. Dry mud caked her left ear, digitalizing forest sounds into conch-shell acoustics. Bird chatter and climbing creatures faded beneath slow, undulating waves crashing in her head.

A strange haze radiated, her vision smudged as if dipped in petroleum jelly. She stumbled over fallen timber and rough terrain, dragging her ravaged body onward. The world blurred, hazy light setting the forest ablaze. She measured time by the sun—Jack's teaching—but now light stung her eyes raw.

Jack, a gifted outdoorsman, had taught her off-grid survival without phones or gadgets. She missed him in moments like these. Her loving father somehow still gave her strength from the great beyond when survival demanded it.

The forest's richness, woodsy moss, wild mushrooms, swaying ferns, sticky pine sap, morning dew, wildflowers, escaped her fractured senses. Breathing through her gaping mouth like a wolf brought new challenges. Her mouth sat bone-dry. Tongue registering something like mildew. If mildew had a taste. Maybe she hallucinated it all. The marauders had ravaged every sense, or maybe the clay from earlier poisoned her mouth.

The sun sailed west, bleeding purple and pink across a cloudy horizon as day yielded to night. Dante stumbled upon a treeless, grassy hill. Billions of stars pricked the black universe and cradled the clearing like an emerald. She couldn't appreciate its beauty. Her world remained blurry and fragmented.

A deep crevice carved the hill's backside. Dante took shelter as wind howled across the landscape, battering stone by stone. The fissure stood immune, a barrier against the elements. She found a patch of silt among river stones and curled up in darkness, neither hot nor cold. Numbness claimed her, yet her teeth chattered as though locked in ice.

Behind closed eyes, assault fragments played endlessly. She drifted in and out during the attack, remembering key details, men hovering above her, then vanishing.

Strangely, these remembered faces differed from the men she'd beheaded. Nothing made sense. Those haunting faces had burned into memory forever. She was losing touch, and then a sinking realization hit, she'd counted over seven marauders. The woman marauder, Messenger of Light, where had they gone?

Only distance mattered now. Usually, she'd count steps, twenty-five thousand per mile. On good days, she managed fifteen miles. Three days, maybe four if lucky, to cover that distance. Fifteen miles in four days moved slower than a snail. They'd catch her for certain.

Camp remained too close. She stumbled through the woods like wounded prey, tripping endlessly, dragging tired feet, resting against trees to preserve precious energy. She'd made tracking easy. For all she knew, they closed in now. Maybe they weren't skilled trackers. Their poor planning suggested as much. Maybe they couldn't survive the wild at all.

She pulled the knife from her satchel, clutching it to her chest. Trying to sit up proved impossible as pain paralyzed her body. She lacked strength to fight or flee. The killing urge had faded. "Let them come," she whimpered.

What would Rory do? This was her first thought of Rory since the attack. "Rory," she croaked, gravel-voiced. Speaking the name brought tears. Dante called it repeatedly, as if her voice held power to resurrect.

Her existence shut down. Heart hammering, sweat seeping from every pore, she panted desperately. Her chest heaved as her body temperature climbed to 104ºF—fatal hour. Her eyes grew heavy as worlds, and just as consciousness slipped, a masked figure in military fatigues snatched her. She slashed wildly, hitting nothing.

The figure overpowered her, twisting her wrist until the blade hit dirt. She screamed in agony but had no strength left. Her body went limp in her captor's arms. Their eyes met briefly before darkness took her.

The masked figure laid her down and grabbed a walkie-talkie. "I've got one. Gonna need help carrying her out," a woman's voice said.

Static crackled against stone walls. A man's voice replied, "Copy. Is she alive?"

"Affirmative. Barely. You were right about the bloody girl in the woods."

Static popped. "I'm always right... What's your 20?"

"Lookout point. Inside the chasm."

"Copy, four clicks out."

"Copy, hurry."

"Can you stabilize her?"

"On it," she said. "Jesus, she's covered in blood."

"I told you. I'm on my way, out."

The masked figure checked Dante's pulse. "You're burning up, girl." She stripped away blood soaked clothes, searching for wounds. Finding the source, the woman removed her mask and began emergency medical care, racing against time to save a stranger's life.

SHC

WHEN THE FIRST catastrophic wave hit the United States, most Americans went about their daily lives without a care in the world. News feeds flashed warnings that no one heeded. Stock markets climbed despite the smoke signals from the East Coast. And even Logan's own station treated the early reports like just another slow news day. The calm before spontaneous human combustion would later seem like a cruel joke. Until the world's abrupt end

Logan sat at his desk in a corner office on the fourth floor, one level below the president of the broadcasting suite. It never made sense to him why they called it a suite when it spanned the entire fifth floor, more of a penthouse really. A deserted penthouse with old cubicles, dusty computers, and a depressing reception area. The only staff employed up there were an assistant and a secretary. "Otherwise, it's a fucking ghost town," he'd griped to Tala one night over cocktails.

In his youth, he never dreamed of becoming an executive for a local news station. Hell, he never saw himself working for anyone, in any capacity. Not in the conventional sense. But here he was, an executive for a small news station in Denver, Colorado, with a base salary of $71,000. He hadn't matched his father's success. Then again, he hadn't served time in prison for a $180 million real estate Ponzi scheme either, like dear old dad. Nor did he have a whole other family and a double life in the Philippines, although sometimes he wished he did.

He'd inherited just two traits from his father: a cheating heart and ambition. Ambition was the nobler of the two. Though Logan had a cutthroat attitude, like his father. Not a $180-million-dollar cutthroat attitude, but heartless, just the same.

He obsessed over the fifth floor, particularly the president of broadcasting position, even though he considered it a rat maze of cubicles and computer monitors and what have you. His corner office had sweeping views that overlooked the parking lot. Every time he gazed out the sprawling windows, he couldn't help thinking his career was floating downstream. Five years ago, $71,000 was fine. Doable, even. But his salary hadn't budged since. Just the occasional bonus here and there. Like the one for that local exposé about a corrupt cop and a strip joint on Broadway employing underage girls. Though he conveniently forgot to mention his own nightly visits to the same establishment.

His desk was laminate wood. Matter of fact, they'd manufactured the entire news station to look like something it could never be. The office furniture screamed bargain basement cheap. Every piece laminated or covered in vinyl or dipped in plastic with fiberboard construction. The kind of stuff you'd find at a liquidation warehouse for a dollar a pound. Even his imitation desk shifted and jittered to the left every time he moved the wrong way.

He often obsessed over a news station he'd once toured in Chicago. That affiliate had Herman Miller and Knoll coming out of the wazoo. Their men's restroom on the second floor had a wall lined with Dyson hand dryers and floor-to-ceiling marble subway tiles. Not the dreary yellow tile and puke brown linoleum they had in Denver.

Chicago's fragrant hand soap made his skin baby silk. And they had Egyptian cotton towels on top of those Dysons. "Boy," he muttered, "they really know how to pamper a guy in Chicago." That was just the beginning. He imagined what treasures awaited in their penthouse. Oh yes, he assured himself, Chicago has a proper penthouse.

Denver was lucky to have paper towels, the kind that evaporated once anything wet came into contact. The restrooms on the fourth floor ran out of toilet paper and paper towels daily. It never failed. He'd get ready to have a serious sit-down but had to hold it because a cardboard carcass hung on the roller. Once, he'd had to rip the carcass from the roller and wipe his ass with it. Now, every time he used the restroom, he paid special attention to certain things, making sure he could take a shit in peace. Or wash his hands. Or play with his hair in the mirror. Pick his teeth. Whatever.

Even the hand soap dried out his skin so badly that between his fingers started to crack and bleed. Whatever chemical compound the soap contained must've been some bargain basement buy one get one buy. Somewhere next to cheap hell. And that's when he realized he was living in cheap hell.

His life was one giant bargain basement from hell. Even bargain basement hell lacked heat. More like freezing, because they'd constructed a fiberboard furnace of fiberboard. And whatever fueled the damn thing was spitting out bargain basement gasoline. The kind that doesn't burn clean. The kind that evaporates before it even ignites. News station life was boiled down to imitation, like a packet of Splenda. Like his career. Like his trajectory.

Logan could see his life ahead of him, whatever was left. He wasn't planning on living forever. At his age, this frightened him the most. Fiberboard would pave his road, leaving him with nothing to wipe his ass with. He spent his days in the office, hoping for a big story to boost his career.

Logan made his first mistake hiring Chloe as his assistant. His fatal mistake was inviting her out for cocktails one evening. They spent the entire night getting hammered at a bar in LoDo before ending up at her studio apartment somewhere in Capitol Hill, where "uptown" should, in his opinion, be called "downtown." As in down, down, downtown. Where the pimps and drug dealers roamed.

They had a few glasses of boxed wine, refrigerated merlot, and before he knew it, they were rolling around naked on her loveseat. He wanted to end his misery right there. Get a gun and end it all before he loses his nerve. That's what he kept thinking as Chloe lay in his arms, crying about some boyfriend, Chip so-and-so, who'd dumped her weeks ago. All he could think was, "Who names their kid Chip?" Like tortilla chip.

He wanted to tell Chloe she'd dodged a bullet. That she was better off. The name alone suggested she might have ended up in the outer boroughs with Chip, playing house in a mobile home or RV campsite in the foothills. And from the looks of her shitty little apartment, she'd skirted that reality already.

Chloe was content with her studio apartment on Capitol Hill. It bothered her little to have what Logan surmised were thrift store furnishings and a free curbside recliner, likely infested with bedbugs. And tchotchke hell raining down upon them.

In truth, Chloe could live this life twice over. Three times over, as long as Chip was by her side. Maybe not marry the guy but live together till the end of days. She would do that. Maybe buy a puppy and name it Chip.

With other guys, she'd had to pretend. Now she thought Chip had ghosted her because she didn't pretend. Maybe she was too comfortable around him. Maybe her jaw clicked too loud when she chewed. It always clicked when she chewed. Or maybe she repulsed him in some other way. Her medicated shampoo, her slender fingers, her whatever. Maybe Chip just got worn down and kicked rocks instead.

She cried for over an hour afterward, going on and on about Chip. How much she missed him, how much she loved him. He spent the rest of the night consoling what he privately called a "delusional girl."

Over the next few months after sleeping together, Chloe's work deteriorated. She never jotted down phone messages. She always ran late. She played sick on Mondays and Fridays like clockwork.

Logan had to remind her of everything—pick up this, contact that person, basic tasks any assistant should handle. She kept forgetting everything, even the simplest duties. She couldn't even differentiate between a fresh salad and an expired one.

In observation, Chloe had no talent—or at the very least, couldn't run a cash register at McDonald's. Sure, she could fly around the office seeming busy, but meanwhile, she destroyed everything in her path like a seagull wandering aimlessly through the air.

The day after their drunken encounter, Chloe made a scene in the employee lounge. She cried and spilled about them sleeping together with the first person she saw. That person told another employee, who told someone else, until the story had traveled the entire fourth floor.

She wasn't living in the same universe as he was. Logan wanted to fire her. But he couldn't. Too many variables complicated the decision. Too many what-ifs. He wasn't brave enough to gamble with his career, just brave enough to have drunken sex with his assistant.

Chloe burst into his office, ripping him from the salad ritual—the one where he sat chewing hard, making angry faces while peering out the window. She startled him, and he gulped and choked on a piece of bacon.

Social cues went straight over her head, too. Logan clearly struggled to breathe. This didn't faze Chloe. She blurted out a mess of words about something while he raised his palm to say, "Can't you see, I'm dying?" Still, she continued as if he were fine. About the only thing he understood was, "You need to call Bill, right now."

Coughing and gasping for air, he guzzled water and waved her off like he was shooing a pesky gnat. He guzzled more water. His eyes bulged and teared. His forehead sweated from all the commotion. It took a few long minutes to compose himself.

In all his years at the station, he had never sat down and had a serious conversation with Bill. Not about business. Only brief exchanges while riding the elevator, usually discussing the weather. There was always something about the weather. Bill was skilled at small talk. Bill could make even a light drizzle expected at noon on Tuesday sound urgent. In the past, Logan had only relayed messages through Bill's assistant and secretary—never Bill himself.

This must be some mistake, he told himself. He straightened his posture, cleared his throat, and dialed Bill's secretary. "Hello Linda, this is Logan." He covered the phone receiver and cleared his throat again. "My assistant gave me a message to call Bill."

His professional voice sounded fake to him, like he was kissing ass. And now that he thought about it, maybe every time he called Linda, it sounded like he was kissing ass.

He heard Linda place the phone away from her mouth, shouting at Bill. "I have Logan on the line." He could hear her shuffling paper. Then she came back on the line and said, "I'm transferring you now."

The phone rang once when Bill picked up. "There's no time for formalities. I'll get straight to the point."

Logan gulped hard. He could feel his blood pressure rise as his heart plummeted. A million scenarios swam inside his brain in a matter of seconds. He couldn't help thinking he might get the boot. Why else would Bill want to talk to him? He cleared his throat, as if the bacon remained stuck. "Yes, please go on."

"There's been some troubling developments on the East Coast," Bill said while Linda helped him with his jacket. Logan could hear a lot of racket on the other end. "I just got off the phone with our affiliates in Atlanta." Bill's tone sounded more like a Texan roaming the oil fields, straw hat, wheat stalk twirling between his teeth. Truth was, Logan wasn't sure Bill was even Texan. He just sounded like a bumpkin.

Holding his breath, gripping every word, Logan said nothing.

"Logan, are you listening?"

Logan snapped out of it. "Yes, I didn't want to interrupt. Please continue."

"Something is happening all over the world. They're calling it SHC, a phenomenon of sorts," Bill said. "It's unbelievable, really. Something out of the Twilight Zone."

"SHC?"

"Spontaneous Human Combustion." Bill's voice carried the weight of a funeral director. Even his usual folksy manner had burned away, leaving something raw and urgent. "My sources tell me it might be a biological attack or something. But nobody knows at this juncture. People are dropping like flies. Burning like flies, more like it."

Logan's fingers trembled as he pulled up the news feeds. Each headline hit like a hammer. "Mass Combustion Events Reported in Major Cities," "CDC Baffled by Spontaneous Human Fires," "Death Toll Mounting as SHC Claims Thousands." The corner office with its bargain basement furniture suddenly felt very small, very far from where he needed to be.

"Logan!"

"Still with you, Bill." He thumbed through news articles and saw a bunch of national alerts. Each one read worse than the last. "Do I have your commitment?"

The fluorescent lights seemed to flicker as Bill spoke, or maybe that was just Logan's imagination playing tricks. Outside his window, the sun still shone on the parking lot. People still walked to their cars. The world still turned, for now. But something in the air had changed, become electric, as if the atmosphere itself was holding its breath.

"Commitment?"

"Yes," Bill raised his voice. "We need all hands on deck."

He stopped scrolling, thinking about what to say next. "What are we talking about here, Bill?"

"We need a crew to cover the story." Bill's voice turned matter-of-fact. "And we want you to head this up. This gets your name chiseled on the front door. I'm sure you understand where I'm going with this. This could be your big moment."

Logan's mind raced past the promotion, past the corner office, past all the Herman Miller furniture in Chicago. For the first time in years, he saw his life clearly. Not through the lens of career advancement or status symbols, but through the simple, terrifying question, *where was Rory right now?*

Logan froze. The phone line fell into cricket-silence. For the first time in a long time, he thought about Rory's safety. And the only person who mattered most was Rory. Maybe he loved his daughter after all. Using a distant tone, he said, "I'll have to call you back, Bill." He didn't bother waiting for a reply. He just hung up.

U-TURN

He called Rory in a panic. The call didn't even ring, it went straight to voicemail. "Damn!" He tried again with the same result. After Tala died, Rory had blocked his number. She'd caught him with another woman mere hours after her mother's death, when the hospital sheets were still warm.

The scene played out like a nightmare in slow motion. A half-naked woman rummaging through their refrigerator, wearing nothing but a thong, in Tala's newly remodeled kitchen. The kitchen where Tala had spent her last good days teaching Rory how to make lumpia. Her hands were still steady enough to roll the delicate wrappers.

That summer, while Rory vacationed with friends, he'd turned their house into his playground. Those precious final weeks, while Rory battled recurring nightmares about her mother dying alone, nightmares so vivid they'd driven her to skip senior year to become her mother's full-time caregiver.

It was Tala who pushed Rory toward normalcy. "Go," she'd insisted, her voice still carrying that musical lilt, even as cancer gnawed at her bones. "I want you to have some normal in your life." She'd cupped Rory's face, looked her straight in the eye. "I will be here when you get back. I'm going to beat this thing, you'll see."

The lie tasted like mercy.

Halfway through the trip, Tala's call shattered everything. The cancer had outsmarted the chemo. It had invaded her lungs like a silent army. "She has weeks left," the doctor said. Rory took the first flight out of Utah, leaving behind half-packed suitcases and broken promises.

For forty-eight hours, Rory became part of the hospital room's architecture. Her feet merged with the strange, speckled tile. She forgot about teeth-brushing, about sleeping. The nurse's station coffee became her lifeline. She watched the sparkle in Tala's eyes dim like a sunset. Their hands clasped together in those final hours, mother and daughter dwelling in their own dark universe. The moment felt transcendent. Precious, even. Though haunting.

Tala slipped into unconsciousness before Rory could say the words that burned in her throat, "I wish I'd spent every waking moment with you." Before she could whisper, "Thank you for loving me." She'd thought those words might give Tala peace, but now they lived in a place where certainty went to die.

Nobody prepares for the afterlife, even when death winks at you. You can't negotiate with it, can't bargain. Despite Tala's brave face, her passing devastated everyone. Two days after the diagnosis, her lungs filled with fluid. She stopped breathing on her own. Her heart gave out at four o'clock, while the afternoon sun painted false promises across the hospital walls.

Grief hit Rory in waves. That initial nightmarish state, seeing her mother's skin turned to parchment, watching the chemo strip away everything that made Tala glow. Even her smile, that last gift, had faded like old photographs.

Rory worked lotion into her mother's hands and feet, even after death had claimed her. It didn't matter that Tala was gone. Rory didn't share her mother's color, and that fact haunted her now more than ever. Tala's skin had glistened like black pearls wrapped in moonlight. Rory wore her father's skin like an ill-fitting suit, and it shamed her. Deep down, she feared her insides would mirror Logan's one day, hollow spaces where love should live.

Introducing Tala as her mother had always sparked an avalanche of questions. Strangers assumed a stepmother, their eyes doing the math that never added up. "Definitely not biological," she'd once overheard at a dinner party, those words cutting like glass. Their faces always registered shock when they learned the truth, that Tala had birthed Rory, had shaped her heart if not her features.

In that cold, dark room, Rory balanced on the knife-edge of tears but never fell. She fought the urge, wearing strength like armor. She had to be her mother's daughter, unbreakable. Tala wouldn't cry at a time like this. But Rory couldn't have been more wrong. If their positions were reversed, Tala would have shattered the sky with her grief.

Inside, Rory was dying. Tala had been so particular about her appearance, treating her hair like silk, her skin like precious jade. Few people earned the right to touch either. Her natural beauty belonged to another era. In another life, she would have been Hollywood royalty, her face launching a thousand dreams.

For hours, Rory combed her mother's hair, painted her nails, as if these small acts of devotion could tether Tala to this life. But no amount of grooming could restore what cancer had stolen. This wasn't the woman who had danced in their kitchen. Who had braided Rory's hair with fingers that knew every curve of her daughter's scalp. Those jewel-brown eyes had lost their light somewhere between diagnosis and goodbye, now flat and sunken. Her skin wrapped nothing but bone and broken promises.

For the first time in her life, Rory needed Logan. And he was nowhere. A father-shaped void in the geography of her grief. She'd left countless messages on his cell phone while at the hospital. Each one more desperate than the last. He never called back. The betrayal brewing inside confused her, a toxic mix of need and hatred. She'd needed him to ease the agony, and thought somehow he could make the pain disappear. But he didn't. He never could. He only added to it, like poison in an open sore.

DECOUPAGE THE HEAVENS

Leaving Tala in that cold, dark room after grooming her was like walking away from the sun. The elevator descent to the lobby felt endless, each floor taking another piece of her heart. Dawn shimmered across the skyline as Rory waited for her Uber outside the hospital, the morning light cruel in its beauty. As warmth touched her skin, she felt Tala's presence radiating from above, as if her mother had already found her place among the stars. She peered at the sky and whispered, "I love you. I always will."

The pain kept bubbling no matter how she tried to swallow it down. She ached for one of Tala's hugs. The kind that smelled of jasmine and safety. The kind that made everything okay. She wanted someone, anyone, to speak Tala into existence again. How beautiful she was. How her kindness changed lives. How the world would spin differently without her. But there was only the icy sidewalk and her shadow for company.

The Uber driver looked about thirty, with eyes that caught hers in the rearview mirror like twin spotlights. "Rory?"

She nodded. The SUV's industrial carpet shampoo scent turned her stomach inside out. "Is it okay if I roll my window down?"

Those bright eyes found her again in the mirror. "Sure, I'll turn the heat up." She edged closer to the window, letting bitter winter air feather across her skin like her mother's forgotten touch.

"How about some music?" He didn't wait for an answer before the radio came alive.

And then "Sweet Dreams" filled the space between them, Tala's song. The soundtrack to countless evenings in their kitchen, her mother swaying as she stirred pots of sinigang, singing into a wooden spoon.

Then, the levy that held her soul at bay broke. Every emotion she'd bottled exploded out of her like shrapnel. She wailed, grief cutting through her with the force of a million knives. The driver calmly pulled to the curb, turned the music low, and sat there with those bright eyes fixed ahead, as if giving her grief the space it demanded.

This wasn't his first encounter with tears. Usually, they came with the midnight crowd, when bars emptied their sorrows into his backseat. LoDo, Denver's drunk capital, had taught him about human vulnerability. He'd spent countless nights scrubbing away the physical evidence of emotional wreckage, vomit, urine, smeared makeup. Sometimes, around 2 a.m., he'd have to call the police when belligerent passengers refused to leave. Both men and women had taken swings at him. The money in LoDo was good, but it cost pieces of his sanity. Now he worked days, trading profit for peace.

He waited, letting her tears run their course. The last thing this girl needed was someone policing her feelings. When her sobs softened to sniffles, he reached into the glove compartment for a box of Kleenex.

"Thank you."

"Take as many as you need."

The car slipped back into traffic. She dabbed at her eyes. "My mom just died, well, not just, but a couple of hours ago." The words tumbled out, as if she needed to justify her breakdown. She didn't want him thinking she was unstable. Not after Logan had once scolded her thirteen-year-old self for crying. "Stop being such a girl," he sneered, wagging his finger. "You're being way too emotional." Since then, she'd learned to hide her tears from men.

Without meeting her eyes in the mirror, he said, "I'm sorry for your loss."

"She was a really good person."

"It's always the good ones, and never the bad ones."

"Right." She sniffled.

"Don't I know it."

Their eyes met in the rearview. "Do you think there's a heaven?"

He hesitated, throat working. As an atheist, he'd never set foot in a church, never sought comfort in promises of an afterlife. He didn't usually get personal with passengers, but there was something about this girl's raw grief that demanded gentleness.

"What do you think?" he deflected carefully.

"I don't know. Part of me thinks there is."

"Wishes are a powerful thing."

"Really?"

"Sure," he continued. "A friend of mine made a vision board."

"What's that?"

"It's a cork board where you tack pictures of what you wish for. Dream house, dream job, whatever you desire. You find pictures and create your future. My friend decoupages magazine clippings of tropical islands onto hers. She had a thing for islands."

"What happened?"

"She's living on an island now. Talks to me sometimes, says she's never been happier. Who knows?" He lifted his hand in a gesture of possibility.

Rory sank deeper into the seat, brow furrowed. If only she'd known about vision boards before, maybe she could have saved her mother, decoupaged her way to a miracle.

The driver sighed, keeping his eyes on the road ahead.

They rode in silence after that, Rory watching the city scroll past her window. She prayed to a heaven she wasn't sure existed, because the possibility of seeing Tala again was the only thing keeping her heart beating. Maybe that's why people went to church in the first place. Not for salvation, but for reunion.

UBER AFFAIR

THE GARAGE DOOR gaped open wound like when the Uber pulled up, the first warning sign. Logan, master of HOA regulations and property values, never left it open. His car sat crooked, straddling the garage and driveway like a drunk trying to find his way home.

The deadbolt turned without resistance. Already unlocked. A trail of clothes marked a path through the foyer toward the staircase, breadcrumbs leading to something Rory wasn't ready to find. She followed anyway, cataloging each piece. Logan's suit jacket , the one Tala had bought him for Christmas, his tie, navy silk, another of Tala's gifts, and then, like a slap, unfamiliar feminine things. A lacy white bra gleamed against the dark carpet, a lighthouse warning of rocks ahead.

Kitchen sounds drew her forward. Later, she'd remember trying to walk quietly, but her feet betrayed her, each step thundering, weighed down by what was coming. The woman stood there, wearing nothing but a lace thong, bent over and searching through the refrigerator in the kitchen where Tala had spent her last good days. The kitchen where mother and daughter had rolled lumpia together, where Tala had taught Rory that food was love made visible. Now this stranger's bare ass pointed at her like an accusation.

"Babe, would you like some eggs?" The woman didn't even turn around.

Rage rose in Rory's throat like bile. An opened bottle of champagne sat on the counter—a celebration. While Tala's body lay cooling in the hospital, they'd been popping corks. Her mind refused to process it. Logan was an asshole, yes, but this? This existed in a universe she'd never imagined possible. "Who are you?"

The woman startled, dropping the egg carton. It exploded across the travertine tiles Tala had chosen, yolks spreading like small suns. She turned, squinting at Rory as if she were an unexpected glare. "Who are you?"

Large breasts with bright nipples confronted Rory's gaze. The woman's skin glowed pink, flushed with recent activity. She looked young—maybe five years older than Rory. Close enough in age to be sisters. The thought made her stomach turn. "I live here!"

A sneer crawled across the woman's face as she sized Rory up. "How cute. Daddy didn't tell me he had a daughter."

"Daddy?" The word tasted like poison.

"Use your imagination." The woman's lips curled.

"Get out of my house!"

The woman paused in her attempt to clean the mess, looking up at Rory through mascara-heavy lashes. "What bothers you most, that I fucked your dad, or I fucked your dad in this house?"

"Both."

"He's a grown man, sweetie."

"He's married."

"Does it look like I care?"

Curses erupted from Rory like lava, each word burning her throat. The woman's eyes danced with something darker than amusement. She abandoned the egg disaster, leaving footprints of yolk and shell across Tala's carefully chosen tiles as she sashayed out.

Rory collapsed at the kitchen island, folding into herself like origami, cheek pressed against the cool marble. Some foolish part of her brain waited for Logan to appear, to explain, to apologize for betraying Tala. But he never came. Not now, not ever.

Heavy footsteps eventually thundered down the staircase—two sets, one lighter than the other. Rory's head snapped up, hope rising like a stupid bird. The foyer filled with harsh echoes, clothes being gathered, whispered words she couldn't quite catch. Then the front door opened and slammed shut with the finality of a coffin lid.

"Dad?" The silence mocked her. "Dad!"

The house held its breath. Then came the garage door's familiar screech, its aluminum track protesting as it completed its cycle with a hollow clang. She raced to the window, but the driveway already sat empty, like her father's promises.

In the kitchen, egg yolks dried on the floor where Tala had once danced while cooking, where she'd taught Rory that love meant staying even when things got messy. Now all that remained were sticky footprints leading nowhere and a half-empty bottle of champagne, celebrating nothing worth remembering.

BLOODLINE

LOGAN RETURNED days later wearing the same suit—the one that had decorated the foyer like fallen leaves. Bloodshot eyes swam in his face, stubble shadowing his jaw. His hair told the story of wherever he'd been: flattened on one side, rebelling against gravity on the other.

He ghosted past Rory without a glance and disappeared into the shower. When he emerged later, he looked assembled but hollow, dark circles cradling his eyes like permanent bruises.

He kept his distance as he gestured for her to sit, his gaze dancing away whenever it accidentally caught hers. His throat worked before words came. "The hospital called me."

All the days left on earth wouldn't wash the rage from her blood. She fixed him with arctic eyes. "She died, dad. And you weren't there."

"I know."

Tears escaped while something deeper broke loose inside her. Her eyes found the floor. "Did you love mom?"

"We were so young."

"Is that a yes?"

"I think so."

"Dad!"

"Should I lie?"

She searched his face for something human. "Do you love me?"

The pause stretched like a wound. His expression twisted as if the question physically hurt. Silence filled the space between them like smoke while tears tracked down her cheeks.

"Dad!"

"You're my daughter."

The words fell like stones. Somehow, in the span of days, she'd become an orphan twice over. Rory stood, legs trembling.

"Does that mean you love me?"

"You're my daughter." As if biology could substitute for feeling.

She kept searching for those empty eyes, though she already knew what she wouldn't find. Some truths hurt less unopened.

"She didn't want cremation."

"I know," he snapped. "We talked."

"What else did you talk about?"

"I know her wishes."

"Did mom know about her?" Rory's finger jabbed toward the front door like an arrow.

"I think she suspected."

"I'll make the arrangements. You don't have to bother with mom anymore."

"You don't have that kind of money."

"I do."

He rolled his eyes. "There's more to it than that. Funeral arrangements are a serious business."

"I'll figure it out," she said. "I have money now."

His brows knitted. "What the hell are you talking about?"

Rory stood there, teeth clenched, eyes wild. "Never mind dad. I've got it."

"No, I want to know what you mean by that."

"Mom has a blood trust," she said. "Given by grandpa."

She'd fumbled the words, bloodline trust was what she'd meant to say.

"Sounds like something your mom made up."

"It means I get everything," she said. "You can stay, but she cannot come back." Another arrow toward the door.

"This is my house," he said. "I say who can stay."

"Mom bought the house with her money."

"That doesn't matter," he said. "It's marital property, or whatever."

"That's not how it works."

He snickered, yanked out his phone, and dove into google. With each scroll, color drained from his face like water. The room seemed to tilt beneath him as his legs went weak. He sank into a chair, eyes glued to the screen that was destroying his certainties.

———

They became strangers sharing walls. Logan and Rory orbited each other like distant planets, their paths crossing only when gravity demanded. They spoke in the language of necessity, oiling the squeaky hinges of coexistence.

He'd vanish for days, losing himself in the arms of women young enough to believe his lies. Their relationship balanced on knife edges. The knowledge that Rory had inherited Tala's estate—the house, everything—ate at him like acid. She even charged him for half the household bills, mortgage-free property be damned.

Paying rent to his daughter carved holes in his pride. He'd contemplate moving out, dreaming of an apartment where he could entertain women without shame. But the thought of friends and family marking him as the father who abandoned his daughter after her mother's death kept him tethered to the house like a ghost.

The estate's completion revealed Tala's secret wealth, each dollar she'd hoarded like dragon's gold. When he'd coveted things—a new car, golf clubs, the Rolex that whispered promises—she'd always say, "We can't afford it," ending each discussion with, "If you want it so bad, then you can pay for it out of your own pocket."

Meanwhile, she'd poured money into the house and her doomsday prepping, even recruiting Larry from two doors down to feed what Logan had dismissed as paranoid delusions.

The financial power shift between father and daughter twisted like a knife. When his EV battery died again after Tala's memorial, the $20,000 repair might as well have been a million. No bank would touch him. Rory had relented and fronted the money—not from kindness, but to avoid playing chauffeur through rush hour traffic. She added loan payments to his monthly obligations like collecting interest on betrayal. After the affair, Rory never softened. She found ways to make Logan pay, calculated down to the penny, as if debt could somehow balance the scales of grief.

EV DREAMS

LOGAN STARED AT HIS PHONE, watching another "not delivered" notification pop up. He'd tried reaching Rory three times now, each attempt met with silence. The news station's parking lot stretched before him, empty, except for a few cars and his EV still tethered to the charging station.

Twenty minutes. That's all it would take to drive home and check on her. But as the thought formed, another pushed it aside: Victoria, his new girlfriend, wouldn't know what was coming. And Rory? Well, she'd been nothing but difficult lately. The word "bitch" floated through his mind, and he was surprised by how little guilt came with it.

The EV needed more charge anyway. More juice to carry him far from whatever disaster was unfolding. And if he was being honest, he knew who he'd rather spend his last days with.

Logan walked to Chloe's desk, carefully choosing his words to avoid raising alarm about the impending doom. His eyes landed on the stack of sticky notes beside her computer screen. He wrote his address on the top sheet, tore it off, and handed it to her.

"What's this?"

Logan forced his brightest smile, as if the world wasn't crumbling around them. He placed a hand on her shoulder. "Rory isn't feeling well."

"Oh, no." Chloe's face fell. "Are you leaving early?"

"Here's the thing, I can't. Bill needs me to cover the story."

"They haven't told me much," she said, lowering her voice. "But everyone's saying it's pretty bad out there."

"People always exaggerate," he said with practiced casualness.

"Do you want me to check on her?"

"You read my mind." His smile came easier now. "I need you to stay with her until this situation settles."

"I can't, my cat's home alone."

"Bring him along."

"Seriously?"

"Sure. Rory's always wanted a cat."

Chloe's eyes lit up at the suggestion. Logan could tell she was eager for any excuse to leave the suffocating office atmosphere. She stuffed her phone and earbuds into her purse, looped the strap over her shoulder, and headed for the elevator when Logan called after her. "Mind checking on Rory first?"

"Yeah, of course."

From his corner office, Logan watched Chloe walk to her car and drive away. Once she disappeared from view, he tried Linda again.

Bill, in what Logan could only assume was a moment of weakness, had decided to board the news helicopter on the rooftop without sharing his destination. Without Bill's inside knowledge and connections, Logan's chances of surviving this event were slim. He begged Linda for Bill's cell number, but she wouldn't budge.

The reality of his situation hit hard. His circle of friends at the station was non-existent. Even the other executives on the fourth floor avoided him like a plague carrier. If he had any shot at surviving this apocalypse, Cathy Stone would be his only chance.

Time ticked away, leaving few options. Through the glass partition, Logan saw Cathy's assistant absorbed in typing, her back turned. He slipped past her desk unnoticed and entered Cathy's office without announcing himself.

The moment she saw him, the color drained from her face. She held up a palm, signaling him to wait. "Hang on, Bill. Logan just walked in, I'll call you back."

Logan could hear Bill's muffled voice still spilling from the phone. "Yes, uh-huh, that's correct... Bill... Bill... listen, I'll have to call you back." Cathy hung up and fixed Logan with a sharp glare. "Is your team ready?"

"No. I don't even know how to prepare."

"Nobody does. You'll have to improvise," she said, her voice tight. "People are dying faster than we can report their findings on SHC."

"SHC?"

"Keep up, Logan." She coughed. "Spontaneous human combustion. It's all over social media."

"Why aren't you heading this up?" he pressed. "You're the senior executive."

"They need me in Chicago. I'm on the next flight out."

"What exactly is SHC?"

"You're not listening," she snapped. "We're running out of time, and I don't have the patience to hold your hand."

"Why should executives risk their lives for a news story?"

"Fine. I accept your resignation."

Logan stood his ground, clapping slowly. "Wake up! Do you think I'm going to risk my life chasing a scoop?"

"That's what we do," she said. "That's how we save lives. When everything goes to hell, we're the eyes and ears on the ground. The public needs to know how to protect themselves from—." She paused, her expression going blank. "From S—H—C."

"Hope?" He studied her face, his voice dropping. "In what world?"

She maintained that empty stare, her mind clearly wrestling with something beyond his grasp. Without another word, she dismissed him with a wave and reached for her phone.

Realizing he'd get nothing more from Cathy, Logan headed to the employee lounge to gather supplies. He'd convinced himself he could outrun SHC. The vending machines offered little beyond junk food. High calories, high fructose corn syrup, sodium, artificial everything. Nothing with real nutritional value.

The counter held a sad display of stale baked goods: donuts, scones, muffins, and bagels. A bowl of dusty bananas and apples sat near the coffee pot. He grabbed the fruit bowl, bought bottled water from the vending machine, and headed for his EV.

After dumping his provisions on the passenger seat, he unplugged the charging cable. Behind the wheel, he checked the battery icon: 52 percent charge, promising a range of 147 miles. It showed the same reading from this morning before he'd plugged in. The charging stations had been unreliable for months now, working one day and failing the next.

The projected range didn't account for weather or speed, factors that could significantly decrease his distance. He'd need to keep it under fifty and forget about air conditioning if he wanted to squeeze out all 147 miles. At least the weather was cooperating, a mild sixty-seven degrees, with thick clouds blocking most of the sun's rays.

FIJI SUNDOWN

Tala built her doomsday bunker over six months, transforming the basement into a fortress against chaos. She wasn't one for conspiracy theories. Those people seemed unhinged, she'd once said. Until the storm that killed the power grid changed everything. Watching thousands go dark while scattered houses kept their lights on made her question what she thought she knew about preparation and paranoia.

Her house sat in a neighborhood of doctors and lawyers, where she existed as a tolerated anomaly. Her sizable inheritance made her acceptable, if not quite welcome. Besides Larry, a light-skinned man of Spanish descent two doors down. She and Rory were the only minorities in this White Slice Americana. She'd paid her dues, or rather, generations before her had paid with chains that wrapped the globe. Blood and whips and chattel and ships, endless ships stuffed with human cargo sailing the Atlantic toward stolen native land, where colonies of white men built a nation on the backs of the very people they despised.

Before the storm, she thought she understood her neighbors. They were obsessed over HOA rules like medieval priests hunting heretics. Logan was one of the zealots. Alongside a retired gynecologist who patrolled with a ruler, measuring grass length as if weeds were a moral failing. Two years earlier, they'd formed a crusade against a tricked-out RV that dared park on their precious streets.

But eight days after the grid died, everything changed. The utility company's announcement about solar flares frying outdated infrastructure, and the great obstacles that stood in the way of buying overseas parts and three-month repairs, sparked something primal. Houses with power became fortresses overnight. Neighbors turned feral and territorial. Even the grass-measuring gynecologist disappeared behind locked doors. Those manicured lawns withered like abandoned dreams.

While they rationed supplies, Tala braved a trip to Walmart. The only store still powered. The scene inside looked like a heist movie's aftermath. Produce section gutted. Staples vanished. Shelves stretching bare for miles. She lasted five minutes before fleeing, but freedom wasn't free. In the parking lot, two men fought over Fiji water near the cart corral. The crack of gunfire followed her to the car. In the rearview mirror, she watched one man curl around his bleeding leg, screams chasing her to the intersection.

A man shot over water when the faucets still ran, at least in her neighborhood. Then the realization hit, maybe other areas had lost water and sewage too. These men weren't crazy, they were desperate. That day birthed a prepper.

The gun debate with Logan stretched weeks. Neither had fired a weapon before. He feared shooting himself during a home invasion more than any intruder. But she wore him down, like water on stone.

Pre-blackout Tala would've laughed at the idea of guns and bunkers. Now she started with essentials, a Glock, rifle, and tactical shotgun. Enough firepower to clear a crowd or defend a home. At the gun range, perfecting her aim, she met Larry.

He carried his fifty years very well. Spanish blood and silver-threaded hair lending him an elegance that set Logan's teeth on edge. Smaller built but powerful in that quiet way that speaks of experience. Tala called him handsome once, and Logan never forgot.

Larry, a retired FBI agent, initially dismissed preppers as paranoid. But Tala's story changed him. Two worlds collided—an ex-FBI agent and nurse anesthetist. United by a shared understanding of how quickly civilization's veneer could crack.

Together they built their apocalypse insurance inside her basement. Freeze-dried food with twenty-five-year shelf life, water stockpiles, mountains of toilet paper, grains, beans, medical supplies with tourniquets, generators, gas masks, IV infusion kits. They agreed to shelter together when society crumbled.

Their relationship stayed platonic, but Logan seethed watching "Mr. Handsome" at family dinners. Tala always seated Larry across from him, forcing Logan to watch him eat with his fingers like some medieval baron at a feast. Worse were his FBI stories: tales of the world's dumbest criminals that filled the house with laughter. Tala's high-pitched cackle, the one Logan hadn't heard since their youth, rang out at Larry's jokes. His women, hanging on every word from this stranger's mouth.

The new family dynamic was killing Logan slowly. He could charm too, once. Before wife and child and mortgage tamed him into something serious and immovable. He remembered being funny, carefree, wild. But domestication had never quite taken root in his DNA, and now he watched another man bring light to eyes that used to shine for him alone.

LARRY OF DOOM

RORY WAS SHOWERING when the first emergency notification flashed on her cell phone at 10:03 a.m. SHC struck different parts of the world at different times. Even Littleton, Colorado, just next door, didn't feel its effects until 10:55 a.m.

More notifications stacked up, her phone flashing like an Armageddon beacon on the kitchen counter. Every five minutes, another alert vibrated against the granite, too far from her reach. Far from the steam and hot water pelting her.

By 11:06 a.m., when she finally checked her phone, notifications had piled up like autumn leaves. She dismissed them, assuming another Amber Alert. Instead, she opened her favorite social media app, her daily obsession. The endless scroll that consumed hours of her life. Today, that addiction would show her the world burning.

The first video stopped her cold. A man in a busy intersection, convulsing like the infected. Red electricity erupted from his body like those crimson flashes that dance between storm clouds. The light show turned violent, reaching skyward. Within seconds, the man became pure light, then fire, then ash. All that remained was a spiral mark on the pavement, a leg standing like the spirit never left the body, and a charred hand waving from the ashes.

She thought it was a prank at first. The footage had that Cloverfield shake, the camera jerking wildly, failing its one job. But after replaying the horror, more videos flooded in. A woman in a wheelchair, burning to death, smoldering into ash except for a single limb. Content creators tagged it "Proof of spontaneous human combustion," but everyone called it SHC. The platform tried deleting the graphic content, but trillions of videos poured in simultaneously, crashing the entire system.

Spontaneous human combustion was new to her. AI search results yielded countless blogs on the topic. The earliest documented case dated to 1641, but modern science dismissed it as impossible without an external ignition source. Human fat burns when exposed, they said, but not spontaneously. The body's 60 percent water content made it implausible. Pure pseudoscience. Though, the "human wick effect" theory gave her the chills.

One blog, "Strange but True," suggested electrolysis could trigger SHC by breaking down water molecules into hydrogen. Maybe that blogger had stumbled onto something. Because SHC was happening, pseudoscience or not, leaving ghost limbs standing in piles of ash across the globe.

As she searched YouTube for more footage, her doorbell camera chimed. Larry stood on her porch, but something was wrong. He stared into the camera, his body seizing and twitching like those SHC zombies.

He froze like a statue, then convulsed, freeze—flail—freeze, as if red electricity coursed through him. His hands opened and closed like claws seeking flesh. His face, charred and bloody, contorted in agony.

Rory ran to the door, hesitating. Larry clearly needed help, but something felt wrong. Before she could decide, he slammed into the door full-force. The wood shuddered in its frame as he battered it with inhuman strength, boom-boom-boom like artillery fire. "Let me in!" he howled, his voice warped and demonic, like something clawing its way from hell—or into it.

Her phone clattered to the floor, landing face-up, the camera feed still recording. "My phone," she whimpered, as if it had landed on Mars instead of three feet away.

She braced herself against the door, heart thundering. Her hands trembled like Larry's, breath coming in ragged gasps. She stayed silent, praying he'd leave, but the assault continued. BAM. BAM. BAM. Even the hinges screamed under the pressure. "It burns!" His demon voice penetrated the door like it was tissue paper.

She clung to the brass and steel framework, her sweaty hands slipping on glossy paint. That door was her whole world now, the only barrier between life and death. She kept her eyes locked on the camera feed, her window into Larry's nightmare.

Inside her head, silence reigned like a recording studio, while just inches away, hell itself raged. In her wildest dreams, she'd never imagined her mother's beloved home might become her tomb.

But Larry's supernatural strength had limits. The booms weakened to thuds, then whispers, then silence. The phone screen went dark from inactivity. She nudged it with her sock-covered toe, but static-proof fabric blocked the connection.

She held her position until her muscles turned to water. When she finally sank to the floor, her fingers still trembled as she dialed 911. Two rings, then dead air. The second try connected her to this message: "You've reached emergency services. All operators are assisting other callers. Please hold."

Beyond the door, an unnatural quiet settled. No wind. No lawnmowers. No leaf blowers in this manicured suburban paradise. The Ring footage showed an empty porch. Poor, psychotic, infected Larry had vanished. But that brought little comfort. She knew he was out there. Maybe trying to chew someone's face off like a zombie movie comes to life.

Fifty-three minutes of hold music later, stress forced her bladder to release. Even with the bathroom steps away, she couldn't leave her post. Amber liquid pooled on travertine tile and trickled toward the kitchen. No amount of courage could move her from that wet spot while Larry prowled the neighborhood.

Chloe's drive to Rory's house revealed an eerily empty world. Traffic had vanished like a Sunday morning dream. Abandoned cars dotted intersections, some still running, windows down, music blaring. A jacked to hell black 4Runner idled at a crosswalk, its engine purring, hyper pop rattling windows. The bass thumping away like a metronome counting down to end days.

COSTCO TOMB

THE HOUSE NUMBERS on Rory's block perched near the garage eave, barely visible in the fading light. Chloe pulled her car around and parked across the street, positioning it perfectly in view of the door camera. Oblivious to the danger lurking nearby, she took her time, adjusting air vents, wiping smudges from the navigation screen, checking her makeup in the rearview mirror, fishing for gum in her purse.

Through the driver's window, Rory's frantic movements went unnoticed. She jumped up and down, desperately mouthing words, trying to catch Chloe's attention before it was too late.

Chloe stepped out, slammed the door, and pressed the alarm. Two sharp honks pierced the quiet street. She locked eyes with Rory, who mouthed a single word: "Run."

"I can't hear you?" Chloe called out, brow furrowed in confusion.

Rory's hands moved like she was trying to reel Chloe in with an invisible rope. She fought to stay calm, screaming would only alert Larry, wherever he was hiding. If Chloe had any chance of survival, she needed to sprint toward the house right now. Every muscle in Rory's body screamed warning signals, but Chloe remained painfully unaware.

Finally, Rory abandoned subtlety. "Run!" she screamed, pointing frantically to Chloe's left.

Before Chloe could turn, an inhuman howl split the air, part human agony, part bestial rage. Fear flooded her system, but instead of choosing flight mode, she froze. Like a deer caught in headlights, she stood rooted to the asphalt, waiting for death to claim her.

Larry's second scream came closer, more guttural, raising goosebumps across her skin. His footfalls thundered against the pavement.

"Run!"

Terror had turned Chloe's legs to concrete. Her hands snapped open, dropping everything. Phone shattering on impact. Keys landing with a metallic ping. The world slowed to half-speed as she finally forced herself forward, but she'd barely gained a few feet when Larry launched himself through the air like some twisted predator, claws extended to snatch her.

He clipped her feet, sending them both tumbling onto the scorching asphalt. Within seconds, he had her pinned. Chloe thrashed, but his strength was beyond human. The hot pavement seared her exposed back as she struggled.

Rory's mind went blank with panic. *She's toast*, she thought. *The girl is dead*. Her eyes darted everywhere at once, searching for a weapon. In desperation, she yanked open the foyer closet.

Her frantic fingers brushed past winter coats and old sneakers before finding her mother's gardening gloves and a rusty trowel. She gripped the tool, then dismissed it, too small and too weak. Above, a golf umbrella caught her eye. Its steel tip glinting. The girl's screams filtered through the door, spurring Rory into action. She grabbed both tools and charged out like a knight entering a jousting tournament.

But as she closed in, her courage evaporated. The left side of Larry's face was simply... gone. Raw brain matter pulsed beneath charred flesh. Bright pus oozing from the burns. SHC had left him unrecognizable except for his dark hair, still flecked with gray.

He swiped at Chloe with blood-dripping teeth, as if trying to devour her. Her bright strawberry hair glinted against the black road. Some of it clutched in Larry's grip where he'd torn it from her scalp.

Rory hurled the trowel with all her might. It bounced off his ruined face with a pathetic clink, barely fazing him. He continued his assault, ignoring her like an annoying insect.

"Stab him!" Chloe screamed.

Rory raised the umbrella high, its steel tip glinting, and brought it down like a lightning bolt. The point punctured Larry's collarbone with a wet crunch. He howled and thrashed, giving Chloe enough space to squirm free.

For a moment, Larry knelt there, vacant and mindless. Blood and saliva dribbled from his mouth as he stared into nothing. But the instant Chloe scrambled to her feet, something switched back on. Rage flooded his eyes with terrible clarity.

Rory and Chloe shared a single glance, reading each other's thoughts. "Run!"

They sprinted toward the house, Rory in the lead. The open doorway seemed to stretch impossibly far, warping reality in this waking nightmare. Larry gained on Chloe with inhuman speed. He leaped again, but this time she dodged his grip by inches.

"It burns!" he shrieked as he hit the ground empty-handed.

Rory crossed the threshold and began closing the door before Chloe made it.

"Don't leave me out here!"

"Hurry!"

Larry face-planted on the road that turned into a skid. Road rash peeling away layers of burned flesh to reveal the raw meat beneath. His eyes bulged from their sockets like a cartoon character, mouth frozen in a silent scream. But the godless infection driving him wouldn't let him stop. He sprang up like a feral animal and resumed the chase.

Chloe slipped through the doorway and ran deeper into the house, searching blindly for sanctuary. She ping-ponged from foyer to kitchen to living room, directionless in her panic. For some inexplicable reason, she yanked open the living room curtains, desperate to track Larry's movements.

Rory secured the locks and watched the Ring camera footage. She saw Larry bypass the porch entirely, heading straight for the living room window. Before she could shout a warning, glass exploded inward. Larry's fist smashed through, sending crystalline shards raining over

Chloe. He latched onto the window frame, feet scrabbling up the siding as he tried to force his way in.

Chloe stood paralyzed, bleeding from dozens of cuts, glass fragments twinkling in her skin like deadly glitter. Her scream seemed to come from somewhere far away.

At that moment, Rory's mother's crisis management training kicked in. Kill Larry. Get to the basement. Simple priorities crystalized through the chaos. She sprinted to the kitchen, grabbed a knife, and found herself back at the broken window with no memory of the journey between.

She stabbed with mechanical precision, blade finding whatever target presented itself. Face. Arms. Hands. Chest. Shoulder. The first strike opened his face from forehead to chin. She screamed as she worked, more butcher than defender now. When the knife found his sternum, his howl shook the walls.

But no matter how much blood sprayed or how deeply she cut, Larry wouldn't retreat. The knife grew slick in her grip. Her hand slid down the blade, opening her palm. Still she stabbed, though it felt like attacking concrete. Her arms burned with exhaustion.

Larry's fingers tangled in her hair. With one final thrust, Rory drove the knife into his eye. He screamed and stumbled backward, the blade still embedded in his eye socket.

He collapsed on the front lawn, thrashing like a landed fish. Rory grabbed Chloe's arm. "We need to go now."

"I'm not going out there again." Chloe yanked free, glass fragments catching the light as they fell from her clothes.

Rory dragged her to the basement door. "We'll be safe down here."

"I'm not going down there! He'll break the door down, and then what?"

"Look." Rory pulled the door wide. "It's reinforced. He can't get in."

The door seemed ordinary from the house side, but its true nature showed on the reverse, a vault door disguised as residential hardware. Steel rivets and latches married to massive hinges. Once inside, Rory secured multiple locks and dropped a steel bar into reinforced catches.

The basement was more of a bunker than living space. Industrial shelving packed with supplies like a personal Costco. Rory guided Chloe to a couch. "I'll get the first aid kit."

Chloe absorbed her surroundings in shocked silence. The basement's oppressive quiet felt like a tomb, as if they'd descended into some post-apocalyptic mausoleum. In the stillness, every horror she'd just experienced played on repeat in her mind.

The adrenaline faded and let her pain flood back. Her head throbbed where Larry had torn out hair and scalp. Her exploring fingers found wetness, blood. The spot felt raw, meaty. She lowered her hand and cried.

Rory focused on treatment rather than comfort. She methodically cleaned wounds and extracted glass, shard by tiny shard. Chloe's face had taken the worst damage. Cuts scattered across the forehead and cheeks. A deep split in her lower lip. Her head sparkled with powdered glass.

Oddly, her knees were pristine despite the struggle on the asphalt. But her elbow showed white fat through the road rash. Worst was the bite on her palm, a chunk of flesh simply gone. The wound resembled ground meat. More concerning was the complete lack of finger movement on that hand.

Rory noticed it while irrigating the wound with saline. Despite obvious pain - Chloe hissing through clenched teeth, breathing like a woman in labor, those fingers never twitched. *Nerve damage*, Rory concluded, drawing on knowledge absorbed from her nurse mother. Larry had severed tendons and nerves with that single bite.

As bandaging progressed, Chloe grew calmer. Her tears slowed to occasional sniffles. She studied Rory with grateful eyes. "You're pretty." The words seemed to surprise them both. Logan was attractive for his age, but she hadn't expected his daughter to be beautiful. The genetics didn't track.

Rory ignored the comment and continued working. Chloe pulled her arm close. "No more, it stings."

"It needs thorough cleaning, or it might get infected." Rory's tone brooked no argument. "Try moving your fingers."

"I'll just wait for the ambulance," Chloe said, dodging the request. "You called them, right?"

Rory saw the denial, the shock setting in. But sugar-coating would help no one. "They're not coming."

"They have to. That's their job."

"Nobody is going to rescue us. We're on our own."

"Give me your phone. I'll call them myself."

"It's upstairs." Rory nodded toward the ceiling. "If you want it, go get it."

Chloe's throat worked as she swallowed. "We can't stay down here forever."

"Have you read the news?"

"Hello," Chloe's eyes rolled. "I work for the news station."

Rory blankly met her eyes, though rage added sparkle.

"Your dad sent me to check on you. Said you were sick."

"Does it look like I'm sick?"

Chloe studied Rory's clear skin, bright eyes, and healthy color. Another of Logan's lies. "No," she admitted. "You don't seem sick."

"How do you not know what's happening out there?" Rory set aside the medical supplies.

"Your dad said it wasn't a big—." Chloe caught herself. Always lies with Logan. She changed course. "Maybe this whole thing will blow over. It always does."

"Tell that to Larry."

"Who's Larry?"

"The guy who attacked you. He used to be my neighbor."

"Is he off his meds or something?"

"He's a really nice person." Rory's voice hardened. "Didn't you see his face? Half his head is missing. Did he look normal?"

Chloe shrugged. "Everything happened so fast, I didn't get a good look."

"If I had my phone, I could show you what I'm talking about," Rory said. "What happened to him is happening worldwide. Most just burn to ash. I've never seen anyone go crazy like that."

Chloe shook her head. "If something like this was happening globally, I would know."

"It's happening. People are dying. They're calling it SHC."

Fresh tears welled in Chloe's eyes. "Mr. Shelby."

Another blank stare befell her.

"My cat." Her voice cracked. "I'm all he has."

"I'm sure he'll be okay." Rory's tone suggested otherwise.

Eventually, exhaustion claimed Chloe. As she slept, Rory's mind raced. Larry was just the beginning. They needed real weapons. Umbrellas and kitchen knives wouldn't cut it against whatever these things were becoming. She'd stabbed him countless times with minimal effect. They'd gotten lucky today.

The gun safe in the corner held their best chance at survival, but Rory couldn't remember the combination. Her mother had made her write it down somewhere in her room. But during her minimalist phase after Tala's death, she'd thrown out so many "unnecessary" things. Had the combination been among them?

She examined the cut on her hand. Clean, not too deep. Full mobility retained. Unlike Chloe's wound, which had barely bled even under saline irrigation. Something was very wrong with that. And now Rory wondered, had Larry's blood entered her system through her own cut? Only time would tell.

Time tells all.

FORTY-EIGHT DARK

Dark days fell upon her. It bore the weight of fire. And high-energy electrons forged in air molecules called sprites. Forty-eight days since SHC annihilated her world. Forty-eight days since her father turned to ash. The business of reducing human flesh and bone to dust was efficient, under a minute, perhaps thirty seconds. Dante couldn't be sure. She hadn't exactly timed Jack's death, too busy trying to save a life already slipping away like smoke through her fingers.

"What did you learn from this, mijita?" Jack would ask whenever they faced setbacks in the wild, where things rarely went according to plan. If he were here now, her answer would be simple, little. She'd learned so little. How does anyone prepare for this level of horror?

What was clear then, and remains now, SHC functioned as an unparalleled killing machine. Bloodthirsty. Unstoppable. A mechanism of fire and sprite, methodically exterminating humans to the brink of extinction.

Her first encounter happened right there in their cabin's kitchen, while eating toast with preserves at the weathered table. The same cozy kitchen surrounded by lush, godless country that Jack loved more than anywhere else on earth. The part that haunted her dreams wasn't just his death, it was her failure. Even now, she believed she could have saved him.

It started with a flash of light. Lightning sparking the horizon. A sprite pinging somewhere in the stretch of wilderness. Then flames. No in-between. He'd been fine a second ago when she'd glanced up to laugh at his stupid joke. But in the heartbeat it took to look back at her toast, everything changed.

She bolted from the table when the flames engulfed Jack. At first, Dante thought the gas stove had caught his sleeve while he cooked breakfast. The kitchen sink sprayer caught her eye first, and she yanked it from the basin to douse the flames. Water showered everywhere at full blast, Jack, the floor, every surface within reach as she desperately aimed at the fire consuming her father.

For all her quick thinking, the kitchen sprayer betrayed her. Water failed her father. The flames devoured it like gasoline, hungry for more. A cast-iron pot gleamed at the bottom of the sink, sparking another idea. Even with the faucet at full blast, filling the pot took an eternity. She worked in frenzied panic, screaming, crying. Full. Half full. Any amount should smother the flame. She needed water, tons of it, fast. More water equals less flame, that's what logic dictated. But logic had no place here. Those angry flames hungered for water like a dying man in the desert.

Nothing could stop SHC. Shoveling water from the sink to the burning body left her winded. Each attempt ending in fresh disaster. She could have emptied an ocean over those flames, and they would have only craved more. The fire refused to die until Jack was no more. Only wet ash remained, drenching the floor in a soup-like consistency. A charred spiral etched into the pine boards marked where her father had stood.

Looking back, after the flame had its way, certain details stood out in stark relief. He never uttered a word. Never screamed. Only silence. Even the roaring flame was mute, as if SHC had hit some cosmic pause button. The air stayed cool. The smell of sterilization lingered, sharp and wrong. No flapping arms. No hopping around. No stop, drop, and fucking roll. No howling at the moon in agony. Just frozen in time. On fire. The only sound had been her screams, screams that still echoed in her dreams, in the dark, in the still, where wolves cried somewhere in the endless reach of godless land.

If a silver lining existed, or a lesson, or a wish upon a fucking star, it would be this: maybe Jack accepted death peacefully, and not at the mercy of an angry inferno. The thought of him suffering tormented her. No, she prayed for a painless passing, as painless as a blaze could be. Because Jackie, known to the world as Jack, deserved better than to agonize over a fiery death. He was a kind man. A loving father. And now he was nothing, but a spiral burned into pine boards, a ghost of ash and memory.

MEXICO CITY

She knew little about her mother and remembered even less. Dante vaguely recalled Lydia placing a birthday cake before her. When she blew the candles out, everything went black. She was three. That was the last birthday cake her mother served. Dante can still picture Lydia's hands. Her arms. But not her face. Every time she tries, it's fuzzy and gray.

The only thing she could conjure were fragments, spliced together like a broken film reel. Her mother might as well be a blurry cartoon character, Dante would never know the difference. The woman living inside her head wasn't the real Lydia, but an apparition.

Dante didn't even own a picture of her mother. Jack was so heartbroken after Lydia abandoned them, he destroyed every portrait. Every memory. It pained him to see his wife's image prancing around the house, taunting him. Crushing his soul daily, by the seconds.

She wanted to travel to Mexico City someday to see her mother's birth land. To smell it. To taste it. To feel the winds of Mexico City toss her hair in a summer sky. In her best dreams, she would encounter her mother during the trip.

How could she differentiate a stranger from her mother? Better yet, did she have enough information to go on? Enough to pinpoint her mother out of a crowd? The answer was yes, with ease, according to Dante.

Jack had dropped the biggest clue to the mystery. He never expected that Lydia would make an unexpected return once Dante entered her teen years. Lydia came back to crush his soul through Dante. Jack noticed the resemblance and pointed it out every chance he got. Dante was Lydia. "Practically a doppelgänger, mijita," he often said.

Even the tone of her voice was an eerie match. When tired or distracted, he sometimes missed Dante's questions. He'd say, "I didn't catch that, Lydia?" The obvious mistake was calling Dante Lydia.

He never realized the slip-up, and Dante never corrected him. Secretly, it delighted her when Jack called her Lydia. Because she was the apparition of her mother. Thanks to Jack.

Jack met Lydia in the small town of Bacalar at nineteen and fell madly in love. It wasn't love at first sight. Chance, and a turn of events, aligned the stars. Enough to bring two very different people, from two very different worlds, together. He won her heart. They married in Mexico City three months later.

Even though they moved to America years later, Mexico City would forever remain her first love. Something she learned from her father. Lydia's father was an archaeologist and scholar of the Mayan civilization. A Spaniard, he later became fascinated by ancient Mexican history while studying abroad, falling for Mexico City and Isabella. Over time, he built a comfortable life inside the walls of love for himself and Isabella, and eventually Lydia. He vowed to never part from a city that gave him so much in return, thus relinquishing all rights and obligations to Spain.

Still, the land of his ancestors would forever call to his heart. It woke him during the night. No matter the distance, and even though a shimmering sea spanned on for thousands of miles, separating him from Spain. His love remained timeless. Impressing upon him that family values and loyalty are just as important as where you choose to rest your heart. And who you choose to give it to.

PIT OF STARS

ONCE SHE COULD DO no more for Jack, she sat at the kitchen table, defeated. Soaked. Hair wild as a witch. Wearing heavy eyes. A terrifying scream escaped and rose skyward. Any passerby in the forest could hear the heartbreak.

She was still gripping the cast-iron pot, still out of breath, when she sat. Once she noticed the pot in hand, tears blinding, she hurled it across the room. It crashed through a windowpane. She buried her face in her hands and wept, looking up occasionally, as though her father would rise from the soot. Dante was determined to sit in that chair for an eternity, never leaving her father's side like a mystical sentry.

A foot stood erect, ghostlike. An arm lay among the ash on the kitchen floor for days. Jack's limbs shone with varnish flare. Something from a toy box. Shellacked like a doll part. When light struck, those appendages took on a toylike sheen. His forearm displayed a clear tattoo: Lydia. Her name in haunting detail.

The flame spared Lydia's name. Dante took it as a sign. The universe spoke. Or, at the very least, her father's dying word, if he could speak. Without doubt, this was his legacy passed down to her. From his mouth to her soul.

Many times, she thought about calling the sheriff. Or the fire department. Or forest rangers. But who would they save, exactly? Deep down, she knew the answer. She was the only person left alive. And she wasn't in danger. At least she didn't seem to think so.

Jack desperately needed help. A resurrection perhaps. Though somewhere in her heart, Dante knew he was gone. He would never return to this place, the earth from which he came. Now, he was star bound. The event was beyond anyone's control. In her head, she kept repeating, *twenty miles from town, twenty miles from nowhere.* Help wouldn't arrive in time under normal circumstances. Her father catching fire and turning to dust was far from normal. No one could help him now. No one.

After he died, she didn't have an appetite. She hungered for nothing. Basic human needs no longer applied, as though her senses burned with him. She couldn't stomach water anymore. Much less look at it. She hated water. Water didn't save her father. Water was at fault.

She couldn't ignore Jack's remains laying in the kitchen. No matter how hard she tried. And waltz past the sink, the one that failed her father, and root through the refrigerator for food. Something horrific happened in this place. Whatever took him, had left her empty and lost.

"Like all things in life, mijita, this too shall pass, because nothing lasts forever. Even heartbreak." After a few days, a sweet sourness hung in the air. Later, she would grow to recognize that smell. Death brought an eerie solitude. She was alone for the first time. Abandoned in the forest.

Dante grabbed a giant black trash bag from underneath the sink and began the slow process of disposing of Jack's leftovers. Doll parts may look fake but carry foul notes in just days. Like stumbling over a deer carcass in the woods. A touch of sweetness lingered there, too. She couldn't identify the sweet fragrance. Overripe pineapple or something fruity. But that couldn't be right. Inaccurate in every way. Her sense of smell was screwy. Maybe it burned up with Jack. She suspected it was all in her head. Maybe the death of Jack wasn't real either. Perhaps none of it existed. It had to be one big nightmare. And she'd wake soon, she assured herself, she'd wake. She'd wake one day to find Jack sitting in his favorite chair.

Jack's remnants were scant. Though those limbs fouled the entire cabin. During the cleaning process, she stopped many times to dry heave. Stomach acid filled her throat, but not much else. Covering her nose and mouth helped little. Soon, she hauled ass to the sink several times to vomit. From there, the acid in her belly ran dry. No saliva or bile would come. So, she spent the rest of time retching away.

Jack and Dante spent a lot of time venturing the woods together. She knew every trail, every stream, every notable landmark. She knew his wishes. While walking through the woods, they talked about many things, including their feelings, beliefs, and politics. Jack constantly contemplated something. Something to discuss. Something to pass down to Dante. He had so much knowledge to share. He sometimes lacked the time to convey everything to her. As though Jack had an expiration date stamped on his forehead. And now that she thinks of it, Jack was right. Time did not favor him. Time quickened him. Time stole him before the age of forty-seven.

On one of those excursions, death became the topic. Her father didn't want a burial. Neither casket nor grave. "Those things only torture the living, mijita." And he wasn't keen on tormenting his only daughter in life or in death. He didn't want her to feel guilty about not visiting his grave regularly. "Live your life, mijita. I want you to be happy, God forbid, if something should ever happen to me."

For him, how he viewed the world, especially concerning death, was this: the spirit no longer inhabits the body. Where it goes from there, he didn't know. Though he had theories. He knew the soul had abandoned the body at death. "If you're missing me, and you need to talk, talk to the sky, mijita. I'll be listening no matter where you are."

PURIFY THE SKY

Dante took time building the fire pit. Arranging each log to form a pyramid. This configuration ensured the heat would disperse evenly. Fast and steady. A righteous burn. Her father taught her the laws of the pit. Similar to the flames that killed him. If she didn't know better, she'd almost think Jack lit his own death. He was gifted enough to incinerate anything, without leaving a trace, including himself.

She stared at the trash bag for a while and didn't set it in the pit right away. She cried for some time. Her eyes never left the bag. In that moment, the entire thing seemed so final. As though she was embracing her father's farewell. Soon enough, when she gains the courage, his molecules will travel toward the ether, forever. Though, nothing could be further from her mind. She wasn't ready to let him go. She would never be ready to let him go.

Yet, as the day drew dark, and the fire reduced to embers, the bag tested her sanity. And it was now, or not at all. She lowered the bag into the pit and watched it curl, and peel away, exposing his arm. Black smoke billowed star bound. Cinder quickly turned to blue flame, concentrating all its efforts on the bag. Hisses and pops shot tiny embers from the pit. A sizzling noise rose and mimicked grilling meat. Every drop of him became fire. He was fire. And she sank to the ground in a moment of sorrow. Flames dancing in her eyes. Heart on fire. Everything set on fire. She screamed as if her heart was burning right alongside her father.

Dante built a fire pit that was true and just. With flames purer than pure. Pure enough to reach the stars.

DIRECT SIGHT OF PACO

AFTER CREMATING whatever remained of Jack, she retrieved a dusty quilt from the hall closet and went to the kitchen and spread it on the floor. Covering the swirl mark. The pattern was still vibrant and intricate. A way to erase death from her eyes.

Once more time had passed, she regained appetite and thirst. Thirst took priority over food. She gulped water ravenously. She bathed in water. Something she thought she'd never do again. Most of it dribbled down her chin and neck, soaking her t-shirt. Her chest clung to wet cotton like glue. The water was so cold and fresh, she starved for a belly full.

Not drinking or eating for days upon days caused her appetite to shrink. The liquid filled quickly, and once she couldn't drink anymore, the hunger melted away. Pushed to the back of her consciousness as a distant afterthought.

In time, the water was no longer plenty, and she ate a little. And soon, she grew exhausted. She slept twelve, sometimes fifteen hours a day. Every ounce of energy drained from her body. Though she forced herself out of bed to get something to eat. Visit the restroom. But she always sought the comforts of bed minutes later. Hibernating in that lifeless room. No tick pitter patter. Ticks always squeezed through the spaces between the timber. Inching along the window sill, hungry for blood. Of any kind. Like SHC. A cabin made of cypress, in the deep woods, still attracting its kind.

With the blankets pulled over her head, insulating herself from the devastation. She kept picturing Jack and the flame. Flame and Jack. Though insulating herself from the memory of Jack failed. SHC tortured her mind. Minute after minute. The second she crawled out from under the blankets, her soul shattered every time she landed eyes on Jack. A picture. His muddy boots sitting near the front door, that's where they always lived. Before SHC. Even now. For all eternity.

What occurred to her, no matter where eyes eventually settle, Jack was there. He was always there. Smiling like a lightbulb. Jack was in the support beams that carried the roof. In the nails that fastened floorboards. Jack was everywhere all at once. Even in the oxygen she breathed. The cabin of Jack became her tomb.

She used the downstairs bathroom to avoid the smell of Jack's aftershave in the upstairs bathroom. Something Paco. Which made her eyes water every time. Sometimes she never made it to the restroom. Instead, she'd crawl right back into bed and bawl. So, she boarded the upstairs bathroom and stuffed towels under the door's threshold to block the scent.

On day fifteen, posthumously, she woke from a nightmare with daylight warming her face. Her cheeks glistened against the dusty light coming in. She took time to realize she had been crying in her sleep.

In her dream, Jack told her to head to Mexico City. "Safest place on earth, mijita." Visiting Mexico City has been her plan since twelve. And she wasn't sure if her subconscious was screwing with her. Or was it possible? Could her father reach her from way out there? From somewhere out in the great whatever one calls it.

Dante was tempted to leave right then. Heed her father's words. Pack only the essentials and head out the door. Never to return. Though she would not go right away. She was in no shape to travel. Even if it meant driving into town. Glenwood Springs was twenty miles down a gravel ridden snaky road. Loaded with massive potholes. And steep hills. Decades of erosion. And so on.

Her father had a Jeep. All tuned up and jacked to hell like Mr.

Universe. It thrived on this abuse, given Jack's preparation, it would perform admirably. The road ahead was perilous. One she could get stuck on. Die on. Stringy curves and loose gravel sent vehicles sailing off a cliff. Even for an experienced driver. The only difference now, and an important one; her father would not be in the passenger seat to guide her. If she veered off the road into oblivion no rescue team would come. That's if she survived.

Glenwood Springs, though small, boasted a strong and growing population of ten thousand. Red brick buildings, smashed together, constructed like row homes. Ran up and down Grand Avenue. It included a grocery store, wilderness to table restaurants, pharmacy, radio station and a sheriff station, among other businesses. At the far edge of town, where Grand Avenue ended, sat a gas station with several pumps, and a three-bay garage.

This gas station, more of a hybrid store, was Humble Traveler. On top of filling people's tanks, it had a video rental section inside. Snacks and drinks. Same as any convenience store. Fresh donuts made daily by five. Car repair, with a full-time mechanic on-site. However, fried chicken ensured their success.

At the back of the store, behind a tiny service counter, sat a galley kitchen equipped with four fryers. Regardless of the time, six to seven people stood in line at the small counter for fried chicken.

Humble Traveler was a popular hangout for the locals. They even set up a few tables outside, where the patriarchs gathered and gabbed. Which they did almost every day, except on Sundays. Humble Traveler closed at noon on that day.

Dante took a decadent shower. Letting hot water open pores and dissolve the anguish within. Campfire still clinging to skin and hair. And she scrubbed and reconditioned a body that hadn't touched soap and water in fifteen days. That long, smokey head of hair turned greasy and lifeless. And required three lathers, and an entire bottle of conditioner before burned pine and decay parted.

She found the skin easier to manage. Somehow, it had a waxy texture to it, almost filmlike. Although, her pits, marred by sweat, delivered a tangy funk. Her teeth had layers of plaque. And a gunky residue that smelled of tobacco, more burned pine and decay. Even though she brushed three times and flossed twice, her mouth still felt unclean. Not convinced her breath was minty enough. Her teeth were not slick at all afterward.

She had never gone this long without changing her clothes. Each clean article she put on bore a chemical fragrance. The laundry detergent was unscented. Before this, she never noticed the smell, as though overexposure made her immune to the unscented flavor. Now she realizes unscented detergent carries a soapy, chemical note.

Her senses were born again. She tasted and smelled everything ten times more intensely. Its psychedelic wonder imbued her with childlike, vibrant senses.

Her cell phone had perched on the dresser for fifteen days. Attracting a coat of dust. Once the flames engulfed Jack, she couldn't bear to look at the phone. While she was brushing tangled, wet hair, she picked up the device with a curious expression. To her surprise, the phone still had a 10 percent charge. The moment she touched the screen, several social media notifications shone. Each notification she pressed took her straight to the app's website. Then displayed an error message: 404 PAGE NOT FOUND.

Some sites had a 🙁, instead of a 404 page.

It wasn't just social media displaying error messages, all reported broken links. Corrupted or something. Out of frustration, she googled, why is there a social media blackout? The search results showed nothing to do with the blackout. She spent time re-wording her question, hoping something would pop up. Minutes had gone by, and she couldn't find an explanation. It wasn't until she searched news feeds dated fifteen days ago the mystery started making sense.

News articles reported error messages too when she tried accessing web content. Terrifying links about SHC flooded the internet. Some displayed information about the death toll, though she couldn't read the entire article because the links were no longer active.

Page after page, death toll and SHC in bright, big lettering, Helvetica font, smashed together, had annihilated the internet. What little information she could read scared her. And for some odd reason, she concluded SHC had to be a virus or deadly flu.

A major contributing factor to her father's death, she assured herself, had to be a deadly contagion. Yet never did she read SHC was a virus or flu. She came to that conclusion on her own. That's what the news was about these days. A new deadly flu strain. A new deadly fungus. Lethal bacteria. Plastic oceans. Melting polar caps, and on.

Scouring the internet made her paranoid all of a sudden. Dante thought Jack might have infected her. Maybe, she wondered, the process hadn't fully kicked in yet. Maybe she would burn alive too. But not right away, not like her father. Her death was stuck on some kind of time release. Taking its sweet ass time before ending her.

When the answers didn't come quick enough, she dialed 911 as fingers trembled. It didn't even ring once before a recorded message blared in her ear. "We are experiencing a high call volume. Please hold for the next available call taker." After the message, everything went silent. No going away to music. No static. Just dead air.

Her phone tracked calls by minutes and seconds. The phone timer confirmed 911 remained connected. She switched the call to the speaker and continued searching the internet. Ten minutes had passed, and dead air filled her ears. Dante became impatient and ended the call. And dialed again. As before, the emergency line played the same prerecorded message.

She ended the call and raced toward Jack's den. Because of the cabin location, "twenty miles from nowhere," Jack liked to tell people. Her father created an emergency call list, for the 'oh, shit moment', tacked to the corkboard in the den.

Jack had bought an expensive shortwave radio. Another way to reach the outside world. If the Wi-Fi went down. The only way they could get a Wi-Fi signal among all the trees was having a satellite dish installed at the peak of the roof.

On stormy days, towering conifers and aspens would sway with vengeance. Often puking snow, and leaves, and pine needles against the satellite dish. Blocking the line of sight caused the signal to vanish.

Sometimes Jack would climb the steep roof to clear the debris from the dish. Except one time he slipped on ice buildup on the aluminum singles, and fell off the roof, and fractured both ankles. Thankfully, he landed on his feet and not on his back. His back wasn't in good shape to begin with. Long after the accident, he didn't bother clearing the dish anymore. "Let nature fix it, mijita" he told Dante over dinner, when the Wi-Fi went down for a third time that day.

OVER?

THE SHERIFF'S emergency line sat first on Jack's list, their radio frequency right next to it. Her eyes stayed glued to each number as she dialed, as though under a spell. When a ringtone chimed in her ear instead of the pre-recorded message, excitement and relief washed over her.

The phone just kept ringing. She let it ring and ring before hanging up. Dialing again did no good. Their radio frequency delivered only crickets in the meadow. At every turn, silence or endless rings.

Jack had scribbled ten numbers on the list in red Sharpie. Not one answered. Not even Humble Traveler picked up. "That's impossible," she said.

Humble Travelers always had someone on duty. It wasn't a Sunday. They kept five to six people working during the week, even more on Saturday. Hell, on Saturdays they'd run out of fried chicken before six. A serious problem dawned on her then.

In utter distress, Dante grabbed the shortwave radio and began transmitting. Finding another frequency was unnecessary, she chose Bonnie's channel. Bonnie lived even farther in the woods, a recluse who shunned cell phones and computers.

She had a curious look about her. Shoulder-length wavy hair with thick streaks of gray. Spooky, clear, colorful eyes, almost machinelike. Her face showed meticulous sculpting, every feature balanced, though age poked through with crow's feet at the corners of eyes and mouth.

She draped herself in crystals, turquoise, and sterling jewelry. "An ex-hippie from the sixties, mijita," were her father's exact words.

Bonnie swore the government was trying to capture her. She'd helped organize political protests around the country. "Sometimes peaceful, sometimes rowdy," she claimed. Bonnie said the government had tagged them as communist.

Her first attempt at reaching Bonnie went nowhere. This wasn't unusual, sometimes it took a few tries before she'd answer. Dante spoke into the receiver, repeating the same phrase. "Janis, this is Ladybug. Come in, over." Bonnie had dubbed her "Ladybug" years ago.

A peculiar phenomenon occurred whenever they'd bump into each other. No matter where they met, Bonnie would spot a ladybug crawling on Dante. This fascinated her to no end.

Mysticism consumed Bonnie's life. She believed nature could determine whether a person was good. "The universe uses nature to warn of impending doom," she'd said over dinner once. "Insects communicate to attract attention." She told Dante the ladybugs were trying to tell her something. "The home you seek lives in you."

Janis was a reference to Joplin, the famous singer. Dante hadn't known who Janis Joplin was until she asked Jack why Bonnie used that code name. She was about to give up when Bonnie's voice burst through, breathless. "Ladybug! This is Janis. Go ahead, over!"

Dante clutched the receiver as though it might vanish. "It's me, Janis! It's Ladybug! Over."

A celebratory scream from Bonnie rang through the static-filled background. Fearing something had happened, Dante transmitted, "Janis! You still there, over?"

"Thank the stars. You're alive. Over."

The word 'alive' hit Dante wrong. Her mind locked in a flashback—Jack bathing in flame. Tears filled her eyes, and she didn't know if they were from sadness or joy. Perhaps both. Another person's voice nourished her soul, yet she said nothing in return.

"Ladybug, over?"

Dante squeezed her eyes shut and held her breath. Telling Bonnie about her father would forever seal the devil's flame. No going back now. "Dad's gone. I couldn't save him, I tried, I swear, but, but—." She stopped transmitting and cried.

"I'm so sorry, honey." Silence filled the radio waves. Bonnie waited, then transmitted, "Honey, you couldn't save him. It's not your fault."

Dante shot back, "Yes, it is."

"It's happening everywhere, honey. They're calling it SHC."

Through half-sobs, Dante transmitted, "What's happening out there? I tried looking but the internet's messed up."

"Nobody knows how it started."

"Is it a virus?"

"I wish I had a better answer for you, honey. We just don't know."

"Am I going to die?"

The radio waves went quiet. Dante stopped crying and straightened up, alert and wide-eyed. She transmitted, "Bonnie! I mean Janis! Are you still there, over?"

"Listen to me carefully, honey. You need to stay away from people. Don't go to town, don't come here. Over."

"Why, over?"

"Do you remember Kippa, over?"

"Yeah, over."

"She thinks some people might be carriers, over."

"How does she know? Over."

"Tom and I were planting root vegetables in the greenhouse. I stood right next to him, tending to purple beets. Out of nowhere, I saw a flash of light at the corner of my eye. When I looked up to find its source, Tom just... went up in flames. Couldn't put the fire out." Dante heard her voice quiver, fighting tears.

"Dad was in the kitchen when it happened." Saying those words felt like driving a nail through her soul. Maybe she was to blame.

Bonnie sniffled and cleared her throat. "If we're carriers, then we need to quarantine. Over."

"For how long, over?"

"I wish I knew the answer to that, honey, over."

"I'm sorry about Tom. Over."
"Thank you. Over."
"Ladybug, over and out."
"Keep in contact. Let me know you're okay. These woods can be a lonely place for us girls. Janis, over and out."

GLUTTON DOWN PROVISIONS

DANTE WENT to the kitchen straight away after speaking with Bonnie. Her father had an important meeting in the city on the 21st. They'd only brought a week's worth of provisions to the cabin. Before the flame came, they'd planned on driving into town to buy whatever they needed at the grocery store. Now, nothing would be so easy. She emptied everything from the kitchen cabinets and fridge, then lined and stacked the leftovers on the table.

She took inventory to see how dire the food situation was. The pantry held one-pound bags of kidney beans. A cup of basmati rice, intended for vegetarian chili. Half-eaten jar of almond butter—it never lasted, being one of her favorite snacks. Oat milk. Two eggs. Irish butter. Three slices of grain bread. From a specialty deli came whipped mozzarella, a cheese her father loved. Canned tomato sauce. Tube of tomato paste. Miniature bottle of mustard, Worcestershire, olive oil. Wild-caught sardines packed in oil. A sleeve of water biscuits. One small package of raw almonds. Two blemished apples. Shriveled banana. Four red onions, God knows why. Two bottles of beer and a half bottle of wine. A couple of elk steaks sitting in the freezer—Jack's favorite. Otherwise, nothing else, with plenty of room to spare.

Over the last few years, Dante had followed a vegetarian lifestyle.

Not out of any grandiose crusade to save the animals or the planet. Rather, the taste. The mere thought of eating veins and fat grossed her out. She didn't consider herself a true vegetarian because she ate cheese and eggs. Although Beth, a close friend, accused her of being an ovo-vegetarian after ordering an omelet with spinach and brie at a restaurant in Park Meadows.

Beth knew Dante didn't eat meat. At first, Dante thought Beth was paying her an insult. Beth's behavior could be cynical and judgmental. Dante scoffed, considering it a joke. Yet Beth sat there looking confused, and said, "Well, you are, aren't you?"

Dante smiled and said, "Yeah, of course." Embarrassed, not knowing what that meant.

Later, after dropping Beth off, she googled ovo-vegetarian while parked in front of Beth's house. After reading the definition, Dante realized she had vegetarian tendencies. She might be a vegetarian or at least a mild version thereof. That's what ovo-vegetarians were, they dabbled in the vegetarian lifestyle but weren't committed to purity. Some even ate bacon. Even she sometimes ate bacon. Which was a no-no.

Five days was too long for something so perishable to last. So, she ate withering fruits and vegetables first. The natural sugar and fiber only kept her full for a short time. Her metabolism sped up in just one hour. The first bite, an apple, jolted her stomach. She was more driven by her senses than logic. She craved more. Much more, as if she were a wolf ravening in a blizzard with no prey in sight. Food was on the brain every moment of the day. She sat in other rooms, just to avoid making eye contact with the kitchen.

That damn swirl mark covered by a dusty blanket made her feel guilty every time she looked at it. And the desire to survive, to stuff her face, to stuff her belly, overpowered all other emotions. Under those circumstances, after going back and forth inside her head, tormenting herself over the shame in her heart, SHC didn't give Jack that luxury. She ate anything, despite portion size. The heart of the wolf won. Just as before. And she made her way back to the kitchen and continued snacking.

She hadn't eaten well in fifteen days, and now her body was catching up, requiring more sustenance. Hour after hour. Tin after tin. She ate crackers, or what remained of them. Irish butter. She cut it in thick slivers, allowing the squares to liquefy on her tongue. This left a thin coat of fat along the gumline, providing a waxy texture.

She even added olive oil to beans, rice, and vegetables. Anything she could, to add saturated fat to her depleting diet. She started eating this way after reading blogs on the internet. Googling How long can you survive without food? One link claimed four days. While another boasted fourteen. The most optimistic blog claimed forty-six days. As long as you drink plenty of water and somehow find a fat source. Saturated fats are the best. An internet source claimed the body metabolized this compound slowly. One blog post provided a spark of hope. Suggesting the forest offers many edible trees for people to eat. Short-term solution. Only use in extreme cases. Near death scenario. She was optimistic for a moment, as though she'd hit the mother lode of knowledge. Acres upon acres of forest surrounded the whole damn cabin. She spent a while thinking about whether people could live by eating tree bark. If only, she thought. But would it digest? That's the real challenge. Would it digest?

Even so, something in the back of her mind told otherwise. Jack was gifted, especially when surviving the wild. He never mentioned eating tree bark. She would have stored that information in her memory forever. Over time, as hunger burrowed deep, dizzy spells knocked her silly. Followed by hunger pangs. Every time she stood, her limbs became unsteady and shaky. Her entire body was rubbery, as though she had run a marathon.

No matter how carefully she planned each sparse meal through portion control, and denying her panza the spoils of gluttony, hunger inevitably won, destroying her remaining willpower. The supplies seemed to vanish before her eyes.

She knew troubling things rose when she reached for the mustard and Worcestershire. Both had sugar and sodium to offer, nothing more. Zero nutritional value. Still, she mixed a strange slurry, adding salt and pepper, and oregano, and basil and from there, feasted.

And she embraced what was to follow, death. Unlike Jack, she worried her molecules wouldn't rise. No kissing stars by fuel from a fire pit. Rather, her trajectory led hell bound. A different fire. In her last hours, her body will decompose into the sofa.

ELK, THE OTHER FOOD GROUP

IN THE WAKE of Jack's death, minor catastrophes erupted everywhere. She had no way of fixing them, either. Or to grieve. Or find closure. SHC was always there, destroying every thought.

Isolation began playing tricks on her. One night, she stayed awake until three o'clock talking to Jack. They even played a game of cards. She won for the first time. From there, Jack visited on the regular. At 11:20 a.m., Jack got Dante drunk. She drank wine and beer. And polished the whiskey bottle hidden in his desk. Jack cheered her on.

Stuck in an empty cabin. Isolated in the forest. Armed with only a cell phone, and little more, set her imagination and paranoia on fire. She may have not burned alongside her father, but her brain was turning to molten glass.

When Jack didn't visit, she would sometimes escape reality by having a good cry. Despite her best efforts to ignore it, the image of her father engulfed in flames toyed with her mind. The cell phone never left her hands. Even when going to the bathroom. And when dreamland called, her subconscious would take over. She clutched the device to her chest in her sleep, as if it were a newborn.

She combed the internet, wishing for good news. A government agency will post updates on SHC. She went google crazy. She googled every word combination she could think of. Using keywords like SHC virus, SHC contagion, SHC death toll. Then she would spell the entire thing out, spontaneous human combustion and on and on. Convinced that a virus caused the world to vanish.

None of her efforts paid off. The internet provided quick results. Though none she could read. The information given was few and inconsequential. Enough to grab the reader's attention. Yet when she held breath and clicked the link, it would display a 404 page.

Over time, the internet was dying. Death wasn't immediate. It stumbled through digital levels like a video game. Then, one day, the internet entered a new phase. Not a black phase, but a white one. On day twenty-three, the internet burned blinding white. Where links pixelated and melted into a milky digital galaxy.

Strangely, the google search engine was operational. Though, once she pressed enter, it led her to a white digital ghost town. The Wi-Fi worked flawlessly. The internet never quit. Just reduced to white pixelation. Then flat white pages. Disintegration.

The same thing happened with the cellular signal. When the internet became useless, Dante called each number on Jack's emergency list three times a day. Plus, every phone number stored in her cell. A barrage of calls started at seven, when daylight peaked its nose through the blinds. Then circling back and revitalizing the call regiment at noon. And ending the last call at eleven.

Days and days of droning ringtones made her ears buzz well after the calls ended, as though her eardrum morphed into a dial tone. But then again, cell service lasted longer than the internet.

At seven, day thirty-three, when she called the sheriff's department, the phone didn't ring once. Instead, a recorded message blared. "We're sorry, we cannot complete your call as dialed." Every single number she dialed, no matter what time of day, this message, or a version, played thereafter.

Day thirty-five tested her vegetarian taste buds on a fundamental level. The last remaining food she couldn't eat. Elk. No matter how bad her tummy growled. The elk steaks belonged to Jack. It would destroy her heart to eat the essence of Jack.

She peeked in once in a while, though. Checking on things. Still frozen solid in the freezer, peering at her, tempting her, looking more edible each day, even tasty.

The notion entered her brain after consuming the last kidney bean. A prelude to bigger troubles ahead. She exhausted the supply of concoctions. She used every ingredient, including all the spices. For breakfast, lunch, and dinner, she ate McCormick's steak seasoning. One teaspoon at a time. And yesterday she ate the last cinnamon stick, which she sucked on the entire day before swallowing it at bedtime after turning out the lights.

From the start, before the flame devoured Jack, Dante weighed 106 pounds. And she never made it a habit to weigh herself, only when they visited the cabin. In the bathroom sat a scale, dreary yellow. Rust eating through the glossy enamel. The scale sat in the far corner, tucked near the sink, facing the shower. When she pulled the cotton curtain back after showering, there it was, staring her down, ready to criticize her weight.

She feared the scale every time eyes landed on it. The scale terrorized her. Her gut twisted over the thought of climbing aboard. Each time she stepped on the scale, fear took over. Her heart hammered away beneath that boney frame. Dante almost passed out a few times when the needle on the meter spit out death. Her eyes worked just fine. 20/20. She didn't need a scale to convince she was turning into a walking corpse. That same corpse haunted her every time she spied herself in the mirror.

She was always checking on things these days, assessing. Reassess her weight. As it stood, 73 1/2 pounds was the end all number. After that, she stopped weighing herself. It wasn't so bad when she lost a pound here and there. But, when she lost four pounds in a day after waking from a nap it frightened the hell out of her. Every day when she woke, she wondered, will I die today? How would I know for sure I'm not already dead? The sickness toyed with her minute after minute.

Wilting away on the sofa. Somewhere between awake and perching death. And all the while still pondering whether to eat elk. To eat Jack. Dante heard a sharp buzz come from the shortwave radio, after the thing went dark for weeks. She scrambled to her feet and sprinted to the den. A high-pitched squeal barreled from her mouth faster than she could comprehend. A tone she hardly recognized, as if a ten-year-old stole her voice box. "This is Ladybug! Read you loud and clear, over!"

"Ladybug, this is Janis, over."

"Go ahead, over." Her famished body was making a serious comeback, as if the belly was stuffed turkey-style. No longer weak. No longer plagued by bone rattle. Bonnie's voice provided a seven-course meal.

"I've got news. Kippa thinks carriers might be immune. They might be both. Not sure how all that stuff works. So far, not one person has died from coming together. They're mobilizing a group to head to Anschutz Medical Center in Aurora. Maybe we can get some answers. Hopefully some of those doctors survived. It's worth a shot. There's nothing left for us here, over."

All that built up anticipation for good news melted. Any ounce of joy sailed into the pit of her gut. Aurora was not her intended journey. Pushing her farther away from where she wanted to go. She had no intention of heading east. Her heart lay south, somewhere in Mexico City.

She couldn't help thinking Lydia might have survived SHC. And in that nanosecond, she decided, "What the hell" she'd give it a shot too. Like Bonnie, like the survivors. She'd go on a journey. Except Mexico City was her white whale.

"I'm not going. I need to find out if mom is still alive. I've got the Jeep. It'll make it, over." Dante pulled up google maps on her phone and typed in Mexico City. The little pinwheel icon whirled, seemingly frozen. She cleared the search bar and typed Mexico City again. The circle of death greeted and never supplied directions.

"Listen to me honey, you going off on your own is dangerous. You're going to get yourself killed. It's not safe out here. This thing, whatever the heck it is, might happen again. We're safer in numbers, over."

"Do you have a map, over?"

"How are you going to fill up that gas-guzzler of yours with nobody working the pumps? You'll run out of gas in a hundred miles. And if you manage to get gas the first time, you might not be so lucky the next, over."

"How are you guys getting gas, over?"

"A girl in our group is an engineer. She made a fuel pump that draws gas from the underground storage tanks, over."

LITTLE BROWN GOD

SHE SAT at her father's desk and leaned way back and thought for a minute. No, she didn't even consider how to get gas while on the road. Her brain was stuck on how the world operated before SHC. Rather than how end days works today. She planned on using Jack's credit card for the trip. Not once did she kick around the idea the banking system had gone kaput? That everything went kaput. Gas pumps included. No, Dante hadn't made a clever plan. She'd wing it, though.

Fake it until you make it, enter her mind, giving her strong confidence to adapt and improvise. Her first job was a disaster and a blessing. She knew nothing about making cappuccinos or lattes, with whip cream, and half and half and almond milk. The liquid was in plastic cups, and tiny green straws emerged from their centers. Cups and straws she swore leached forever chemicals into the drinks. Infecting people over time with cancer if they drank out of those vessels every day of their lives. Which seemed to be the case. Although her father mentioned excessive sugar levels would cause kidney failure and diabetes first.

Her poor performance initially didn't matter. She made far more mistakes than the average person. When an employee asked her if she could work at the cold station, confident as she was, she said "Sure." She messed up so badly. Mixing drinks crazily with whatever she could get her hands on. Never using the right ingredients for anything. Not only was she in the weeds most of the time, but re-fire hell too. Customers demanded she remake their drinks because they tasted awful. It's too sweet. It's not sweet enough. The espresso tastes sour. And she didn't disagree. She imagined the drinks tasted awful. Way worse than customers could put into words.

On the receiving end, at the end of the service counter, where customers impatiently waited for their concoctions to come to the window. Her initial excitement soured as every drink she served was screwed to hell. Various liquids brimming. Slathered in fingerprints. Streaks crying like a crazy science experiment. Customers bitched non-stop, as if the entire world had just gone up in smoke. One customer yelled at her and called her an "Incompetent brown little twit." The brown part she understood, but she had to google twit because she didn't even know what that word meant.

Day after day, she worked at the hot station and had similar results. She was driven by the need to get it right. To the level between somewhere or bust. She never quit. And she learned from her mistakes. Improving in a matter of weeks.

Soon, after another customer had a meltdown because the espresso was too cold, Dante left little brown twit status in the rearview mirror. And elevated to god status. A customer nicknamed her that. After she made a mocha with many sugar-free flavorings and almond milk in under thirty seconds. Once the woman received her drink so fast, her eyes grew toward the ceiling. She pointed a long, bedazzled nail at Dante and said, "You are a god."

THE TASTE OF HOME

"Do you have a map, over?"

Dante heard Bonnie groan, as though she forgot to stop transmitting. "No, over."

"Does the used bookstore on Grand Avenue have one, over?"

"Check Humble Traveler first. They seem to have everything, over."

"I hope you receive some good news in Aurora. Over."

"Listen honey, be careful in town. Someone finally answered the sheriff's station radio a few weeks back. She said her name was Sarah Walter. Never heard of her. She claimed to rent the Meyers's place on the river. Airbnb, I guess. I didn't know the Meyers rented the place, you know how Mr. Meyers can get. That old goat. Something odd about the whole thing, over."

"Okay, I'll keep a lookout. Love you, Bonnie, over and out."

"Oh, sweet girl. Don't let your guard down for a second and don't trust anyone. Kippa said survivors are doing horrible things, preying on women, killing folks. Things like this make people unpredictable. They'll do anything to survive. Janis, I mean, oh the hell with it, Bonnie, over and out."

Several hunting rifles lay in Jack's closet. His favorite rifle was the

Anschütz. It was small, light, and powerful. Silky smooth bolt action that glides with zero effort. And fast. Straight follow-up. She simply had to point and shoot. In the corner, the polished wood and cold steel gleamed, barrel aimed at the ceiling. She looped the Anschütz strap over her shoulder and dumped the rest of the ammo into a satchel hanging on a hook.

On the other side of the room, sat a red duffle, perched at the edge of a chair. This was his hunting bag. He packed a headlight, waterproof matches, knife, water filter, Vaseline, cotton balls, and compass for emergencies. But no map. Jack lost his favorite map four months ago on an overgrown trail. Somewhere south of the cabin.

The cabin provided only a handful of supplies for the Jeep. Among the things she packed were a sweater, underwear, sanitary products, a waterproof parka, socks, a toothbrush, and other essentials. Two five-gallon jerry cans, full of gasoline, sat on the hitch gate before the trip. Jack did this whenever he planned to hunt.

Despite packing everything and having it ready to go, she remained. Something inside herself wanted to hold off a while longer. It wasn't until the forty-eighth day that the power went out. This sort of thing happened occasionally around these parts. And would return within forty-eight hours. Though she couldn't count on it this time. At minimum, she hoped the power outage wasn't caused by SHC.

She again, was stuck with hard choices to make. A generator sat in the crawl space beneath the cabin. The only problem is it needed fuel to stay alive. Bad idea. Gas was a rare commodity now, and she would not waste it on keeping the lights on. Or refrigerate bare shelves. She needed every drop of gasoline to reach Mexico City.

Dante locked everything up, just as her father showed her how, as though preparing for a long winter. She took a hard look around while facing the cabin. In her heart, she already left. But fond memories tied her to this place for all time. Whatever time remained. The ones where her father showed her how to hunt and fish and survive a godless land. Where he transformed a shy, unsure of herself girl into a strong woman. And he did it with love and kindness. One day, she promised herself, she'd make it back this way. Home is home.

But before she left, she cooked the elk steaks. It's better to travel the country on a full stomach than an empty one. One never knows. This might be the last thing she ever ate. The elk were juicy, plentiful, and good.

FRIED CHICKEN DREAMS

THE JEEP'S massive tires crunched and whined as it bit down on the gravel road. Puking pebbles and silt out the rear like a dust storm. She steered, mindful. Easing through twisty turns, as though she were docking a giant yacht. She navigated around every hill, deep pothole, and other deadly features of the road. Driving twenty-five miles an hour the entire way brought her to the edge of town under an hour.

The first building she came upon was Humble Traveler. From where she stood, brick buildings and pointy roofs were visible above the trees. Watching the small town gently rise from the lush forest thrilled her, as if she had touched down on a new planet.

Trapped in the woods for forty-eight days, and having zero contact with the outside world made her lose touch with reality. She felt like an avatar from a video game. An avatar just released into the sequel. Nothing seemed real to her. Who knows, maybe she was dead and just didn't know it yet.

She parked the Jeep in front of the gas pump and got out. The digital display on the pump flashed digital black: $40.02. Two other vehicles occupied pumps at the far end of the station. Unoccupied, as though the drivers went inside to pay for gas or pick up fried chicken for dinner on their way home. That was a good sign, she assured herself. Everything appears to function correctly.

Another encouraging sight was a pristine, vintage pickup, parked near the entrance. It belonged to Dennis, what's his face, she thought. The guy who always wore the same flannel shirt and work denim and steel toe boots. Long beard. Full head of white hair but thinning on top. Always the comedian. Telling dirty jokes when ringing customer's items at the register. Some being on the cruder side. Man or woman didn't matter. He told everyone the same jokes.

Jack thought Dennis was a pervert. Telling those jokes to young girls. Or women. Or whoever walked through the door. Despite Jack's disapproval. Dante found his jokes entertaining. Some were original. Though she agreed with Jack's assessment. Dennis was a pervert.

Although, one glaring, horrifying truth came into view. From across the way, lying on pavement at the main entrance, was a swirl mark. Large enough to be human. One of the gas pumps was blocking her view, and she couldn't get a good look. Her vantage point prevented her from seeing body parts emerge from the ash.

The convenient store had windows that reached the sidewalk to the roofline and wrapped the length of the store. A three-car garage attached to the side of the building had a bay still open, with a rusty blue beetle on a lift.

Beer neon signs blinked and pulsed in the windows alongside advertisements for vodka and whiskey. Lottery signage showing the latest jackpot. One nearing a billion dollars. Beyond the cluttered glass lay pitch-black, as though someone had cut the lights. That profound darkness was like looking into the abyss of a black hole.

The mere idea of strolling past the front door and descending into darkness, a darkness filled with so much uncertainty, electrocuted her heart. Dante remembered what Bonnie told her, "Trust no one". She grabbed the Anschütz from the Jeep, loaded a round, and crept toward the entrance with the barrel pointing dead ahead.

A few yards away, a burned hand emerged from the ash. Dante tiptoed around the mound and pulled the door open. She propped it with one foot and steadied her aim. Peeling the door wide had the same results of breaking the seal of a tomb. Retched odors jetted out and made her gag while fresh air sucked inward like a vacuum.

Angry flies buzzed around her head and escaped through the opening. The repulsive smell disrupted her senses, clouding her judgment. The smell of death flooded her mouth. A tangy scent was there, too. The effect grew stronger the more time she spent in the doorway.

Not willing to relinquish the Anschütz, she clung to it as a lifeline, while her body quivered in disgust. Dante fought back waves of nausea, gagging several times to avoid throwing up. Within seconds, chunks of elk splattered against the linoleum at high-speed. Glistening stop light red.

Going from daylight to darkness blinded her. Her vision cleared only after her eyes adjusted. "Hello," vomit stretching from her mouth. Her voice echoed through the store with hollow acoustics, as though she were in an auditorium. As soon as she said hello, she realized it sounded wrong. Not the introduction she aimed for. The tone wasn't authoritative enough. It depicted her growing internal fear. Reading more like I'm scared and alone.

The only thing that answered her call was silence. An eerie emptiness settled in as she regained sight. Despite the store's many windows, it remained dark inside. Welcoming ice cold blackness like the dark side of the moon.

And that horrendous smell had plagued every step. Somewhere in the distance, music played. She couldn't pinpoint the sound's origin. It poured in from every which way. With the butt of the rifle tucked at the crook of her arm, she swung the barrel from right to left. Scanning each aisle in the darkness. Eyeing for signs of life. "Hello!" This time, her tone sounded frightful and trigger-happy. The store gobbled up her voice like a vacuum. As the seconds tolled, the nothingness settled into all those empty spaces once again.

Fastened to the rifle was a night scope. Her father never hunted at night. And it confused Dante; he bought the scope, anyway. According to Jack, night vision gave him the eyes of an eagle, especially during the day. It did a good job of filtering out sun glare. Locating wildlife within the dense foliage was easier this way.

Dante peered through the scope to guide each step while nausea tugged at her, as though vomit built a mansion inside her throat. She walked behind the crash register first. Thinking a red switch would start the gas pumps. She remembered a movie from a few years ago where an actor did the same thing and succeeded. Yet, a swirl mark, and ash, and a ghost leg stood tall behind the register. Defying gravity. More doll parts.

She was certain the leg belonged to the comedian, Dennis. She mused that, in this dark, comedic reality, the information was priceless. An opportunity missed, so to speak. The most hilarious jokes always come from depressing topics. Even if Dennis were alive, he wouldn't be able to stop himself from telling another crude-spirited joke. A leg standing on its own without a master. Now that's funny. No doubt he'd cleverly work this into a sexual punchline.

She ditched finding a secret button to the gas pump. And crept out from behind the register, not wanting to disturb Dennis's parts. Exploring each aisle only ushered more despair. Everywhere she turned, more ghost parts rose from ash.

A foot here. An arm over there. At the corner, a hand, fingers outstretched as though clawing it way out of the ash. There were matching pairs among some mounds. Some just had a pile of soot. Black patches invaded Humble Traveler as though the entire town sought shelter. It made no sense. Death circles outnumbered candy and goodies.

EYES IN THE DARK

PUKING elk onto the pavement stripped her of precious nutrients. What little remained in her gut was gone. The enormous choice of sweets and trail mixes made her feel guilty for even considering food. She should have slapped herself for thinking about feasting among the dead. But her eyes kept drifting to those gummies. Her mouth watered for something salty.

In the corner, a stainless nacho cheese dispenser beckoned. Cheese. What about the cheese? A little couldn't hurt. Even though starving and weak, and her mouth watered for junk food. She couldn't bring herself to feast among the dead. Though tempted. Though the thought soured like the meal before her.

Another lesson learned. No matter how awful the smell, she got used to it pretty quick. After the gag reflexes settle. And seeing any food on an empty tank lowered her dignity, her standards. Though Jack would disagree. He'd say with that sarcastic grin, "Mijita, what the hell are you waiting for? Dig in." Her survival meant everything to that man. Her survival was Jack's entire existence.

Deep down, she wanted to rip open that package of gummy bears and shove every delicious one down her throat, including the green ones. She hated green ones. But today, she'd love them just as much as the red bears.

She pictured herself tilting her head to the side, lining her mouth to the nozzle and pumping nacho cheese right down her gullet. And she might have given in after a few more minutes of staring temptation in the eye. Except the grocery store popped into her head like someone had flipped on all the lights. Yes, she would drive there and feast properly. But if she consumed high calories and sugar now, she'd crash for sure. Then what?

Opening the front door created a wind tunnel effect again. The gust kicked hard against her body, her hair whipping and snapping in the wind. Her face felt cool and wet. She glided fingers across her cheek and realized she had been crying.

The number of tears told her she must have cried through her entire venture. Some hellish walkabout through a macabre land. Doused in human flesh and body parts. More like the land of doll parts rising from the depths of some ashy hell.

Through all the carnage, Dante had almost forgotten why she stopped at Humble Traveler. The damn map. It came to her the moment she locked eyes on the pumps. She hadn't noticed a map section while inside. Important errands on her to-do list had vanished from her mind, as though someone hit factory reset, and replaced all brain activity with death. And Jack succumbed to the flame. He burned for eternity in her mind.

Exploring Humble Traveler again would not come easy. Easier than the first visit, she promised herself. She had gained special insight this time. She knew what lay beyond the glass door. Dante contemplated whether she needed a map. After quick deliberation, her father's apparition nagged her from the afterlife. "Prepare for the unexpected, mijita." Straight to the heart of it all, his voice rang inside her head. "Over prepare, over, over prepare, until your back breaks and bleeds from the burden, mijita."

She went back inside and searched the place over. Near the register, sitting on the counter next to the Bic lighters, stood a plastic display of maps. She shouldered her weapon and stole a Bic from the display, casting a slender flame. An orange hue glowed and flickered and whirred. The flame danced among state maps, national parks, trails, and camping guides, until at last, her eager eyes stumbled upon a United States map. A map of Mexico wasn't required. She only needed enough information to get to the border. Dante had planned this trip in her mind a million times. Only in her imagination, it played out differently.

The goal had been to board a plane. Arriving at her destination three hours and twenty-three minutes later, weather permitting. It never crossed her mind to plan a road trip. Not once. She knew Mexico City lay way down south. And looking at the map, she'd cross the Mexican border through New Mexico. It offered the fastest route from Glenwood.

To her surprise, the gas pump still worked. She used her father's credit card to allow the sale, topped off the tank and headed for the grocery. After forty-eight days, the banking system still functioned. When she climbed into the Jeep, death followed her. The smell had seeped through her clothes, penetrating skin, going bone deep. Her hair reeked of it. She smelled only rotting flesh, as if her nose were buried in a morgue. She could taste the sour meat at the back of her throat. She would have never noticed, had it not been for the brand-new upholstery. Fresh from the factory, plastics and metals vying with death. Death won.

The Jeep made its way down Grand Avenue. Black swirls of death rose everywhere her eyes landed. On the sidewalk. The corner of the street. Even in the middle of the crosswalk. Cars stalled at various streetlights, preserved for all time. Some veered to the side of the road at angles, coasting to full stops at the curb. She passed a convertible with its top down. It belonged to Mayor Williams. No doubt in her mind. No mistaking that car for any other. And sitting on the driver's seat, glinting against the tan leather, was a pile of soot. A ghost leg lodged and protruded from the gas pedal. SHC had stolen the mayor while shifting gears.

Automobiles lined the parking lot of the grocery store. Six, she counted. Good news was scarce these days, and she'd take a win whenever the occasion called for it. If SHC had shopped on a Sunday afternoon or Friday night, it would have found the grocery store packed. She recognized some cars belonging to employees. On her approach, she saw the automatic doors stuck halfway. Unlike the gas station, the grocery store had splashes of dull light running along the perimeter. She gained a sweeping view of the interior.

She stood at the entrance for a time. Silence reigned. The town collapsed all around her. Every shop. Every business. Every house she could see, hollowed. Not a stir from an animal or bird, just gutted like an elk during snow season.

Dante listened through the small opening, trying to detect anyone rustling around inside. She stuck her head between the doors and sniffed the air. One way to detect the dead. It smelled like a grocery store. The produce section wafted up her nose. Bananas or something fruity.

With the Anschütz pointing inward, she snuck inside. And just as she readied herself to venture into another ashy hell, she caught a small figure darting past her peripheral vision.

Dante saw the figure sprinting in the distance. "Wait!" She bolted down Grand Avenue in heated pursuit. The tiny figure ran into the pharmacy on 12th street.

That little sprint had done her in by the time she reached the pharmacy. Her lungs burned. She starved for air, stealing whatever she could through her mouth. Eyes gone wild and hunkered from exhaustion at the doorway. Trying to slow her breathing as her heart hammered away. That short run had tested her ability to flee in a dire situation. In those forty-eight days, she hadn't jogged once. Her fitness level had gone to hell.

The pharmacy was darker than the gas station. No windows. She heard something scuttle around inside, knocking over items as it moved. "Hello!" She waited in the doorway, hoping someone would reply. But no one did.

Every little noise fell silent. "Shit," she whispered. The moment she walked past the threshold, sterilized air swam up her nose. She couldn't decipher the smell. Rubbing alcohol or something antiseptic.

The good news was prescription medicine filled her senses instead of rotting flesh. No one seemed to have died in the pharmacy. At least that's what her senses told her. But who could tell with all the chemicals playing mayhem.

In a quick, uniform fashion, she scoured each aisle, peering through the scope. Hunting the tiny figure from the street. Within seconds, her heart sunk to the floor. Cowering at the end of an aisle, near the Band-Aids and gauze, was a white-haired child, a girl. Hair down to her shoulders. Night vision did not provide a clear image. Everything appeared as silhouettes. Gray outlines. White-out on certain objects. The girl child being one of those white images. Except her eyes. They shimmered in the dark and glowed like a creature from another dimension.

Dante reached for the girl. "I won't hurt you." Still spying through the scope with a sharp eye.

She saw the girl glare at her. "Mommy," her raspy tone sounded as though she had drunk nothing for days.

"My name is Dante. What's yours?"

The girl didn't answer. Dante could see her tiny chest and shoulders expand and contract like a scared rabbit. "Do you want something to drink?"

The girl just stared off into the distance, catatonic. As though she didn't understand a word. "Mommy," then the girl collapsed.

"Hey!" Dante nudged her. The girl lay still and lifeless for a few seconds. "Oh, my God!"

Dante looped the rifle around her chest, scooped up the girl, carried her outside, and laid her on the sidewalk. She needed to examine her where the light was better.

The girl breathed heavy and fast. Dante forced her eyelids open. What stared back was a wall of ivory. Her eyes had rolled to the back of her head. She looked like a baby doll with those pouty, chapped lips and big round eyes, alabaster skin and blond hair.

Dante didn't recognize the child. She looked nothing like anyone from town, especially with that stone-blond hair. Old blood crusted the girl's lips, now turned flaky. Dante did a quick skin test, something Jack had taught her. She pinched and pulled her skin taut, as gentle as she could, to see how fast the girl's skin would rebound. It never laid flat. Instead, it held a scrunched form.

In her quick assessment, Dante determined the girl was severely dehydrated. The best place to treat her was back at the grocery store. The grocery store ensured safety. Plenty of food and water. The girl needed electrolytes fast. She carried her to the entrance and laid her on gray rubber mats.

Wasting no time, showing little care for her own safety, she sprinted inside with one thing on her mind, the girl. "Help!" Her voice didn't travel far, nor produce an echo. The high ceilings and every reaching expanse swallowed it up. The coolers and coffin freezers twinkled like candlelight and hummed along, circulating cold air. Certain coolers had built thick condensation on the glass. Light flooded the area, enough to see the store's layout, though everything in the middle remained dim. Dante headed for the drink aisle and forwent a clean sweep of the grocery store. She saw a case of bottled water sitting on the floor. In seconds, she had removed the plastic wrap and yanked a bottle free. In her passing, she spied a section dedicated to sports drinks. Yet, she shot past it and went for the door. With all her energy focused on aiding the girl, she blocked out the racket erupting somewhere in the back of the store.

It wasn't until she changed her mind and circled back to the sports drinks when she heard people talking. "Hello!" She stood there attentively, expecting a reply. But the voices continued jabbering away. She swore a few were laughing, as though a party was reaching its pinnacle. Dante armed the Anschütz. Once again, aiming the barrel at anything perceived as dangerous. Stealthy footsteps edged closer and closer toward the back, passing the humming coolers.

The noise grew louder when she reached a massive entrance leading to the stockroom. Plastic curtains hung on the threshold. Each strip swayed back and forth as if a steady breeze moved about.

The plastic curtains, once clear, now milky, blocked her view of what lay on the other side. Now that she was within earshot, she heard a woman's voice say, "I love you, Bill." She crept through the opening. "Hello!" The woman continued talking while other voices joined the conversation.

Large metal rafters and industrial shelving took up valuable real estate in the stockroom. It overflowed with supplies. Packed to the ceiling. Pallets of overstock swamped the floor with no place left to go.

No one appeared nearby. The stockroom bore a dangerous aura. A lethal aura. An office trailer stood at the very back. The window shades were drawn. The front door ajar. Warm light spilled from the door and cast a path. Many voices erupted from the office trailer in a deafening stir. A damn party going on. But she couldn't see one human silhouette moving about inside.

She lowered her weapon and approached the doorway. "Hello!" Dante entered the office, expecting to see people packed together in a cramped space, dancing away. She found only disappointment, just a couch, some odds and ends, and a TV. An employee break room.

A legendary game show blared on the TV. She rarely watched television, yet she recognized this one. All the contestants wore clothing that belonged to an older decade, much older, the eighties. Big hair and fluorescent attire and parachute pants. The picture quality wasn't crystal clear. Broadcasting an orange fuzzy, vintage feel. It seemed pre-recorded or stuck on a televised loop.

Even though the volume was cranked to oblivion and beyond, and her ears hurt, the show captivated her. Hypnotized her. People laughing. People cheering. Celebrating the win. Hissing and booing when a contestant lost. She even smiled when the game show host cracked a corny joke.

Standing there watching the program felt surreal. Like a dream, a nightmare, a reality she could not wake from. No, she didn't want to turn it off. She wanted to savor every second. In her gut, she knew it was only a matter of time before the TV would pixelate and go white, or black, or whatever, like the internet did. Her eyes had front row seats to the end of modern technology, to civilization, to humanity. Was technology humanity, though?

She grabbed the remote and turned the volume down low. Stashed the Anschütz behind the love seat, away from a child's reach. Then collected the girl from the gray rubber mats. Dante laid her gently on the couch. Pulled up a chair. Tried to dribble water into her mouth, a little at a time. The liquid refused to go down, trickling out from the corners of her cracked, baby doll lips. The girl remained unconscious and panting fast. Her little chest went up and down, faster and faster. Her little heart was moving as if running a marathon.

Dante didn't want to force water down her throat, afraid the girl might choke to death. She peeled the girl's eyelids open again, only to meet a full white-out. Even her eyeballs were dry with crust jammed in the corners. In all her nineteen years, living a sheltered life, nothing could have prepared her for this.

Every thought in her brain stalled. She searched her memory bank for a solution. The girl needed treatment from a hospital. A doctor. Or at the very least, a nurse. Those professionals would know what to do. But she damn well knew that world was long gone. No one was coming to rescue the girl. The girl's life was now in her hands.

Dante was an only child. She had no experience with small children. The only brief encounter came from her cousin Marie. Marie was the only person she knew who had a baby, Oscar. Already a toddler by the time Dante got to hold him. All the other times she saw Oscar were on FaceTime or Facebook. Whenever Marie had free time to post the latest stuff.

She recalled Marie administering a pink medicine to Oscar for a cold or viral infection. Dante was more traumatized by watching Marie shove the medicine down the boy's throat. He was so tiny, but mighty. Marie struggled to keep his head still. Oscar was flailing and screaming and biting. The whole mess sounded a lot like waterboarding. The noises roaring from him were beastly. Erupting in horrid gurgling sounds. Gasping and gagging. Unknown rattles that seemed torturous and grim. Child abuse escalated to attempted murder vibes.

In those few seconds, just thinking about little Oscar's ordeal, she remembered an important detail that seemed inconsequential at the time. Marie got Oscar to swallow the medication by using a plastic syringe. She used the syringe like a tiny squirt gun. And shot the pink liquid down his throat.

The pharmacy was pitch-black, and the girl's health reached a golden hour. Peering through the night vision would waste precious time. She might never find a plastic syringe without proper lighting. Jack's red duffel bag had a high-lumen flashlight. Powerful enough to set the place ablaze.

She dashed through the aisles and out the front door. The moment her feet touched the parking lot blacktop, a sudden dumbfounded expression fell upon her. Dante furrowed her brows, as though confused and lost. Looking to the right, then left, then back again. From there, she interrogated herself, whether she had parked the Jeep in front of the grocery store. She sprinted to Grand Avenue. And ran eyes up and down the street to locate the Jeep. Thinking she had parked someplace else. But it had vanished.

Gasping for air, she slumped down on the edge of the curb. Her eyes skimmed the road with frantic energy, as though the Jeep would reappear. "Why did you leave the keys in the ignition?" she muttered. "Stupid, stupid, stupid." Pounding her fist against her skull. She lowered her head and began weeping.

Bonnie had warned her. Bonnie told her about Sarah something. Sarah what's her face. Sarah, who gives a fuck? Fuck, fuckin Sarah. Hope all the tires fall off and she nosedives off a fucking cliff—that one, that Sarah.

She had loaded her entire existence and means of survival in the Jeep. All the ammo. Cell phone bursting with pictures of Jack. Of her life. Credit card. Survival kit. First aid. The whole damn lot—gone. A single bullet loaded the chamber. Now, she was otherwise defenseless. No way to protect the girl. Or herself.

LIQUID IN A BOTTLE

SHE WIPED her tears and went back inside. After a quick search, she found an end-cap loaded with hardware items on aisle five. A Duracell lantern sat on the top shelf alongside flashlights. The third shelf held a siphoning kit. This contraption interested her greatly. It came with a slender, clear PVC hose, long enough to reach the back of the girl's throat. If the syringe failed, the siphoning kit would make a successful backup. She could funnel the liquid easier. That's all that mattered now. Hydrate the child. Do what it takes to save the girl.

Dante powered the lantern and made her way through the grocery store. The lantern lit her path with a hazy incandescence, as if she'd fallen into the depths of purgatory. The floor was littered with unopened beer cans, Snapple, and other beverages sitting upright on the linoleum. Some of the bottle caps had tiny teeth marks embedded in them. When she came upon the snack section, chips and candy and Little Debbie cakes painted the floor in the same fashion, as if a critter had scavenged for food. One Little Debbie package had the same size teeth marks on it, small enough to belong to a child. She pictured the girl playing hell, trying to peel wrappers and pry caps with those glass-like fingers, eventually giving up and using her tiny teeth instead. Bite her way through. The girl had bitten her way through the entire store.

Everything dialed down to how well one could bite their way through a problem.

The pharmacy contained many goodies. She looked for the pink medicine behind the counter, just in case, but couldn't locate it. Every bottle was solid white or transparent brown, labeled with ingredients and drug names that might as well have been written in Latin. Researching each bottle proved impossible. Dante found a plastic syringe near the register, sitting in a box. In one aisle, she picked up a package of baby Tylenol and a bottle of Pedialyte. Her father always packed a bottle when he went hunting. He swore by the stuff, claiming it hydrated him better than water.

When Dante returned to the breakroom, the girl hadn't moved an inch. Her face looked flushed, as if running a fever, followed by labored breathing that wouldn't quit. Her tiny chest rose and collapsed quicker than before. She eased the syringe into the girl's mouth and began squeezing the liquid down her throat. The girl, though unconscious, sucked on the syringe as though it were a bottle or sippy cup.

Someone had left a cell phone charging in the break room, still fully charged, still keeping accurate time, she hoped anyway. It wouldn't surprise her if that was unreliable too. The phone was locked with a password, but Dante could tap the screen to display time and date without one.

At every hour, Dante administered one syringe loaded with Pedialyte. The girl drank each time with little trouble. Sometimes she bit down on the syringe and wouldn't let go. During those moments, Dante backed off and waited for her to settle before removing it. Their first encounter had been chaotic, and considering the girl's rough condition, Dante hadn't concerned herself with little details.

Now that she lay there on the couch, Dante could get a better look at her. That stone-blond hair ratted. Baby diamonds in her earlobes. Her pristine tee shirt, once stark white, had yellowed over forty-eight days. Filthy, though not from food. Dante was confident the girl hadn't eaten for some time. She may have wandered the wild, perhaps.

Her pink jumper was in worse condition than the shirt. Clumps of dried mud and pine needles stuck to the soles of her shoes. She smelled like pee and poo. Dante checked to see if she'd soiled herself but found nothing. If she'd eaten and drunk, even a little, there would be evidence.

Despite the smell and dirty clothes, the girl seemed well cared for. At first glance, her teeth appeared fake, blinding white. Everything she wore looked expensive and tailored. Those Louis Vuitton shoes with that iconic LV print. The diamonds were genuine, Dante knew enough to tell. Who the hell did this girl belong to? What boggled her mind even more was how the girl had survived this long on her own.

FOOLISH GAMES

DANTE HATED herself for being so careless, so stupid. *Why did I leave the keys in the ignition?* One name shined brightly in her mind, Sarah. She obsessed over the Jeep and her cell phone. Especially her cell phone. She didn't own a picture of her mother, and now she had nothing tangible of her father. She had recorded her entire life on that phone. Pictures she could never duplicate because of the cloud, as she assumed, went poof in that mysterious sky. And the fucking map.

Jack's cell phone was back at the cabin. She'd placed it in a drawer for safekeeping before she left. That was the only valuable thing worth going back to. Many vehicles were available to Sarah, the town had become a graveyard of cars. Yet Sarah didn't have the means to gas them up. Best guess, that's why she stole the Jeep. She couldn't figure out the gas dilemma either. Dante wondered how long Sarah watched her drive into town before springing into action. If she was watching Dante, then Sarah surely saw the girl running around town too. *What kind of person does that to a child?*

The power was bound to fail. They couldn't live in the grocery store forever. *The good news, we have survivors. The bad news, they'll steal whatever they can get their hands on. Maybe kill for the lint in a stranger's pocket.*

Dante realized survivors would get the same idea as she. It was a matter of time before others came to forage the town. To pick it clean. Soon, others would come. Soon, she might have to fight for her life. And now the girl's life too.

On the third day, after painstakingly feeding her jugs of Pedialyte one syringe at a time, the girl woke. She tried to sit up but struggled. Dante intervened and assisted her. The girl seemed terrified of her new surroundings, casting eyes all over the place, all at once. Dante's presence overwhelmed her, compelling her to scoot to the other side of the couch, far from reach.

Dante smiled and said in a comforting tone, "Are you hungry?" The girl sat there for a moment, glaring, not saying a word. "You must be hungry. How about we eat together?"

The girl stared at Dante. Tears welled. Her entire face was bright red and puckered, as though she'd eaten something spicy. "Mommy!" She crumbled into herself and sobbed. Dante sat next to her and put her arms around the girl child. "I want mommy," the girl said while crying.

Dante had no clue how to defuse the situation or how to interact with her. She needed to think of something quick. The girl's cries grew louder by the second, releasing all those horrible feelings built up inside. Weeks' worth. Even forty-eight days' worth of trauma caused by abandonment. Dante did not lie well. She was terrible at it, couldn't keep a straight face, occasionally giggling while telling a lie.

Though Dante had many talents. Her best was having a wild imagination. She was an amazing storyteller, plucking them from the sky, or the heavens, or wherever as though she was reading them out of a book. "I spoke to your mommy on the phone. Do you want to know what she told me?"

The girl stopped crying. Still sniffling, rubbing her little red nose. "What did she say?"

Scrunching her face and searching for the right thing to say. Now that the girl used more words than mommy, Dante distinctly heard an accent. An English one, she believed. "She wants me to babysit you for a while. Do you know what babysit means?"

The girl furiously scrubbed her eyes. "Yeah." She started playing with Dante's fingers. "Where's Sarah?"

Mentioning that name was like a gut punch. "Sarah?" Dante said, anger filling that tone, making her response sound aggressive.

The girl gave Dante a look, as though suspicious. "Where is she?"

"Oh, she had to go home. It was an emergency, I think. I'm taking her place. But don't worry, Sarah is okay. She wanted me to tell you that everything is going to be just fine." Dante swallowed hard and closed her eyes. The girl moved on from her hands and started picking at Dante's fingernails.

"What about Cecil?"

"Cecil is great. Your mommy is great, everybody is great."

"Who's going to feed him?"

Dante realized the girl was extremely smart and articulate. And she wouldn't fool. If she started asking the girl a lot of questions, specifically ones she should technically already know, the girl's age, her name, her mother's name, who the hell Cecil was. Not knowing any of this stuff could blow her cover. The girl might cry her little eyes out indefinitely, for all time even.

"Sarah's going to feed him. She took him home with her." Dante brightened her tone. "Hey, you know what? I just thought of something. Do you like playing games?" The girl nodded eagerly. "Have you ever played the guessing game?" The girl shook her head. "I ask you a question, and you answer it, even if I already know the answer. Then you ask me a question, and I'll answer it. If you guess right, then I'll give you a surprise. Okay?"

Her eyes lit up. She shot up and nodded her head repeatedly. "What's the surprise?"

Dante's eyes moved toward the ceiling, embroiled in deep thought. "How about—"

The girl started bouncing up and down on the couch. "Roller skates!"

"Ooh, I don't know about that. You might get hurt."

The girl laughed. "That's what mommy says."

"Mommies are always right."

The girl squeezed Dante's hand. "Tell me."

"You can have anything you want in the store."

The girl frowned. She let go of Dante's hand. "A real surprise."

"You can have anything you want in this whole town, anything. If you see something you want, then you can have it." Little did she know, later, she would redact that statement and school Grace on the ins and outs of perpetual borrowing.

"Roller skates?"

Dante groaned. "Yes, roller skates too." She doubted there was any chance of that happening. Not in this town. Or so she hoped not. Nothing like teaching a kid how to roller skate down the sidewalk, surrounded by ghost limbs and piles of ash that used to be people.

The girl started bouncing again. "Me first, me first."

"Okay, I'm waiting."

"Mommy's favorites, favorites, favorites."

"You. Your mommy's favorite."

"No."

"You're not her favorite?"

"No, her favorites."

"I give up."

"Mommy puts her favorites on, like this," the girl said, while running her fingers under the bags of her eyes. "I'm not supposed to touch."

For a second, Dante felt bewildered. Maybe the girl was talking about her mother putting on makeup, or something cosmetic. A cream perhaps.

"Okay, my turn. What's your name?"

"Grace!"

"That's a cool name. How old are you?"

"It's my turn. What's your name?"

"Dante."

"I'm six." Grace held her fingers in the air.

HYDROGENATED WORLD

FOR BEING SIX, Grace looked younger. Scaled down. Before she woke, Dante had time to investigate the grocery store. She'd ventured outside and walked around town, though never wandering too far. Unexplained, interesting developments emerged. No one had perished in the grocery aisles.

The grocery store played out differently than the Humble Traveler. Everyone seemed to have died right where they stood at the gas station. The same thing occurred on Grand Avenue. Same with her father. But in the grocery store, everyone died in the walk-in freezer. Six total.

In the produce section, Dante found apples and pears and other fruit carcasses strewn about. Cantaloupe and watermelon and potatoes moldy with bite marks and deep wounds. A produce knife was present. Large. White plastic handle. Sitting on the floor next to a shriveled mango.

Only fruit closest to the edge of each produce display was missing. She imagined Grace ate the ones within reach. Even the bananas hanging on a rack were half-eaten, peel and all. Grace's tiny, glass-like fingers probably could not peel a banana. Then, when she ran out of stuff to eat, she moved on to the bins with melons. The stock of melons sat at floor level. She vividly saw Grace's progression through the store, as if watching a movie. Anything placed at her eye level was game. No matter how hard she tried, her little hands couldn't cut through the thick rind of melons. The fruit placed higher on the display was untouched, with hairy mold spidering out. Preserved. For all time, like some nuclear fallout.

Almost all the produce was inedible by now. And the edible ones, past the cusp of ripeness. The apple she ate had grainy flesh, its skin wrinkled and rubbery. The stockroom's walk-in cooler bulged with produce. The cool air and being locked inside a dark metal box must have stopped the aging process. From lettuce to apples, and anything between, rested in the cooler, just as ripe as the day the grocery store received it.

Dante and her father ate clean, although he adored red meat. Elk. The grocery store stocked its shelves as if it knew end days were approaching. She saw brightly packaged, affordable, ready-to-eat meals everywhere. Ones that boasted an appealing tagline: healthy meal for the whole family. Despite its unhealthiness. Many had popular cartoon characters, at a child's eye level, as a hook, line and sinker.

Most everything on the shelves was junk. Over-processed. Loaded with sugar and sodium. Powders and borderline potions and hydrogenated this and that. Corn syrup, high fructose, ungodly amounts. Way more than recommended daily allowance. Dante doubted the produce would last forever. A new shipment of fresh, healthy options would not waltz through the front door on a magic carpet either. This, she accepted, was the new normal. Six months ago, not a chance in hell. Today, fake food was looking mighty fine, mighty fine.

CREATURES LOVE ROT

AT EVERY TURN, SHC challenged their existence to remain on earth. Toyed with her daily. Coffin freezers located smack in the middle of the store up and quit one day. She first noticed the failure when water pooled and made an island. Those coffin cases no longer spit vapor frost from the lip, the kind that slowly threaded up toward the ceiling.

It took days and countless shopping carts to clear soggy bags of vegetables and fruits and ice cream tubs and lasagna and Mexican-inspired cuisines. Cuisines from around the world.

Cart by cart, she disposed of everything into the trash compactor outback. Dante poured gasoline between loads. The smell of fuel gave her a headache that refused to go away. Tunneling her brain, her sanity.

It got so monotonous and bad she woke to the machine droning inside her ears, though she wasn't anywhere near. Her clothes were now combustible. Controlled fire would soon follow. She learned this from Jack. Way before SHC.

Dante refused to stop. She feared the god-awful smell. Maggots and bears and wolves and mountain lions would soon come. Rotting meat lures the creatures of the forest. Then what, she tells herself. Then what?

Then the perimeter coolers quit. Rinse repeat, rinse repeat, her exhausted body tells her. Strangely, the electricity stayed on in certain areas of the store. The walk-in coolers in the stockroom still worked.

Though the freezers quit. Night after night, she tended to the upkeep. One day, she sat and leaned against the trash compactor and cried for a good while. Its industrial metal teeth no longer chewed. No longer accepted any of her offerings.

What would she and Grace do without the grocery store? She spent more days hauling full shopping carts to dumpsters behind businesses on Main Street—some far from the grocery store. The kind that locked tight with metal braces to keep bears from getting in. More gasoline. Controlled fire followed. "Leave no trace, mijita," Jack often said.

Their survival would meet a quick end once wildlife started wandering into town from the smell of rotting food. If anything, SHC taught her fire doesn't burn every molecule. It leaves behind residuals. Like her. Like Grace. Limbs. Bits and pieces of flesh.

Then came the rudimentary barriers. She constructed each one around the compactor and dumpsters to prevent wildlife from clawing their way in. Hoping they would get bored and wander off. Or head back to the forest.

But would they come, she wondered most days. Would they come? Did she do enough? Truth was, time would tell. Their bodies required similar things the creatures of the forest did. Maybe by then, they would combust like everything else.

YELLOW SILENCE

RORY WOKE, not knowing the time of day. Her senses were whacky. The basement wore a cloak of darkness no matter the hour. Night after night, Chloe would wake from nightmares and scream in terror. She went on like this twice, sometimes three times, during the witching hour. Ripping Rory from a deep sleep each time. Then, afterward, once Chloe settled, Rory would just lie there for how long? She did not know. Staring into the black abyss. She could see dark wood beams crisscrossed the house's foundation. Running this way and that. Groaning underneath the weight of the house.

Chloe's nightmares had escalated to the point of being unmanageable. And lack of sleep was the perfect breeding ground for delirium or psychosis. Her dreams always included Larry, attacking her or some variation thereof, and sometimes the cat was there too, Mr. Shelby. Rory wasn't sure if Mr. Shelby was being murdered by Larry. If Larry murdered Chloe and Mr. Shelby together in the darkness. When Rory asked further about the nightmares, Chloe refused to elaborate. "It's too scary to talk about," she said. "I don't want to think about it because it might happen. You never know."

And Chloe wasn't looking too good either. Her hand wasn't looking real these days. The bite oozed a rich golden mucus mixed with merlot.

Her blood had stolen the color of merlot. Other issues also demanded attention. Chloe had a constant fever of 102º.

And, thankfully, Tala had prepared for this day. Well, maybe not this day. Maybe a mild version of this day. One without SHC and a zombie. Though, could Larry fit the definition of zombie? Rory almost wanted to laugh just thinking about what her mother would say.

Tala had created a solid medical emergency station in the basement. She had prepared for any injury one might befall. Including injuries that required antibiotics. Though, a slight problem existed. Rory could have located the medication instructions if not distracted by her phone. The day Tala had told her where to look.

The complete drug inventory sat on the third shelf, next to the banana bags. Tala's nickname for the yellow saline IV bags. A mixture of vitamins, minerals and electrolytes. Tala had even broken it down into layman's terms, so Rory knew which drugs were used to treat just about everything. She had tucked these instructions neatly inside a manila envelope next to the banana bags.

So, with no knowledge, Rory fed Chloe a low dose of amoxicillin. Out of all the medications, Amoxicillin stood out to her. She had had to take amoxicillin once to treat an abscess tooth. If amoxicillin had fixed her abscess, then it must fix serious hand injuries too.

Yet, if Tala were still alive, and saw a ¼ palm missing, a ¼ palm bitten off, she would have taken drastic measures. That sort of injury landed on the fourth tier. The medical shelving system had five tiers. First tier, bumps, and bruises. "Nothing to whine about," Tala often said. Though, the 4th tier was most definitely something to cry about. And Tala would have fed Chloe a steady, heavy dose of cephalexin—on the fourth shelf. Alongside an even bigger dose of morphine.

KISS MR. SHELBY

Day one was deathly silent living under the whispers of the house. No conversation to be had. What was there to talk about, anyway? For what does the damned offer the damned, really? Most of the time, Chloe sat balled up. Knees to chest. Arms wrapped around herself, rocking, dreaming of better days. Eyes glued to the wall. Eyes glued elsewhere. Somewhere beyond this reality. And doing her best not to lock eyes on Rory.

At first, Rory had slept on a cot near the sofa, where Chloe permanently rooted herself. After the first night, and being ripped from her sleep many times, Rory moved the cot far east of the basement. She hoped by doing this, she could escape Chloe's night terrors. But she didn't escape. The only way she'd escape those screams, those night terrors, would be to pack it up, and move to the next-door neighbor's basement, Jill's.

Chloe remained planted to that sofa, and immovable. Only leaving her circle of protection for quick bathroom breaks. Rory heard Chloe sobbing in there. Rambling to herself. Words Rory couldn't make out. Her bathroom rants seemed psychotic. She knew Chloe used the bathroom for emotional release. Away from prying eyes. Building herself another circle of protection. Chloe traveled from circle to circle. The only person Chloe was fooling was herself.

Sure, Chloe freshened herself right up afterward. Rory heard the bathroom sink running. The water splashing around in the basin. Chloe even gargled water. And then would saunter back to the couch as though perfectly fine, composed. Pretending she was resilient to whatever ran rampant in these parts. Chin up. Head held high. Posture straight. An attitude that suggested the world wasn't falling apart, just in transition. For how long? Not relevant. What comes next? And what comes after that? Now that's the genuine concern. The devil is in the details. Mysterious, uncharted, so irrelevant.

Freeze-dried food came in a wide variety. Meals that included Asian fusions, Italian, Mexican. Breakfast items such as eggs, apple cream of wheat. Rory loved the mango habanero chili. She ate it for breakfast. It prepared easily. Tear open the package. Dump the contents into a bowl. Add boiling water and voilà, you've got a hot meal.

Her mom had left nothing out of the equation when constructing the bunker. Coffee, green tea, wine, beer, etc. Rory tried coaxing Chloe to eat something, but she passed on most everything offered. The only thing she partook of was a cup of green tea.

Rory watched Chloe's hands trembling as she held her tea cup. They'd been doing this dance for days now, stealing glances when the other wasn't looking, finding excuses to move closer on the couch. The basement's shadows played tricks, but Rory could swear Chloe's pupils dilated whenever their fingers accidentally brushed during meal prep.

"Tell me about your mom," Chloe had said earlier, and Rory noticed how she leaned in. How her voice dropped to that intimate register that made the hair on Rory's arms stand up. But whenever Logan's name came up, Chloe would fold into herself, become smaller somehow. Rory had attributed it to fear of him, but now she wondered if it had been guilt all along.

The basement's ventilation system wheezed above them like a dying animal. Rory had never noticed before how the shadows from the overhead pipes created bars across the floor, their own private prison. The bourbon bottle between them caught the light, throwing amber reflections that danced across Chloe's tear-streaked face like accusations.

Each time the heat kicked on, the pipes would gurgle and vibrate, reminding them of the world above. Of Mr. Shelby, waiting. Of Larry, possibly still alive. Of all the things they were hiding from down here, not just SHC but their own truths, fermenting in the artificial light like the emergency rations on Tala's carefully organized shelves.

Bourbon seemed to loosen Chloe up. Rory slipped it into her green tea. She had learned the hot tea and liquor trick from Logan. If it loosened him up, it was bound to affect Chloe similarly.

The days before the affair. Way before the cancer. Before Logan turned into a stranger living in the house. Someone she barely recognized. After a rough day at the office, Logan would come home and fix himself hot tea and bourbon with lemon. Claiming hot tea was a perfect catalyst to intoxication. Or better yet, embalming the mind. He enjoyed embalming the mind daily.

Her father was always stuck inside his head. A prisoner of his own thoughts. Liquor fixed that illness. He reached a new, positive level after his fourth drink. He was funny and very likable, just add liquor. Rory loved this side of him. Tala, not so much.

Her parents were once in love, she told herself. Something had transformed between Tala and Logan once she turned fifteen. They still slept in the same bed. Went on vacations together. Carried on as married couples do. Yet, a vast chasm existed. Rory saw it. Anyone who knew them saw it. Except them. Just as Chloe wasn't fooling anyone, neither were her parents.

Dilution is a curious thing. Dilution from the past. From life. From goodness. Parting from the light and entering darkness is easier than one thinks. Never a clear path ahead, still, they forge ahead, for miles and miles, until the eyes adjust. The eyes grow resilient in any environment. And embrace the horror once unseen.

Rory poured herself a cup too, and another, and onward they went. First one always went down slowly. Burning on its way down. Drinking lightning, Logan once said. Then warming the insides. Tingling sensation flowing outward. Toasting skin to a rich glow. The second, the third and the fourth, effortless. Getting drunk was effortless after the first shot.

Chloe matched drink for drink. Soon the basement took on a whole new vibe. The air was no longer musty and dreary. The heaviness lifted. A light shone down the barrel of a gun. Thirty minutes prior, the room had lacked the current brightness. Everything went poppy.

Pretty soon, Rory grabbed the bottle and placed it on the coffee table. She plopped down next to Chloe and filled their glasses to the brim. No splash of green tea required. Joyous eyes beamed while a sly grin rose on her face. Rory raised a cup high. "Larry's gone."

Chloe lifted a brow and let out a distorted snicker. No, a celebration was not in order. Their survival was not a guarantee. Chloe gave Rory a dirty look. With all the joy wiped from her face, Rory lowered her cup. "I didn't mean it that way. I just meant cheers, Larry's gone."

Chloe stared off into space again, wearing guilt, and finished Rory's sentence for her, by saying, "He's dead. You stabbed him to death."

Rory said nothing and sipped more bourbon. Eyes traveling the room. Chloe set her drink down. "There must be someone we can call. The National Guard. FEMA. They can't leave us here to die."

When Chloe mentioned FEMA, Rory rolled her eyes. This was a very telling sign. Larry must have concussed Chloe during the attack. Rory hadn't a clue how the other stuff worked in a national emergency. But even she knew FEMA was false hope. They hadn't saved them during the blackout, FEMA hadn't saved anyone. They were the last to respond to the blackout. Many months after the grid was repaired.

Even Ms. Craddock complained about FEMA in EMI class. The district created EMI curriculum to prepare for disasters but focused intensely on school shootings. And how to survive one. "It's not a matter of if, but when, boys and girls," she'd say while polishing the lens of her glasses. "Take a good look around you. Would you take a bullet for one of your classmates? I'm being very serious now. This is the world boys and girls. Wake up. This is the new normal."

People considered everything the new normal. Ice caps are melting. Shut up and get used to the new normal. Her coming-of-age memoir would no doubt include many layers of the new normal.

"This is the safest place." Rory slammed more bourbon. She grabbed Chloe's cup. Filled it. Liquor dripped all over and handed it back. "I don't think it's safe to go upstairs right now. We should wait. Larry could still be up there. There's a good chance he might be alive."

Chloe stared at the amber liquid in her cup for a good while. Hesitant at first. And then took a long swig. She looked at Rory with tears forming in her eyes. "Mr. Shelby needs his medicine. He's very ill. You don't understand. I can't stay here any longer."

Rory didn't know how to respond. And the way things were going, Chloe wouldn't last long in captivity. She might lose her shit way before rescue. If rescue was still possible. She was one bathroom break away from suicide. Or liable to run out the door on a death wish. All to save her cat. Yes, things in the basement were at a tipping point. And for the first time in quite a while, Rory didn't want to be alone. Not at end days. "Safety in numbers, boys and girls," Ms. Craddock once said.

If safety in numbers improved chances of surviving an active shooter, then surely this way of thinking could apply to this situation. SHC was way worse. Surviving another wild attack by one of those things was slim. Added to one simple reality, Chloe might be the last living person on her block. Perhaps in the city. Hell, the entire state. The entire planet. Rory placed her hand on Chloe's shoulder. "We'll go tomorrow."

Chloe sprang to life and said, "Are you serious right now? You'd really go with me?"

"Yes," Rory smiled, eyes jilting around from intoxication. "But once we get him, we come back here. Where it's safe."

For Chloe, that last part wasn't an accurate statement. Beauty was often subjective by whoever bore the correct color lens. The basement, or better yet, the bunker, clashed with her logic. What if Logan somehow survived and wandered his way back home? She refused to spend her remaining days with him. Whatever that entailed.

Chloe's eyes took a long stroll around the room. Her face spelled desperation. Fleeting and lost. Traveling far beyond the walls to someplace safe. Chloe refused to disguise her true feelings. Rory saw guilt or dread, or both, oozing from her, as though Chloe had just been handed a life sentence. "I can't do that."

Rory had not expected her response. Arguing about it would do no good. Her words, especially her tone, carried a finality to it. Not open to discussion or interpretation. Don't bother weighing the pros and cons.

Zilch. That's it. Rory panicked. And had nothing to bargain with. She was at the mercy of Chloe. "Then where? We need someplace safe to go."

"My apartment. It's a secured building."

The idea was ludicrous. Borderline psycho. Rory could see it now. Locked inside a building full of those things running around. They wouldn't last a millisecond. More importantly, Rory realized Chloe might be a liability. But who's not a liability these days? "Let's get the cat first."

"Mr. Shelby." Chloe interrupted with piercing eyes. In a direct way, setting the record straight. Implying Rory was downplaying the cat's status. He was no mere cat. Far from it. Mr. Shelby had transcended from animal to helpless baby long ago. And Rory needed to steer her way back to reality and recognize Mr. Shelby's importance.

"Yeah, Mr. Shelby. Then we'll decide where to go next."

Chloe hugged Rory tight and prolonged the embrace. It lasted a little too long. She squeezed so tight that Rory gasped. "You don't know what this means to me." Chloe pulled back and locked eyes on Rory.

They both sat there, inspecting each other again, stealing more glances, as if something was happening between them. Chloe wore desperate eyes, or lust. Rory couldn't tell which.

Before either of them caught on. Clueless that their bodies drew in like tractor beams. Their faces magnetized. Chloe suddenly kissed Rory. Rory did not pull away. Her eyes were confused at first.

When Chloe's lips met hers, Rory's first thought wasn't about the sweetness, or the softness. It was about her mother's perfume bottle, still sitting on the bathroom counter upstairs. How Tala would spritz it twice before date nights with Logan, back when they still had those. The same scent Rory had smelled on that young woman in their kitchen, hours after her mother's death. And now here she was, tasting bourbon on another woman's lips, becoming part of her own family's cycle of secrets.

The kiss deepened, and Rory felt herself splitting in two. One part floating away toward something that felt like freedom. The other part was anchored by the weight of history, of patterns repeating themselves in this underground shelter while the world burned above.

Surprised. Still kissing. Still stuck in the moment. They embraced.

Pulse racing, blood pumping fast. Fused together as one. Working their way up toward the heavens. And just when losing themselves seemed positive, Chloe pulled free. "I can't."

Rory looked as though embarrassed. She sat there, speechless. Trying to unpack what had just happened. "I slept with Logan." Everything inside Rory just melted to the floor. Her face, once lustrous, now turned dark and angry.

The words hit Rory like a sucker punch. But it was the way Chloe said them, like ripping off a bandage, quick and practiced. That really twisted the knife. How many times had Chloe rehearsed this confession in the bathroom during her "emotional releases"? How many times had she gargled away the taste of guilt along with the tap water?

Rory's mind raced back through every interaction between Logan and Chloe. Logan never invited Chloe to the house, but her name filled it from time to time. The way he'd lean against the doorframe when Chloe called him. How he'd offer to help with her car troubles. All those little moments Rory had dismissed as her father's awkward attempts at being a kind boss now reformed themselves into something darker, more deliberate.

"You're a lunatic!" The words burst from Rory's mouth before she could stop them, and she realized she wasn't just speaking to Chloe anymore. She was speaking to Logan, to that half-naked woman in the kitchen, to every person who'd ever thought they could replace her mother. To herself, for almost becoming another link in this chain of betrayals.

No longer able to look Rory in the eyes. "I'm not proud of it."

"Him?"

"I don't know." Her face shone like a child in deep shit. "My boyfriend cheated on me. I wasn't in a good place," she quickly rephrased. "He made me feel special."

Rory couldn't bear to look at her anymore. She got up and went to the cot and lay down. Chloe sprang up, hands intertwined, fidgeting. She cast eyes in Rory's direction. She could see Rory lying on the cot, staring up at the ceiling. Using a sweet tone, she said, "You're still coming with me, aren't you?"

Rory turned her back on Chloe and faced the wall and said nothing. "I'm sorry! I really am."

The only thing afforded to her was bitter silence. The room now deflated, and hollow. A whooshing noise from the air ventilation system kicked on. Lights casting a concentrated glow down below. A low buzzing sound, high above. Electricity coursing through every track with a snap, making its way to every bulb.

"Please talk to me. I'm scared." Chloe's voice cracked on the last word, but Rory kept her back turned, counting the cinder blocks in the wall. One, two, three... like counting the months since her mother died. Four, five, six... like counting the empty bourbon bottles Logan left around the house. Seven, eight, nine... like counting the lies that had led them here.

The ventilation system still hummed its mechanical lullaby. Somewhere upstairs, a floorboard creaked, the house settling, or something worse. Rory felt Chloe's presence behind her like a shadow, waiting. The same way that half-naked woman had waited in their kitchen, expecting... what? Forgiveness? Understanding?

Rory pressed her forehead against the cold wall. Tomorrow they would have to go upstairs, face whatever was left of their world. Face Mr. Shelby, face Larry, if he was still there. Face all the things they'd done to survive. But tonight, in this basement that her mother had built to protect them, Rory would let the silence do what she couldn't—tell the truth about how some betrayals cut too deep for words.

SHE CAN DANCE

RORY LAY THERE, filled with frustration and confusion. She found boys appealing, at least she thought she did. But holding onto that idea after kissing Chloe felt like a mistake. Something shifted within her in the moments that followed the kiss. The thrill of kissing a girl was stronger than anything she had experienced with boys. With three boyfriends in her past, none had ignited any real excitement. One had gone through the motions but never reached all the bases.

Kissing boys felt mechanical and detached. It lacked the spark that should go along with a real coming-of-age experience. Instead, it felt drawn-out and tedious, marked by endless self-reflection and disappointments in herself. Was she not doing it right? Or were they? It struck her that they often seemed oblivious to the significance of their actions. The thought crossed her mind more than once, especially after a date ended and her boyfriend drove away into the dark.

Making out with boys felt devoid of emotion. She forced herself to believe she should feel something. The boys were always charged with energy, eager to engage, their minds racing. But for her, it was the opposite. She'd prefer the discomfort of a dental procedure. At least that would provide a real sensation.

She had no real comparisons until now. Chloe had opened up a new perspective. Kissing boys was like consuming a bowl of steel-cut oats, mealy and tasteless. The process was about getting through it, no matter how uninspiring, while trying to wash away the unpleasant aftertaste.

In contrast, kissing girls was akin to indulging in rich chocolate truffles. Everything melted and blended to create a delightful symphony, bursting with flavors. The thought of Chloe being intimate with her father unsettled her deeply. The mere idea of sharing the same kisses and intimacy with the same woman as him was enough to churn her stomach.

Rory fought against sleep, continuing to process her thoughts, replaying the events of the evening over and over. The kiss kept resurfacing in her mind, intertwining with memories of her father's betrayal and her loving mother. Why did her mother have to leave? Why not him? She wouldn't miss him. Not now and certainly not in some hypothetical future. But now, she felt a void, she craved another kiss. To feel the warmth, the heartbeat of another person.

Chloe's sobs echoed in the background, searching for comfort on the sofa, curled inward. The sounds from the bathroom punctuated the silence, her distress evident. The alcohol had loosened her up but led to shaky breaths instead of quiet tears and sniffs and whimpers filling the space.

The night was marked by an unending cycle of sniffles, as if her nose were a faucet. Rory could almost hear every tear that hit the floor. At least Chloe wasn't crying like she had in the bathroom. Amid the emotional turmoil, an odd sense of calm began to emerge. The bourbon was racing through her, making the room feel turned upside down, dark and disorienting, like everything was slipping down a deep abyss.

RESCUE ME

RORY WOKE IN A HANGOVER PANIC, the time of day elusive. For all she knew, midnight still reigned. The basement lay soundless and empty, void of its typical symphony of creaks and groans, settling joists, the roar of the furnace, Chloe's sniffles.

A veil of light ran the length of the room, bleaching out the couch from her position. Her head throbbed as though ready to burst, her mouth desert-dry, throat scratchy. That ravenous thirst screamed for attention.

When she got to her feet, the earth wobbled beneath her. She stood cockeyed, as if the floor had tilted. Looking at the couch, Rory realized she didn't even know Chloe's life to make such judgments. Between all the crazy bullshit going on, it had never come up in conversation. Why hadn't she asked about her life? She cradled the side of her head.

"Hey, are you awake?" Her voice cracked. She waited for a response, still holding her head. When Chloe didn't answer, Rory stumbled toward the couch. "Hey." She crossed over the barrier of light and found the couch empty, its cushions square. No indentations or creases marked the foam and held its original form. Virtually untouched. Chloe had not slept on the couch.

She started toward the bathroom when movement caught her eye, the basement stairs, where another stream of light cast down from above. Each step sparkled with dust motes. Around the corner, the upstairs door gaped wide open, unleashed. The first step buckled and cracked under her weight. "Hey," she called out, her voice barely a whisper.

Each step felt like walking on broken glass as she ascended. At the landing, a piercing kitchen light blinded her. She shielded her eyes against the assault. "Hey." The word came out muffled and raw, her voice box betraying her.

Her ears rang in ultra-sensitive mode, every noise amplified to torture. The world had changed while she slept, and now she had to face a brutal calculation, Larry ranked highest in the pecking order, with Chloe a close second. And here she was, contemplating a suicide mission for a sick cat. Mr. Shelby without his medication, he'd die within the week. No getting around it.

Try telling that to Chloe, the girl who'd lost her grip on reality. Emergency services had vanished. Hospitals too. Which meant veterinarians and prescriptions were a pipe dream. Soon, very soon, the cat would swallow his last pill, his last drop of elixir. Then what? Pretty sure vets didn't make house calls during the apocalypse.

Yet nothing seemed to faze people anymore. Household pets reigned supreme while corpses littered the streets. Are you blind? Can't you see? The dead are peaceful at last, comfortable in the afterburner of SHC. Nature taking its course. Stop the theatrics. Plug your nose and breathe through your mouth, the smell will fade. Eventually. Small mercy that little remains to decompose.

After some reflection, considering recent evidence, maybe a vet would come. Maybe they'd channel through the dead that lay about like rapids in a mighty river, all to save Mr. Shelby. The dead might wither, as they should, but the living still clung to their delusions of normalcy.

Rory approached the broken window. In the middle of thick green grass lay a pile of ash and a single arm, the kitchen knife glinting in the black swirled patch, Larry. He'd finally burned up like the others. Across the street, Chloe's parking spot sat empty. Her tiny red car was gone. But her purse contents remained scattered across the pavement. The blood-stained white umbrella was still lying in the street.

The front door stood wide open, leaving the house exposed to whatever roamed outside. Chloe must have torn out of here like she had demons on her heels. Rory walked to the end of the driveway and surveyed the block.

Under normal circumstances, the neighborhood would be alive at this hour. Joggers in trendy athletic wear. Neomammas prancing in pairs or triplets, monopolizing the road with their monster-truck strollers and platform sneakers. Landscapers bouncing between houses like circus performers, their leaf blowers and lawnmowers a constant symphony. Delivery vans racing porch to porch.

Now, no-man's-land welcomed her gaze. No passing cars. No people. Not a stir. Just a brilliant spring sky that didn't give a damn about what happened below. A perfect day. The air hung still and cool against her skin, greenery sparkling in the light.

Beauty meant nothing. Her heart started racing, dizziness making her knees shake. A tingling sensation ran amuck throughout her body, tickling the back of her neck. The neighborhood seemed to shrink, collapsing in on her, tightening its grip. Squeezing and squeezing, stealing the air from her lungs.

She ran back inside, slammed the front door, and locked it. Her hands trembling, she grabbed a glass from the kitchen cupboard and filled it with water, guzzling it down in seconds. She sank to the floor and sat there until her heart slowed, until her breathing reduced to a murmur.

Alone. During all the chaos, she hadn't checked her text messages. Not that she had many friends anymore. A year ago, sure, before her mother's diagnosis. Autumn and Becca had been her closest friends then. But between the chemo and radiation, friendship lost its importance. She'd stopped responding to texts, to posts, eventually blocking their numbers. As Tala's cancer progressed, Rory had ghosted them all.

Her phone lay on the carpet, surrounded by a pool of dried blood. The broken window loomed above it, bloody fingerprints and smear marks transforming Tala's beautiful home into a slaughterhouse. All the hallmarks of a gruesome crime scene.

Perspective matters, even in times like these. Yes, she'd stabbed him in the eye. In his chest. Everywhere, really, concentrated on his upper half. It wasn't like she'd kept count. Who tallies each blow during a struggle, except maybe a serial killer? Besides, SHC had taken his life in the end, not her. It was just cleaning up loose ends, reclaiming bodies that had tried to coast under death's radar. Righting a cosmic miscalculation.

Phone in hand, she returned to the basement and latched the door. She'd wait for Chloe to return. Somewhere in her mind, she believed Chloe would come to her senses. Sooner rather than later. Before the soup congealed. Surely, all the horrors of SHC would guide her back.

Five days passed. Then eight. Then eleven. Day twelve hit Rory hard, reality crashing down, Chloe might be dead. Or living her best life with Mr. Shelby riding shotgun. Rory pictured Chloe's little red car cruising down the highway, top down - never mind it wasn't a convertible. That's how she saw it. Red hair whipping in the wind, the cat perched beside her in a tuxedo and sunglasses, like some twisted Thelma and Louise. But she questioned this fantasy. Death seemed more likely than alive. Yes, likely indeed.

She was lying on the cot, staring past the rafters, when her phone chimed in the distance. She'd left it on the coffee table before her last bathroom run. Weeks without human contact had drained her hope, leaving her convinced she was the last person alive. Reality had become a bitter pill to swallow.

She sprinted to the phone, hands shaking as she opened the message.

Bruce: r u there? r u alive

Her heart skipped. Another living person.

Rory: Still here R U ok

Bruce: hungry thou

Rory: I have

Bruce: no car weak

Rory: Where r u

Bruce: home

Rory: wheres ur mom n dad

Bruce: never came home

Her pulse quickened. The thought of venturing outside, where the world closed in and stole her breath, made her pause. Her mother's station wagon sat in the garage, gassed up and ready. Bruce lived just two miles away. A five-minute drive, tops. Yet panic painted it as a journey across the planet. While she wrestled with her fear, another text lit up her screen.

Bruce: tbh scared

"Fuck." She tossed the phone onto the couch. It chimed again, and guilt drove her to pick it back up. The weight of his vulnerability crushed her resistance.

Rory: Omw

Bruce: mcds? 🍔

Rory: lol

Bruce: 🙃

Bruce hadn't crossed her mind in ages. Truth be told, none of her high school friends had. When she'd first met him, his name alone had intrigued her. The only Bruce she'd known was Bruce Wayne.

Batman's Bruce carried mystery and trouble on his shoulders, orphaned at eight in that fictional Gotham. But her Bruce? He wore different qualities when no one watched. Sure, he fit the teenage boy template, outgoing, charming enough to draw people in. But there was something else. An innocence about him, bordering on naive. Tall and strong for his age, fast on the field. People set high bars for him based on looks alone.

His nature ran deeper than that surface calm. That's how Rory saw him. Easy to talk to about anything. Nothing seemed to rattle him. He moved through life like everything would fall into place when it needed to.

She bolted up the stairs, unlatched the door, and ran to her bedroom. The room became chaos in seconds, drawers dumped, shelves cleared, her life scattered across the carpet. Papers, photos, clothes, shoes, stuffed animals, Mardi Gras beads, all of it searching for one thing, the combination to the gun safe.

She'd written it on yellow paper. But where? Time ticked against her, Bruce might be starving. She'd have to go without a gun. Once she delivered food, she could come back and search properly.

Grabbing her backpack from the floor, she headed to the kitchen. Another knife came off the magnetic strip before she descended to gather supplies. Packages of mango habanero chili, hot cereals, mac and cheese, anything that might help went into the bag. Essential items followed as she steeled herself for the garage.

Before leaving, she taped a note to the front door. Just in case Chloe returned during her rescue mission. Despite sleeping with Logan and then kissing her, bigger concerns demanded attention now.

Her world, the entire planet, had deteriorated in days. Standing at the edge of her driveway, peering into a ghost town, frightened her more than anything else had.

After Tala passed, Rory had cut herself off from the world. Grief convinced her she was better alone. Life could steal anyone you loved in seconds, that's what she'd learned from Tala's death. She used to believe her mother was invincible, eternal. Cancer proved otherwise.

In a world teeming with people, she'd shunned human contact, hiding behind social media. Now, with barely anyone left, her theory about everything being wiped out crumbled. She needed people. The irony wasn't lost on her.

THE ANTS MARCH FREE

THE JUDGE WHACKED his gavel against the polished podium, brandishing an angry, plump finger at Dan Poole. Thunder echoed through the courtroom. "Counselor! Advise your client to answer my question, or I'll rule with contempt!"

The lawyer whispered in Dan's ear, but Dan's death glare never wavered from the judge. He looked ready to storm the bench and beat the man to death with his own gavel.

A sarcastic smirk crossed his face. "Not guilty." His lawyer leaned in again, this time with a longer whispered conference.

"The court accepts your plea and will set the matter for a pretrial conference a month from today." The judge waved the clerk over. "Schedule it on the docket?" Their whispered exchange was lost to Dan and his lawyer. The judge cleared his throat and nodded. "Fine. September twenty-first at nine-thirty a.m."

That damning finger pointed at Dan again. "The next time I ask you a question, sir, you better answer." Dan didn't flinch. Didn't react. Just held that cold, defiant glare.

His jumpsuit washed him out, pale skin colliding with dull gray fabric. He bore a skeletal appearance, as if he'd done hard time, though in reality he'd never spent a full night in jail. His last stint, eight hours. His latest encounter, picked up at 10:33 a.m., home by dinner.

The judge gave him another disgusted look, then sighed. "Have it your way, Mr. Poole. Bail amount set at twenty thousand dollars."

The district attorney sprang up. "Your Honor! The state requests a hundred thousand bail be set. All the victims fear for their lives." She jabbed a finger toward Dan. "They fear the defendant will retaliate."

Dan's attorney stood. "Your Honor, my client is an upstanding citizen. Not a flight risk. He's a pillar of the community, a youth pastor."

"Pillar?" The district attorney interrupted. "Your Honor, Mr. Poole knows each victim's address. They fear he'll try to silence them."

Dan's attorney raised his hand, but the judge cut in. "Mr. Poole is not a flight risk. Bail set at twenty thousand. That's my final ruling." The gavel cracked down. "Take Mr. Poole to holding."

The Pooles had their grip on this farming community since the 1900s. They owned most of the land acquired during the Depression. Corn planted in May and alfalfa in August kept their wealth intact. Only two Pooles remained now, Dan and his grandmother.

Grandma got Dan out of jail. Loyal in that regard. Then he went to Wednesday mass at Twelve Apostles. At the entrance, Sister Ivy stopped him, her warm smile bursting with luminous joy. "Brother Dan, we are so blessed you could make it tonight." She clasped her hands together, rubbing them anxiously. "We'll hear a great sermon tonight. Bless it be the Lord." Her eyes went skyward as though devouring something delicious.

Dan gripped her hands, his smile turning grotesque. "Bless it be the Lord, Sister. Your loyalty has not gone unnoticed. The Lord's blessings upon you."

Sister Ivy beamed brighter. "Your accusers are deeply troubled. The enemy is upon them, and we must pray for their salvation." Her hand soared skyward, eyes closing in fervent prayer. "The devil will test your faith by imprisoning you for ten days. But you will receive eternal life as a reward." He bowed his head. "Today is the tenth day. The Lord keeps his promises. Amen."

He squeezed her hands tighter. Dan hadn't served ten days, but

Sister Ivy didn't need to know that. His smile vanished, replaced by stern authority. "Amen, Sister. The Lord is merciful."

Dan marched down the main aisle like a conquering king. Pew after pew, he waved and made eye contact, his smile broadening with each nod. Halfway to the front row, something magnificent caught his eye, precious Sister Gomer, sitting alone. He couldn't resist sliding in beside her.

Her long blond hair smelled of ivory soap, overwhelming his senses. The handed-down floral dress, when she sat, revealed an inch of mauve stocking above her ankle. He fixed his gaze on the pulpit, awaiting the twelfth apostle.

Sister Gomer's eyes darted everywhere, to Brother Dan, to the couple before them, to the four people on her left, to those sitting closer to the pulpit on the right. Everyone stared ahead, entranced, awaiting their leader's arrival.

Excitement rippled through the congregation as the twelfth apostle mounted the stage. A woman in the back leaped up, hands reaching skyward. "Praise be, Praise be!"

The twelfth apostle silenced her with a subtle flick of his wrist, like a czar commanding his subjects. He ruled with gestures, a wave, a disapproving nod, a commanding finger. Such power needed no words, only blind devotion.

At the pulpit, he stood silent. Straight posture. Squared shoulders. Fire in his eyes as he surveyed his flock. Not a cough nor sniffle broke the silence.

The audience sat mesmerized. A woman wept with joy. He drew a deep breath, held it, released it with a whistle. "Shall we pray, brothers and sisters?"

Heads bowed, eyes closed. "Lord, give me strength. The celestial knowledge to lead your flock. I am your vessel. My lips are yours, my tongue yours, my mind yours, my whole being yours and yours alone."

"Give him the power, Lord!" a man shouted. Another broke into tongues, possessed syllables pouring forth in impossible combinations.

A woman's voice cut through, prophesying birds in fields, seas of blood, fish raining from the sky. The rest was babel.

Brother Dan sat with lowered head, eyes closed in apparent

devotion. The twelfth apostle voice reached heavenward. "Brothers, sisters. We are a pinhole at the farthest reaches of space. Glass half full, not empty. Old becomes new after their passing. Light only shines once, never to return!" His voice rose on those last words. "The tree sways in darkness but always sleeps." People sprang from their seats, hands raised.

"Caterpillars die young only to take flight the next day. Ants build mausoleums underneath the ground, big enough to rule the planet. Women carry their offspring to deliver clones to the world. Big Brother monitors us from the moon."

The twelfth apostle's voice cut off mid-sentence, as if unplugged. Tiny explosions of light danced around the room like misfired camera flashes.

The congregation fell silent. No whispers, no praises, no tongues. Just void. Dan kept his eyes closed despite the growing brightness, waiting for their leader to continue.

The twelfth apostle often fell into trances during sermons, gathering thoughts or receiving divine messages. Only a woman's scream made Dan look up.

Fire greeted every direction. His eyes bathed in flames. The twelfth apostle stood at the pulpit, hands still reaching skyward, engulfed. Left, right, ahead, everywhere fire danced. The church and its congregation transformed into living torches, each person frozen in their final pose, trapped in this earthly hell.

He dashed for the aisle as another scream pierced the air. Sister Gomer covered her mouth, she who'd sat beside him moments ago now stood trapped in a different pew, boxed in by burning bodies. Unlike the others, the flames hadn't touched her. Terror etched her face, orange light dancing in her eyes.

"Climb over!" Dan shouted, running toward her. She stood rooted, immobile. He mounted the facing pew, reaching out. "Take my hand!" Fear blazed brighter than the flames in her eyes. She shook her head, frozen.

Brother Dan grabbed her arm, trying to pull her free. Panic-stricken, Sister Gomer tore away, knocking over one of the burning bodies. It shattered into ash. Her screams intensified as she thrashed in the pew, though no flame touched her. Ash coated her, turning blond hair gray.

One by one, the bodies crumbled, leaving scattered limbs. Dan helped Sister Gomer to an empty pew, checking her over. "Are you hurt? Did you get burned?"

She sat dazed, silent. He wiped ash from her face, expecting raw flesh or burns beneath. Her skin remained cool, flawless.

The fire should have consumed the church, heated the air. Instead, the temperature had dropped. No smoke filled their lungs. *Where there's smoke, there's fire, isn't that how it goes?* Not here. Not in the billions of cases worldwide.

Everything had unraveled so fast, he'd thought only of saving the screaming girl. A vision of beauty he was smitten for. They sat together, staring at the pulpit where their leader had stood.

The silence stretched until Sister Gomer turned to him, her voice distant. "My brother once tried to light a cigarette on the gas stove. He stuck his nose this close to the burner, cigarette glued to his lips. But it wouldn't light, not right away." She tucked her hair behind her ears. "He got impatient, turned the knob all the way up and poof. The burner exploded in his face. Burned his eyebrows. Singed his bangs to the scalp."

"That's enough, sister," Brother Dan interrupted, but she raised her voice.

"His hair smelled like a stinky fart. The sick-to-your-stomach kind. The whole kitchen reeked of burned hair. Have you ever smelled a body on fire before?"

Fear glinted in his eyes. "No."

She met his gaze. "Me either. But don't you think it would smell terrible? Maybe twice as bad as burning hair?"

He straightened. "I suppose."

She gathered his hands in hers, her skin young and warm. "I can't smell anything. Do you smell anything?"

"The air smells sanitized," he said, bewildered by his own words.

Her attention drifted, wonder, or horror, or redemption, sparkling in her eyes. "Yes, the air is pure now. This is not a tragedy. We are witnessing a miracle from the Lord."

Brother Dan stood. "Yes, I suppose."

Sister Gomer rose beside him and whispered, "The Lord chose you as the next apostle... Praise the Lord."

LIGHT IN OPEN AIR

RORY PARKED on Bruce's lawn, near the front steps. The engine idled, as a precaution. She peered through each window, waiting for some maniac to emerge. Another wave of panic hit, her heart stuck on full throttle, making her head sway.

Air vanished from her lungs. She gasped but sprung a mighty leak at the same time. The world started closing in, just like before. Her hands trembled, everything inside going berserk.

The drive over had revealed a city on pause. Cars scattered across roads. Fast-food drive-throughs packed with empty vehicles. Piles of soot everywhere, on streets, sidewalks, gas stations. Body parts rose from ash like macabre sculptures.

Among all the remains she'd passed, one leg still wore desert combat boots. Otherwise, no clothes, or shoes. Just purses and wallets and phones marked the ash. Body parts and more ash. Ash and more parts, wherever her eyes landed.

She'd spotted a golden retriever and a small brown dog prancing through the business district, leashes rattling against pavement as they played. No owners in sight. The tiny one looked like a toy lion, complete with mane.

Rory: I'm here. Open the door

Bruce: K

The next minute stretched eternal, though not quite her longest. That belonged to her mother. The second, her father's affair. The third to Larry, and the fourth to Chloe.

She bolted from the car, backpack in hand, and ran inside. Once in, Rory shoved Bruce aside, slammed the door, and locked the deadbolt. Her paranoia triggered something in him, concern or fear. Maybe both. Still lethargic and subdued, as if running on empty, he asked in a frail voice, "Is someone chasing you?"

She glared at him, breathing hard. "I hope not."

He embraced her, his nose buried in her hair. Her herbal shampoo filled his senses. "I can't believe you're alive."

The hug felt hollow, his body bony against hers. She caught a whiff of body odor, but bigger concerns pressed. "Do you remember Larry?"

Bruce released her. "There's more people alive?"

Rory's expression darkened. "He tried to kill us."

His eyes widened, hopeful, glossing over the word 'kill.' "Us?"

She slipped the backpack from her shoulder. "Don't ask, it's a story."

He stumbled to the sofa and collapsed. "I thought I was the only one left. Until you."

Rory followed, dumping her pack onto the coffee table. "Keep an eye out for the psycho ones."

Bruce's attention was fixed on the food, everything else forgotten. Hunger glazed his eyes as if facing a feast. "Uh-huh." He grabbed a freeze-dried package and tore it open.

"That's the best one." He dumped the powder into his mouth, devouring it. "Add boiling water first!"

He kept eating, hands trembling, body shaking, swallowing, grunting. Fine wrinkles had sunk into his eyes, aging him twenty years. Greasy hair twisted wild. Pompadour gone ratty. Downy hair sprouted on chin and upper lip. His bathrobe draped over t-shirt and boxers. Clothes he'd clearly lived in since the world ended.

Rory returned with hot water and a Pyrex bowl, placing a spoon in his hand. "Stop eating. Let me fix it right. You might get sick."

He stopped chewing, guilty as a kid caught with cookie dough. She dumped ingredients into the bowl and stirred. "Seen any neighbors? Crazy ones running around?"

"Haven't left the house since... you know."

"Maybe we should drive—shit!" Rory sprang up, eyes wide. She lurched toward the front door, then turned slowly. "You're certain no one's outside?"

Bruce stood. "Yeah. What's wrong?"

She stared at the door, fear bubbling up, blood racing, throat tight. "I didn't turn the car off. Keys are still inside."

Her look said everything, one he knew well, packed with an unspoken request. "I'll go." He swayed there, sunken eyes in his pale face, body trembling. A soldier struggling to stand.

"I'll get the keys. You need to eat." He staggered forward, colorless as paper. "Sit! You need your strength."

Time resumed where they'd left off, as if the apocalypse held no power over them. Seeing him again awakened dormant feelings, nonexistent minutes ago. Rory helped him to bed, the food making him drowsy.

"Can I lie next to you?" He shifted over, making space. They slept wrapped in each other as the house settled around them.

Wind howled against siding and roofline, creaking and whistling like a ship's hull in deep water. A storm swept in from the north. The sky lit with sprites pinging off clouds, one after another. Thunder rattled the foundation, burrowing through sheetrock to where they lay.

The elements tore Rory from her dream. She sat up, momentarily lost. It took a minute to adjust, to remember she wasn't in the basement anymore. She'd dreamed of her mother trying to tell her something important, but the words came muted, hazy. Sitting in darkness as rain pelted glass, reality hit, the traditional notion of home had vanished. Not in this new world.

Bruce was home. Not that place on Irwin Street. Home hadn't been home since Tala died and her father abandoned her. She'd wasted so much energy clinging to emptiness, prolonging the inevitable. Tala's home needed rest. A structure, a house, or apartment or penthouse, isn't inherently home just because you hold the deed.

It belonged to others first. Their tribe, their lineage, their heart.

Blood and soul transformed the space. Without those things, a home is just an arrangement of concrete, brick, and wood. Who sleeps beside you matters more than the roof above. They were both orphaned now, like Bruce Wayne. They were all orphans. The new world had orphaned its survivors. Except unlike Wayne's parents, SHC claimed all lives, not just the innocent.

After that first night, Bruce's strength returned, color flooding back. Rory hadn't planned for a lengthy stay. She'd meant to drop off food and leave, maybe convince him to join her in the basement. Everything would be saved then. They'd ride out end days, or their last days, in the bunker with plenty of food, water, and weapons, if she ever found that safe combination. Still, their current supplies wouldn't last. Maybe another day.

"We should leave tomorrow," she said.

"What if my parents come back and I'm not here?"

Rory wrapped her arms around him, smiling without conviction. "We are coming back." The smile told more than she meant. "We have plenty of time to do whatever we want."

Having her around made him self-conscious. Bruce could smell himself now. Her clean scent made his stronger. He stepped back. "I haven't showered in a couple days." Truth was, he hadn't showered since SHC began. Too embarrassed to admit he'd spent days and nights surfing the internet and social media, hunting updates on SHC like everyone else still alive. Countless videos of spontaneous human combustion. Sleepless nights waiting for parents who never returned.

Terror flashed across Rory's face, she didn't want to be alone. "Do you want to take one with me?" He said. She searched his eyes, trying to read his thoughts. "I'm stupid."

She covered his mouth. "Yes."

The bathroom became a study in awkward body language. Accidental bumps reaching for things. Twisted lips. Darting eyes. They stood staring. Each waiting for the other to move. Usually, Rory had no problem with boys seeing her in swimwear at the pool. They lusted over her body and she knew it from the attention she received.

But this was different, seeing a boy in high-def nakedness was new to her. Bruce smiled. "I'll go first." He stripped bare, covering himself. Rory's face went poker-blank, unreadable. "Maybe this was a bad idea."

She quietly undressed, folding clothes on the counter. No covering up. What's the point? Eventually, they'd see everything.

His build was average, proportional. Unlike social media men, Bruce lacked that sculpted look of endless burpees and thousand-pound lifts. He was imperfect. She liked that. Even with missed meals, he kept cute love handles. "Hot or cold?" he asked, turning on the water. "Medium?"

Her smile came uneasy. "Warm, I guess."

They stayed until the water ran cold. He washed her back, long fingers kneading, sending shivers down her spine. When she asked if he'd showered with a girl before, he said no. He never asked her the same. Maybe her inexperience showed clearly enough.

The kiss happened while drying off. One moment routine motions, the next, passion. Bodies pressed close. Strange moment. She'd fantasized about the perfect boy, perfect first time. This beats imagination. No parents interrupting. House to themselves, apocalyptic mood right. Yet nothing stirred inside. No sparks. No movement. Nothing. Unlike with Chloe.

Things were progressing for Bruce, she felt him rising against her skin. She envied that response. Why hadn't her body risen for him?

When she stopped, confusion and hurt crossed his face, triggering guilt. His skin glowed with excitement. She felt awful, turning him on then pulling back. It confused her too. A year ago, boys were everything. Liking girls that way had never crossed her mind.

All those locker room moments with naked girls, never once thinking 'she's hot' or 'I'd kiss her.' A woman's body had been as unremarkable as an elbow or knee. No thrills examining the same sex. What was happening to her?

Still, kissing Chloe had been, as Mr. Schmidt would quote, 'the face that launched a thousand ships.' Chloe was her Helen. Not worth going to war over, that seemed a stretch. Though never feeling that way again, with anyone, forever? Loneliness might make war seem rational. Maybe Menelaus had a point about Helen.

Sleep wouldn't come. She lay overthinking, eyes fixed somewhere up there, just up there, planning next moves. After the shower, Bruce had gone quiet, almost stoic. She'd overcompensated with small talk, fighting awkwardness. What she wanted was to rewind time. Return to that shower moment, finish right. The way it should have gone.

That moment held beauty. Despite lacking sexual interest, being intertwined with him brought comfort. She hadn't connected like this in so long. Rory needed deeper connection, like with her mother. What were the odds of finding the perfect guy at the end of the world?

Bruce was all those things. Sweet, caring. First asking her shower temperature preference. Her comfort mattered more than his. Who does that, honestly? Except a mother who loves you.

Rory shed her clothes. Bruce still slept. She lay across him, kissing. He woke startled. "What are you doing?"

Another kiss. "I want to be with you."

His eyes found hers in the dark. "I don't want you to do something you don't want." She answered with more kisses. He returned them. Everything flowed from there.

Reality shattered first time myths. Kissing topped the evening. The act itself? Anticlimactic. Okay, at best. Nerves didn't help. It didn't last long, mere minutes.

Movies painted different pictures, couples igniting sparks, heat rising, beds rocking. Worlds turning inside out or right side up. Who knew? Lustful sounds filling rooms. Afterward, sharing cigarettes, lying side by side in blissful exhaustion. Bruce stayed gentle but inexperienced. His body was softer than hers.

Truth felt more like checking boxes. Get it done. Get through it. That mindset. Relief came after, holding onto virginity stressed girls differently. So much pressure. So much pressure.

Surprisingly, it wasn't horrible. Nothing like the horror stories girls traded about their first time. She remembered Kate, short for Katherine, saying, "It hurts so fucking bad. It's like you're being ripped apart."

Looking back, maybe Kate wasn't ready. Or lied. Or maybe her first guy was just an asshole who ignored her body and feelings. Because Bruce hadn't ripped her apart. Uncomfortable? Yes. Pressure? Yes. Torn apart? Not quite. That description sounded more like what a guy would say. Rory was ready, that made the difference. She trusted Bruce.

He seemed satisfied enough for both of them. That would do for now. Best part? She felt closer than before. They'd shared something. She couldn't name it. Still, something existed there. Both had lowered their guard, revealing hidden pieces. Things locked away from the outside world and prying eyes.

They held each other, still naked, still vulnerable. Her mind spun wild, overthinking every detail. One thought dominated, they hadn't used protection. Sex Ed 101, never, ever, under any circumstance, skip the condom. Never, ever, period, end of story. "Lock that down," her mother had said. After Rory's first period, Tala gave the talk, among other things.

Tala spoke blunt, too direct. Rory had turned bright red, half-listening, blocking the gross stuff. But two points stuck. One, sex was normal. Natural, even. Everyone should practice often. Do it well. Could become amazing with the right person. Two, always wrap it before you pack it, her exact words. She'd even dressed a medical device with a condom to demonstrate.

STDs at world's end, now there's a nightmare. Fear pressed her to ask, though her mother would've killed her for waiting this long. "I'm your first, right?"

Bruce's voice came subdued, drifting toward sleep. "Yeah."

His answer eased her somewhat. Her gut feeling about his virginity seemed right, given his bedroom inexperience. She'd guided him through certain moments. Still, who could really know? Bruce might be an inexperienced little Romeo.

But her greatest fear waited. Getting pregnant before SHC was life-altering, even with modern medicine. Now? Pure hell. "You didn't..." She paused, drawing a long breath. "You were careful, right?"

His voice came drowsy. "You know I wouldn't do that."

She squeezed her eyes shut, held her breath. "Are you a hundred percent positive?"

He turned to his side. "Yeah."

Bruce drifted off in her arms, but Rory lay wired, sleepless. A thought nagged, there might be a tiny chance. Her first time, no condom. Just her luck. A microscopic embryo probably spinning to life right now as she lay here.

Ms. Ramsey, the sex ed instructor, haunted her thoughts. "Now girls, it only takes one sperm to fertilize the egg. It's ridiculously small. The smallest cell in the body. Sperm always finds a way. Those little suckers are smart and determined. Don't let it happen to you. It's best to wait for marriage. You don't want a baby destroying your teenage bodies. Believe me, they will. Pregnancy is not a good look for young girls."

Regret flooded her brain. Her heart pounded harder. How could she be so reckless?

CREDIT CARD, NOT REQUIRED

MORNING LIGHT FOUND Rory watching Bruce sleep. Her face scrunched in concentration, brows collided like a crash. Something churned behind those intense eyes, those slightly curled lips. He caught it instantly, laying his hands over hers. "Are you okay?"

She sprang from bed, still naked. "Yeah. Are you okay?" Her tone betrayed her. Frustrated or maybe tired. Sunlight caught her body, transforming her into something from a museum, marble chiseled into Greek form. Ethereal, he thought.

Questions circled as she pulled on her bra. "Was I the first person you tried texting?"

He narrowed his eyes. "No. I tried all our friends. But no one texted back."

Rory sat, head lowered. "Why didn't you text me first?"

Bruce knelt before her, lifting her chin until their eyes met. "If our friends died, sure, I'd be really sad. But you? That's different. If you died, that would have killed me. I didn't want to know."

She ran fingers through his hair. "Oh." Yes, that was enough. That was Bruce.

"I love you. I can't help it," he said, kissing her. She smiled, kissed back.

Outside, approaching the car, Rory felt different. Her heart stayed steady. The world didn't close in anymore. She could breathe deep, hold air without drowning in abandonment. Maybe Bruce's presence had cured her claustrophobia.

He held the gun flat. "Where should we put this?"

Tala had taught Rory everything about guns, but they still scared her. Thank god for Bruce's dad owning one. "Put it in the glove box."

Bruce played tough, pretending to tuck it in his waistband. "You mean I shouldn't just stick it here? That's how cops do it on TV."

She snorted. "Aren't you afraid you'll shoot your, umm." Her eyes dropped pointedly. "You know what I mean."

His smile vanished as he carefully stored the gun away.

The gas gauge showed half-empty. "Should we try to get gas? Think it'll work?"

His face puckered. "I don't think so. But we'll see."

Bruce cracked jokes as they drove, until the shopping center silenced him. His arm swung like a pointer, suggesting body parts rising from soot, sidewalks, crosswalks, cars. The plaza surely held more. Beings from another realm in suburban hell.

Disbelief and excitement poured from him like a kid at some alien zoo. "Look at that one. Nasty. Do you see it? That leg looks fake." Her face stayed grim, silent.

A convenience store with pumps appeared, setting off Rory's internal alarm. The street held scattered cars, but the store lot stood empty. Swept clean.

She remembered 12:33 p.m., when Larry attacked. But when had SHC struck? "What time did it happen?"

Bruce stayed fixed on the dead. "Who knows. Why?"

She jabbed his side. "Look."

His glare turned angry. "What the hell."

"Will you look?"

He flashed his palms. "Yeah, I see. Let's stop there."

"There are no cars, even at the pumps. Don't you think that's strange?"

"So. SHC hit when they weren't busy, probably in the morning."

"There should be at least one car. What about employees?"

"Some people can't afford cars, Rory."

"I'm serious."

"I am too. Maybe an employee survived, got out. If it were me, I wouldn't stick around. Last place anyone wants to die is at work."

"Like you know what work is?"

"Hey, I had a summer job."

"Uh-huh?"

His ruffled hair fell back in place. He had a way of making things sound plausible, eyes fixed on her, expression serious. She smiled, brushing strands from his face. "You need a haircut."

At pump one, he offered his credit card. "Try mine first."

She rolled her eyes. "I can pay for gas."

"I have to earn my keep somehow."

Rory snorted. "Keep it. You'll need it."

"For what? Machine might not work anyway."

"I need a pregnancy test."

"I told you I wouldn't do that to you."

"I know. Just want to be extra sure."

"Doubt they carry stuff like—."

"They do. Check the condoms. And no, it wasn't for me."

"I'm not saying nothing." Bruce leaped out, howling like a wolf, making wild animal sounds. Letting off steam.

"This is crazy! Nobody is here. We're the only ones left alive. Can you believe it?"

He couldn't be more wrong. Rory still thought of Chloe. Surely others survived. Look at them, just two miles apart, both alive. The odds favored more survivors. How many remained to be seen.

They could stay the course now. She'd fixed what needed fixing and refused to repeat her mistakes with Chloe. Forward movement was required. They wouldn't last if they didn't work as one brain, toward one goal.

The world stretched empty, but they were running out of places to run. What remained needed people to function. What if someone fell ill, needed a doctor? Prescriptions? Food? Tala always said health and medicine first, everything else last. Nothing lasts forever. Soon they'd need to survive off the land.

Rory knew nothing about hunting, fishing, or growing food. Bruce probably didn't either. Her knowledge of water came from faucets, drink stations, and bottles. Beyond that? Paper-thin understanding. See-through.

The credit card reader displayed a spinning hourglass. "Please work," she prayed quietly.

When the screen advanced to ZIP code entry, then flashed SELECT GRADE, her heart lifted. "It worked!"

Something glinted at the building's corner, like sunlight striking a mirror. Bruce trudged back, hands raised. "Doors are locked."

Rory searched for the flash, ignoring him. "Did you see that?"

Bruce kept his pace. "See what?"

Her voice wavered, uncertain. "I thought I saw something flash over there."

He leaned on the rear bumper, scanning for life. Rory edged closer. "Let's drive—."

Thunder cracked from the convenience store's side. Bruce's head exploded. Blood, brain matter, and skull fragments splattered across Rory's face. Bright red blood glimmered, unreal. She gasped like someone had thrown scalding water in her face. Her mind slowed, unable to process. Eyes wide, expression blank.

Bruce stood jittering, android-like, still propped against the fender. Strange noises escaped his gnarled mouth. "err... err..."

Rory's scream pierced the sky. His body folded, hitting the pavement with a thud. Another crack echoed off cinderblock. She flinched, arms outstretched, fingers splayed to shield her face. The bullet whispered past her arm, shattering the rear window.

She turned toward the gunfire. A man knelt by the building, fumbling with a jammed rifle. She didn't recognize the malfunction, she'd never paid enough attention during Tala's lessons.

The gun came from the glove box. She aimed and squeezed, channeling every action movie she and Bruce had watched. Brock, last name unnecessary, too famous. And Susan Mallory, that dazzling warrior-symbol. Their showdowns, where good triumphed until the villain fell bloody.

Clack, clack, clack. Bullets sparked off cinderblock and pavement until the man howled. "You bitch!" Blood poured through his fingers where the bullet struck his thigh.

Everything inside her seized. The earth shifted. Her knees went weak, sun-drunk. She slumped against the car, gun still aimed. Hands trembling and sweating. "Help me!" the man screamed, again and again. She watched with vengeful eyes until he fell silent.

Minutes later, she approached. Dilated eyes stared skyward, blood pooling around his leg. The Quick Mart vest blazed orange against his baby-faced, bald head. Keys hung from his belt.

Rory loomed over him, expression distant. Playing dead? She couldn't risk it. She had to finish it. Gun to chest, click. Again, click. Again, click. Faster, harder, her finger moved, an inferno building. "We stole nothing. We paid for the gas. We paid, we paid!"

She cradled Bruce's bloody head, smoothing his dark hair. No tears came. Not since her mother's death. Her foundation already shook. She'd cry later, outside a rest stop on I70 westbound to Glenwood Springs. For now, tears just blurred her vision.

Time passed. Blood soaked her legs, concrete numbing her. A golden shape approached like a mirage. The retriever from the business district, leash trailing. It sat beside her, licking dried blood from her face with its rough tongue.

The dog's silver tag read: CHARLIE. "Charlie? Is that your name?" Two quick barks. "Charlie." Another bark, pawing her chest. "Hmm. You don't look like a Charlie to me." More barking. "Are you hungry?"

She laid Bruce's head on the blacktop as if he were napping. "I won't be long," she whispered.

Inside the store, she fed Charlie puppy chow and gave him water. In the bathroom she held a pregnancy test and thought of Bruce, of babies. What kind of mother could she be now? What person raises a child in this world? A narcissist.

Yet she wanted his baby, wanted him living through his child. This morning, motherhood had terrified her. Now...who knows. Like Bruce said on the car ride here, who knows.

No one had told her pregnancy tests need time, weeks, to show accurate results. Hormone levels take time to rise. She'd need a gynecologist. In four weeks. Maybe five. She'd washed blood from face and arms. It had pooled in her ears, her nose. Bruce's blood had found every hiding place. Skull fragments tangled in her hair. Cool tap water couldn't calm her flushed skin. She trembled, tears threatening as the negative test result stared back.

CAVIAR SPA

In the weeks following Sarah's theft of the Jeep, after nursing Grace back to health at the grocery store, Dante and Grace fell into a comfortable routine in the employee lounge beyond the stockroom. She cared for Grace completely, from brushing teeth to entertainment. Constant upkeep.

Two blocks down from Grand Avenue, on 8th and Pitkin, stood a bungalow with a glossy black door. A tarnished brass knocker centered it. Dormer windows lined the walls, and a wraparound veranda embraced the house. Above, a small attic held a pink bedroom overlooking both street and backyard.

Decades had passed, but the pink bedroom remained preserved like a time capsule. A pink canopy bed, ruffles undulating around carved mahogany. Not princess-themed but decorated with cute bears sporting clovers and rainbows on their bellies.

This was William Gates' home. Climbing the three quick steps to 801 Pitkin Avenue, Dante hoped William had survived SHC. She knew this home intimately. William and Jack had been close friends.

They'd spent countless evenings in the cozy dining room playing cards. After meals, the three would clear the table and play cards deep into night, sometimes until dawn. Outside, black streets would shimmer under the porch lights of vibrant bungalows dotting Pitkin Avenue's green spaces.

William had adored Dante. She reminded him of Dione, his late daughter. He lived alone since Julia, his ex-wife, left him two years after Dione's death from glioblastoma. They'd separated first, hoping space and time would bring closure, allowing them reconnection. It never did.

His final communication from Julia came by courier, divorce papers in a slender legal envelope. Her note, paper-clipped to the stack, read in familiar scrawl:

Please forgive me. I still love you. You will always be my first love. But I love our daughter more. I cannot easily forget, my heart won't let me. She had your eyes. I don't have the courage to look into those eyes every morning when I wake. A daily reminder of what we once had and what we lost, love Julia.

The front door stood unlocked. Following her usual precaution, Dante had Grace wait on the porch swing. When she pushed the door wide, signs of interrupted life greeted her, a mug beside a carton of orange juice, a dinner plate with crumpled napkin on the kitchen table. Breakfast, she imagined. William's breakfast.

The house's shotgun layout offered everything at a glance. From the front door, her gaze swept to the rear kitchen table. The open floor plan revealed all, even from the porch.

William had never left messes. Always fastidious, always cleaning as he went. This untidy kitchen kindled hope, perhaps he still lived. William would never ignore dirty dishes or let juice spoil.

Yet emptiness pressed in, the air thick and stale as if circulation had ceased months ago. The bungalow's age seeped through the floorboards, how old, she couldn't say. But during their card games, century-old odors would crawl up through oak planks, earth from ancient dig sites, mildew and limestone. Undisturbed until now.

Damp plaster scented the air like a crypt. She knew that smell from touring the Ramses II Exhibit with her father at the Denver Museum. William's house carried that same tomb-like aroma, excavated stone, sand, and tobacco.

She lifted the juice carton, lukewarm. Coffee grounds fled a dark brown ring at the bottom of the mug. On the plate, scrambled eggs hosted writhing maggots. The half-eaten toast looked plastic. She lifted it, sniffed. No visible mold, but stale yeast overwhelmed.

"William." Her voice cracked, nervous. The name echoed louder in her ears than the empty house. She waited, knowing no answer would come.

Through the window, she watched Grace swing back and forth, singing or talking to herself. Her sounds muffled through glass and siding, the words indistinct.

"Are you okay?" Dante called through the doorway.

Grace swung faster, avoiding eye contact. "Yeah."

Dante stepped onto the porch. "Are you sure?"

Grace giggled. "I'm lovely."

Dante smiled despite herself. "Okay. Just checking."

Since her recovery, Grace had adopted "lovely" as her universal descriptor. Everything earned that label, regardless of significance. This gifted, peculiar child could describe the apocalypse itself as lovely. Morning to night, lovely ruled her world. The word should have grated on Dante, yet Grace's presence transformed their dark reality into something approaching loveliness. At least someone found beauty in this new world.

What Dante hadn't expected, couldn't have anticipated, was how deeply Grace had rooted inside her heart. This stranger, in mere weeks, had worked her way in with charisma and cleverness. Dante would scoop her up, squeeze too tight, because the girl was that irresistible. Her observations barrel out funny and sharp. Simply put, Grace made it impossible not to love her. Her innocence, her genuine kindness sparked something fierce in Dante, a protective instinct bordering on obsession.

"We can swing later. Let's get you cleaned up." Grace hopped down, slipping her small hand into Dante's.

In the bathroom, Dante drew water while unpacking grocery bags of toiletries. All "borrowed" from the store's endless shelves. Grace's mud-caked fingernails suggested outdoor adventures. Among the supplies, Dante found the pink medicine bottle. Grace no longer needed it, but Dante carried it everywhere. Just in case.

The bath water turned murky brown. Debris floated up, pine

needles, grass clippings, black sticky sap. "Did you go into the woods?" Dante asked, noting Grace's smoke-scented hair.

"No." Simple answer, complex implications. After several scrubs, the truth became clear, this was Grace's first real bath in a long time.

Their fingernails needed attention. The unkempt state bothered Dante, reminding her of her father's words: "Everything lies in the little realm now, mijita. Until your house is packed with little things." He'd been right. Human bodies demanded countless small maintenance, things taken for granted. Now each simple item became a treasure hunt in this new world.

Grace sat perfectly still during the nail trimming, fingers splayed elegantly on the tub's rim like a salon client. A stranger's intimate care didn't faze her, naked or not, no matter. It struck Dante, Grace was used to strangers providing everything, including personal care. Yet she showed no spite or entitlement. Her heart remained beautiful, even if her circumstances hadn't been.

She wouldn't leave Dante's side now, tangling in her legs, fear of abandonment. Evident after Sarah's betrayal. After Grace's second hair washing, Dante showered while the girl played with plastic ducks from the pharmacy. Hideous things she'd insisted on having. Their purpose mystified Dante, but they kept Grace entertained. That was enough.

Wrapped in fluffy towels, their heads turbaned like spa-goers, they waited while their clothes tumbled in William's washing machine. At the kitchen table, they shared an impromptu feast, Spanish tuna, Dijon mustard, and gourmet crackers. No mayonnaise for Grace, one of her rare dislikes.

Grace's knowledge of Dijon surprised Dante, but even more surprising was William's pantry, Russian caviar, at least the Cyrillic script suggested so. And a bottle of Krug 1982 in the fridge. Dante knew little about champagne, but the elegant black label with gold lettering spoke of expense. Even the cork showed artistry.

They sat in comfortable silence, this odd pair in their towels, picking at delicacies while the washer hummed. A scene from another life, Dante thought. The kind of peaceful moment that had vanished with SHC. Yet here they were, creating their own version of normal.

Grace arranged her crackers in precise patterns, something Dante had noticed she often did with food. Organization amid chaos. The girl's methodical movements reminded Dante of William, his careful card-playing, his meticulous housekeeping. The thought squeezed her heart.

The house held echoes of William everywhere. His reading glasses on the side table, bookmarked novel beside them. His slippers tucked under a chair, his calendar still marking appointments that would never be kept. All these little signs of life interrupted, preserved like his daughter's pink room upstairs.

Dante watched Grace lick mustard from her fingers, proper table manners forgotten in childhood satisfaction. The girl's presence had transformed this house of memories into something alive again. Not lovely, perhaps, Dante smiled at the thought, but living. They were making their own kind of family in the ruins of others'.

The washer buzzed. Soon they'd need to move on, continue their search for other survivors. But for now, in their towel turbans with their fancy lunch, they could pretend this was just another day. That William might walk through the door any moment, ready for a game of cards. That the world hadn't ended, leaving them to find new ways to begin.

Grace looked up, catching Dante's gaze. "This is lovely," she said, and for once, Dante didn't mind the word at all.

LIMES AND PAPER UMBRELLAS

WILLIAM'S PANTRY spoke of peculiar tastes, far from bachelor fare. The champagne waited as celebration, for the day Dione would beat cancer. Julia had called it a fool's errand.

The doctors had delivered their death sentence while William and Julia sat side by side. "I have bad news," the doctor said, as if they'd merely misplaced a chart. No, Julia thought, this is far worse than bad news. Those words echoed from William's ears to hers.

Julia found nothing ambiguous in their robotic frankness. They predicted Dione's death nearly to the week. William refused to accept their "expert opinions," as he called them, sneering at medical certainty.

When Julia told her college friend Liz about the diagnosis, the response crushed her.

"Oh Julia, I'm so sorry. Did they give you a time frame?"

"Six or seven months," Julia sobbed.

Keyboard clicks filled the silence as Liz multitasked. "Well, that must give you some comfort, don't you think?"

Julia's tears stopped cold. "What the hell are you talking about?"

"What I wouldn't give to know my time of death. Given months, I'd quit my job, find a tropical beach. Take out an obscene loan, live my best life. Look at Bob, he worked himself to death at fifty-five, heart attack at his desk. They called it a widow maker. Can you believe it? Just like that, game over. This is an opportunity. Look at the bright side. Take my advice."

The bright side blared in Julia's head like a foghorn. Bright side? She'd like to bright side Liz right across the face. "Fuck the bright side, Liz. Why don't you bright side yourself?" She hung up, their friendship ending there.

Cruel as Liz was, glacial truth lived in her words. She had a way of forcing perspective, though she never applied such logic to her own messy life. Julia absorbed those heartless words. She could give Dione the best six, seven, even ten months possible. Whatever time remained, she wouldn't waste a second.

Their savings had grown substantial over the years. Not mega-wealth, but enough for comfort. They could have bought the expensive house, the zip code, the fancy cars and foreign vacations. None of it appealed. They loved their bungalow life, first as two, then three. Until cancer ripped good from their hands.

Money was their tool. Yet when they needed its power most, it failed them. Somewhere in their minds, they believed money could fix Dione. Right to the end. William threw more at specialists, experts, hospitals, trials. More, more, more. As if enough money could wake them from this nightmare.

It started with headaches. Paralyzing pain that forced Dione into dark spaces where noise and smells couldn't reach. Light triggered agony. Even cooking odors became enemies. They stopped cooking. Boarded windows. Replaced bulbs with special ten-watt technology for migraine sufferers. The bulbs failed Dione. Everything failed Dione.

They lived in darkness, shuffling through blackness, surviving on bland food like applesauce, Jell-O, low-sodium crackers. Even the smell of water sickened her. IV drips became her lifeline.

Double vision came next. Balance failed. Nausea ruled her days. Arms and legs lost sensation, betraying her control.

No, Dione couldn't travel. Not to Niagara Falls, not to Paris, not around the block. Their cherished bungalow became a tomb, dark and tasteless and odorless and soundless, obedient torture.

What destroyed Julia most, what stole her last shred of dignity, was the relief she felt when Dione passed. Not a relief for herself. Not for the light or taste or sound returning. Relief that her daughter's suffering ended. She and William watched those eyes close forever.

That relief crushed her. Shamed her. Julia compressed into herself. What kind of mother feels relief at her child's death? Her tormented brain fired wild neurons, paths her daughter would never travel again. Think. Live. Marry. Bear children, if she chose. Fly to Paris. Live her best life, like Liz could with her fucking beach cocktails and paper umbrellas and fresh mint and lime rims.

Liz's narcissistic brain firing neurons everywhere, wild and free. Something her daughter could never do again. Live a happy childhood. Get married. Have children of her own, if she chose. Fly to goddamn Paris. Live her best life, like Liz could and would, if she only had the fucking funds. On some goddamn beach at world's end, lounging with cocktails, tiny paper umbrellas and fresh mint and lime-rimmed glasses. Carcass out, or whatever the latest fucking trend. Martinis dirty all day long. Highballs, yeah to highballs. Having a grand old time while pinkies salute the sky and party balloons drift down to empty dance floors.

Living the best life. The only life. Living wherever, whatever. High-rise to trailer park to tent on the street, doesn't matter. Like life is grand and happy as long as you pack enough Xanax bars for the trip back. And how's it all supposed to go? How it truly goes? Like nobody ever said life wasn't fair. Maybe you're not applying yourself. Not focused on the bigger picture. The actual picture. That you must work harder or smarter or just work until your fingers bleed and your heart gives out. Until your bones disintegrate to dust. From dust to flesh, back down again from where you came. Doesn't matter. Maybe someday you'll find happiness right where the cure for cancer resides.

That mysterious tunnel waiting. Down that endless corridor with its bright light finale. Where strangers greet you - some dead relative you never met, but never the one you truly love. The one you brought into this world. The one who stole your heart the moment she entered this realm, when you first sank your eyes into her, onto her. And all along you'd tethered yourself to another world, the one after this one. The one you spent your whole life preparing for, crying for, dying for.

What would a ten-year-old do in Paris anyway? They want bikes and amusement parks and woods where giants roam and pixies soar. Sleepovers and birthday cakes drowning in sprinkles. Late movies and cereal bowls overflowing with rainbows and goodness and life fully lived. Where old crosses over at a rightful age.

These thoughts clouded Julia as she locked that glossy black door at 801 Pitkin Avenue one final time.

BROOK OVER GRACE

ALMOST EVERYTHING in the fridge had soured. On the kitchen table sat a wicker bowl filled with playing cards and a tangled mess of keys. Car keys looped through the chaos. Through the kitchen window, she spotted a small garden nestled against the garage. Tomato plants reached skyward, lush leaves sprouting from a planter box.

She waltzed out to the backyard, Grace in tow, to inspect the garage and William's SUV. The pile of ash stopped them both. Despite uncertainty, she knew William lay among the soot. Nothing defining stood out. Minimal clues. Too little left behind. Still, probability favored him.

A bulging kitchen trash bag sat tipped over beside the ash. That's how William left this world, she imagined. On his way to throw the trash. Everything spontaneous in the land of doll parts. Frozen and preserved for all time in the exact spot and last moments of doing everyday shit. Never think twice about how your life will end. Where it will end. With whom. Doing what, precisely? You better hope it's good and clean and not naughty. Or your mother or wife or husband or whoever you decide to lay your head next to will pass out from embarrassment and shock. Wondering who the hell you were in the first place. Nothing like the profile on Facebook or selfies you portray. The ones where you wear a white smile and promising eyes and brushed hair. Nose free of boogers. One would hope. Or pray it doesn't show when the flash goes off.

Get a wild hair to walk the dog, proof you're dead. Take a Sunday stroll down the block, times up, poof, you're dead. Like those souls on Mount Vesuvius. Calcified by boiling volcanic ash, preserved through ages. Putting the kibosh on their morning rituals. To any routine in a twenty-mile radius, for that matter. Poof, everything ceases to exist, in an instant. Just like SHC. SHC on a grander scale, though, by the billions.

Dante sent Grace back into the bungalow while she rummaged through the garage. The SUV fired up right away, full tank humming. How many miles would it travel? Anyone's guess. Late-model Scout, according to the hallmark on the dash. Older vehicles burned gas, lots of it. Resources were plentiful now. Extracting it from underground storage tanks, that's the real pickle. Burn what you've got, but please, don't burn too fast. You're liable to go up in smoke.

A week into using William's bungalow, Dante believed he would have approved. If still alive. It might please him knowing Dione's things gave new life, brought joy to another child.

The pink room had been caked in years of dust. Undisturbed. Dante ran her finger along the dresser top, collecting gray matter. She sneezed repeatedly as particles danced in the morning light.

Many shops lined Grand Avenue as they walked downtown. Grace noticed Bob's Used Emporium, Jack's kind of place. Her supernatural ability to eye the smallest things zeroed in on roller skates displayed in the window. Grace about died when she saw them. Dante about shit herself.

That promise came back to haunt her. The skates looked filthy. Boiled leather, size ten maybe. Man's skates with worn orange wheels and toe stops. Probably from some roller rink's rental fleet. Grace pointed and screamed, "Those are Lovely!"

Dante placed hands on her shoulders. "You can skate for a little while, but we can't take them home."

Their new home being 801 Pitkin. Grace's lips pursed, eyes narrowed. "You promised."

"I don't have money, and we don't steal. We only borrow, remember? We talked about this."

Like 'lovely,' 'borrow' became this century's tag word. One Dante used repeatedly when they needed anything not theirs.

She'd tried the barter method first, trading personal items. That lasted two hours. Grace cried after trading her ducks for some strange toy from the grocery store. Soon they had nothing left to trade. The Dante system quickly turned to borrowing.

The bungalow on Pitkin borrowed. Until they moved on. Or the electricity finally cut out. Which it would, eventually. Food and hygiene products, borrowed. Not like they could replace item for item. Even item for like item. Someday, down a long dark road, they'd pay for it. Way later. When the world got pieced back together. Maybe never. One can never be too sure about these things. Optics dominated. Borrowing instead of taking whatever they pleased insulated them from the apocalypse's full assault. Insulated Grace. She was raising Grace, or trying like hell to, as though SHC never happened. As if living in an abandoned town, all by themselves, was an average Monday.

"Without laws and morals set in place, then what do you have left?"

Grace smiled big. "I forget sometimes."

Dante tickled her. "It's impossible to remember everything, even for me." Grace screamed and laughed. Dante kneeled to eye level. "What do we do when we enter a store?"

Grace squeezed her eyes shut. "Cover my eyes, hands out."

"That's right, now give me your hand. And don't let go, not for anything."

They entered the Emporium when a horrendous smell knocked them sideways. Grace whimpered. "Ewh, it stinks."

Dante shushed her, recognizing that familiar odor. But she wouldn't leave Grace outside alone on Grand Avenue. Not again. Never again. Last time she'd instructed Grace to wait on the sidewalk while canvasing a store, she'd freaked out. Abandoning Grace traumatized her. PTSD, or whatever the hell they call it. Sarah abandoned her, forcing her to survive alone in a small town that felt enormous to a little girl. A giant town for any one person. Dante squeezed her hand for comfort. Grace signaled back, squeezing twice in short intervals. Like hand morse code.

If such a thing existed. Her way of saying I understand, or I'm okay, without words.

Dante grabbed the skates from the window. They scuttled back to the street where she positioned them on the sidewalk, lifted Grace's dangling legs, and plopped her feet in. They wheeled around the block a few times, but Grace kept slipping out. Especially on tight turns or changing direction. No matter how tight Dante tied them, those little feet wiggled free. Grace quit twenty minutes later, bored. She wanted to skate alone. Frustration set in. Dante wasn't pushing fast enough, hadn't turned when Grace wanted, the right way, her way.

That night, after walking back from the Emporium, Grace asked about her mother again. She wanted to go home. Where her things were. Where Sarah was. And Cecil, her dog. Dante didn't fault her for that. She wanted the same. Things to go back to the way they were, well, with major changes. The old world was far from perfect.

Still, Grace wasn't anything like Dante expected. Kind and agreeable most times. Appreciative and quick to excite over small things. I think Grace knows everybody's dead, including her mother, Dante convinced herself. Convinced herself they played the same game. Though Grace played a better one.

Grace was nothing like Brook Hart, a girl from school. A somewhat friend. An only child, like Grace. Brook approached life differently. Maybe given enough time, age, Grace would have ended up just like her. Something inside Dante thought maybe Brook was born rotten. Always getting her way and rarely compromises. The word no wasn't part of her genetic makeup. Likely stricken from her vocabulary at birth.

Hearing no drove Brook nuts, ignited her. Usually collapsed into tantrums or fits of rage. Most everyone gave in to her demands. Even the nutty ones. Once, she demanded a special chair in class, claiming her posture looked imperfect in wooden school chairs. Vanity is bliss. The appearance of droopy posture alone demanded better seating. Better yet, give her God's throne. I'm sure God won't mind. Add more pillows too. The seat's a little firm. In the end, the school caved. Not a request, but a command, a duty. How could the school be so reckless in the first place?

Brook Hart was a total bitch. Dripping in couture. Never off the rack. At least not department store racks. Brandishing names from

Milan and Paris designers, who's who, Dante had never heard of. Names she wouldn't know, couldn't know, not on her budget. Brook declared she'd never be caught dead in such rags, repeating it a million times. As if her first statement wasn't enough.

She looked like a real-life Barbie. Minus the blond hair. Brook had multicolor. Ice pink transitioning to purple at the shoulder, then aquamarine, then pale yellow. Like a snow cone. Her designer hair treatment cost four thousand dollars, she bragged. Now that Dante thought about it, she didn't know Brook's natural color.

Nothing about her looked real. Nails, hair smooth as silk. Wiglike. Slender body. No dimples or curves. Straight and stiff. Why, in God's name, would Brook befriend me, out of everyone? Dante often wondered. They were intersecting lines headed in the wrong directions. Wrong equation. Wrong solution. Totally. The end. People branded her intersection line "Macy's" on a good day. Brook's intersection line custom-made whatever. A name she couldn't even pronounce.

Dante's father made decent money. Contractor for a prestigious developer. Specialized in the industrial sector. Large-scale projects. They lived middle-class. Private school. He never seemed to worry about money. But they didn't have Hart wealth. The Harts had stupid rich stamped on their foreheads. I don't give a fuck kind of money. Brook knew it too. Used it to her advantage. Even exploited it when the occasion rose. And the occasion always rose.

They had a live-in chef who prepared all meals. She'd bring Japanese sashimi for lunch, the whole setup. That wasn't even the strangest thing. Once she brought a pale tiny bird wrapped in pig bladder or lamb bladder. Dante couldn't remember which. The sad little thing looked boiled to hell and emaciated. The meat oozed juices as Brook delicately transferred it to a white plate. Hit with a splat, just like that. A pale lifeless bird on bone-white-china for all to see. Open for interpretation. Brook ate every bit. Called it a delicacy. When rich people eat something cruel and bizarre, it's instantly elevated to delicacy status.

No, Grace was nothing like Brook. Though Grace consumed Spanish tuna, Dijon mustard, and later caviar. Not a typical diet for a six-year-old, now is it?

FOOL'S PANCAKES

THE TAIL END of summer sweltered into record heat. Soon, autumn would dust the town in ember and gold. Trees turning the color of fire, shedding another year from their limbs. Another year lost. Right down the tubes. What once was clearing the way for new blood. Winter would tiptoe over the summit shortly after, when the surrounding forest cried its haunting cry, before the last leaf plummeted to earth.

Dante and Jack spent one Hanukkah at the cabin. Thick snow. Faithful snow that seemed to fall for weeks. Frigid temperatures crept and ate window panes. Enough to funnel clouds of frost from nose and mouth. Enough to deprive lungs of precious oxygen the moment they stepped outside. Something loads of burning pine couldn't cure. No matter how many logs fed the fireplace.

Wind navigated through trees like a canoe skimming rapids. A biting chill that penetrated skin and froze bone-marrow. Muscle crystallized from inside out. No, winter wouldn't provide mercy for those living around these parts. Dante knew it. But could Grace and she last the winter? Better to deal with the devil you know than a stranger. If they left now and got stuck somewhere else during winter, she wouldn't know the landscape. Predicting challenges proved impossible. Whether by daylight or nightfall. Nightfall would be their lamp. Their salvation.

Dante scraped pancakes onto Grace's plate. Grace sighed and picked at it. "There's no chips."

Dante piled pancakes onto her own plate. "You saw me use the last yesterday."

She kept poking with her fork, wearing a frown. "What about the store?"

Dante ate a few bites. Then a mouthful. "Nothing left on the shelf. You know this."

Grace shook her head. "No, the back has things, lots of things."

She set her fork down and peered at Grace. "Climbing the rafters is dangerous. I could get hurt. You could get hurt. Something could fall. Anything could happen. Best not to risk it."

Grace held her fingers out like spread talons and mashed them together. "What about the claw thing?"

Dante continued eating. "I don't know how to drive a forklift. Don't even know where the keys are."

A lie. She'd found them a week back, sitting on the battery charging station near the cardboard compactor. Red label: FORKLIFT. While Grace obsessed over a glossy reindeer poking from shrink-wrapped Christmas decorations high in the rafters, Dante had scooped them up.

"Now drink the rest."

Grace made a face. "It tastes funny."

The only milk left came from the powdered kind. Three weeks ago, they'd finished the evaporated milk. No other choices remained. Everything was spoiled now. "I know, but you need the nutrients."

Unsure if that was true. She still used the same line anyway, as with most things Grace ate. Everything sparse and nutrient-driven or discussed or pleaded. Nutrients always snuck into the conversation.

Grace stood on a chair beside Dante, helping rinse dishes, when loud knocking rattled the brass knocker. They froze and fell silent. Dante waited. Maybe they'd imagined it. The knock grew louder. This time, a man's voice. Deep and resonant.

"Anyone home? Hello." He banged again, hard. Cop knock.

That's what William said during card night when the pizza guy knocked. "The guy beats the door like a cop."

They looked at each other, searching their eyes. Inside her head, she heard Bonnie say, "Don't trust anyone."

Dante helped Grace down. "Stay behind me, do you hear me?"

She pressed a finger to her lips, gesturing silence. Grace's little face gleamed with terror. She nodded. Dante grabbed the Anschütz from the gun rack mounted high on the living room wall. Away from Grace's reach. She cycled the bolt to chamber a round and paced to the front door. Grace clung to her left leg. With authority carrying through her tone: "Who are you? I don't recognize your voice."

The man, still deep-voiced, said, "Ma'am, my name is James." His voice mighty enough to smash doors and walls. She'd forgotten to lock the front door. He could enter as he pleased, if he wanted. If he tried.

Dante leveled the Anschütz at the door. "What do you want, James?"

He cleared his throat. "I need food and water. For my dog and me, ma'am."

Grace tightened her grip, severing circulation to Dante's leg. Dante's adrenaline pumped hard alongside Grace's. She felt the child trembling. Her little heart beating a million miles. "There's a grocery store down the way."

"Ma'am, I've been walking for a while. I don't think I can make it."

Dante peered down at Grace. Confronting him now, rather than risk bumping into him at the grocery or elsewhere, seemed best. Surely he lived on the outskirts. Or knew someone who did. He hadn't bust the door down. His voice, though very deep, wasn't threatening. "Where do you live, James?"

"I'm out at Doc Peter's place. Fifteen miles up the road, ma'am."

Doc Peters was the town doctor. Dante knew him as Doc. The whole town called him that. "What's his goat's name?"

The man paused. Long, uncomfortable silence. "Ma'am?"

Dante's voice grew louder. "His goat. What's his name?"

Another pause. "Ma'am, I'm not looking for any trouble."

"What's his name?!"

He cleared his throat again. "Ma'am, I never seen Doc have a goat. If he does, I never saw it."

Dante sighed with reprieve. The answer was enough. Doc didn't own a goat.

"Open the door, slowly."

She watched the knob turn. The door swung wide, Dante still aiming dead center. James took one look at the rifle pointed at his head and cowered. Palms held high and flat. Fingers spread. Everything spread, as to say, I surrender, don't shoot. "I'm not here to hurt anybody. I just want food."

James had a dog at his side. The canine sat at attention, like a foo dog guarding treasure. Thick salt and pepper fur, and a white mane and giant paws. It towered. And easily half the size of James. Its eyes stole the color of Caribbean waters. It bore an eerie similarity to a wolf. However, it showed clear signs of domestication. Dante recognized this dog, Ajax. Ajax belonged to Doc. Ajax recognized Dante. His haunting, icy blue gaze locked on her, and his tail thumped the floor in excited response.

The man that cowered before her was very handsome. Movie star beauty. Muscular shoulders. His entire being seemed chiseled and well defined. Dark eyes and dark hair and dark skin. Hands as mighty as the claw of an excavator. Kindness radiated from his eyes. A gentleness encircling.

His face looked worn to bits, as though he hadn't slept for days. Those mighty hands trembled high in the air. James's lips looked parched and cracked. Dante lowered the weapon. "I won't shoot."

He hesitated to lower his hands. And stood there for a minute, frozen in place. "I don't want any trouble, ma'am."

Her eyes moved from James to the dog. Then the dog to James. Going back and forth. The second Grace locked eyes on Ajax, she barreled toward the dog. "Puppy!"

Dante reached for Grace, trying to yank her back. "Grace, no."

It was too late. Grace threw her arms around Ajax's neck in seconds. Ajax didn't move. Didn't bark. And remained stoic. And let the child dangle from his neck. James lowered his hands and looked at the dog and Grace. "Don't worry, ma'am, he's good with kids. He won't bite."

Grace peered up at James. "What's his name?"

James tried to smile but was too weak or too nervous to see it all the way through. "His name is Ajax."

She gazed face to snout with the dog. "Your name is Ajax?" As if the dog could reply.

Grace clung to Ajax as love and joy beamed from those eyes of hers. She looked tiny compared to Ajax. Doll like. Dante set the rifle on the rack and apologized. "Please, sit. You must be tired." She chose her words carefully. From what Dante saw, in his current condition, he looked desperate, as though lost in the woods for months.

He entered the bungalow, lumbering each step. Dante could see his hands still trembling. James peered at the sofa as though his weary bones required rest. And stood instead. He looked uncomfortable. Unsure what to do with himself. And unsure how to interact with people again. Surrounded by a strange land. Civilization perhaps. Surrounded by strangers. Two strangers. In a strange home. It all seemed alien to him somehow. A girl with a kid was a glorious sight to see these days.

She knew James wouldn't make the first move toward anything. In any direction. If she didn't coax him along, he might stand in that same spot for days. Dante headed for the kitchen and waved him over. "Have a seat at the table. I'm sure you're hungry."

He looked at her wearing a hungry face. A face that would readily eat anything. Bark from a tree, perhaps. Still, he remained stoic and unmoved. He turned to face Ajax and Grace. "Ajax needs food. He's gone too long without."

Dante pulled a chair out from under the table. "We'll feed him too." James sat at the table. His attention centered on the dog and Grace the whole time.

A week ago, Dante drove the Scout to the grocery. And loaded up on canned vegetables. But broke down and added Italian inspired meals to the pile. Rice and dry beans, flour, yeast, and other goods.

Grace and Dante ate the fresh produce in the walk-in cooler first. Yet, they couldn't consume fast enough before most fruits and vegetables turned black and inedible. She rescued two large honey crisps from the spoiled bunch. Dante put the apples in the refrigerator to stop the aging process, or so she hoped.

Every day, she checked the apples for any signs of decay, treating them as priceless, as though the apples were the last produce on earth.

And likely the last apples on earth to pass her lips. Fruit in the new world was a delicacy.

Eggs and meat or any perishable soured. All the major staples just vanished. Now, they relied on instant. Or ready to eat meals. Meals that came from a tin or box or vacuum seal. Dante came across a baking book tucked away in a kitchen drawer. She thumbed through the book and found a recipe for homemade bread. Baking utensils infected the kitchen. In the hall closet, she uncovered more baking books. Dante surmised William enjoyed baking. Little did she know, Julia was the true owner of those cookbooks.

She set a glass of water before him. And James soaked it up quickly, like dry soil. "We have ravioli from a can?"

Water seemed to invigorate him. And ignite a fire within. He gave her that same look of desperation. "I'll eat whatever you have."

Dante saw his hands continue to shake. At first, she fished a can of ravioli from the pantry, then grabbed one more, for extra measure. And a can of spaghetti and meatballs for Ajax. She cut a few thick slices from the loaf of bread on the counter and piled it on his plate.

While James gobbled warm ravioli and bread, Dante fed Ajax. Dante filled a bowl with water and placed it on the floor next to the plate of spaghetti and meatballs. Once Ajax licked the plate clean with his massive tongue and lapped up water, he wandered through the house, nose to floor, sniffing every inch.

Grace wouldn't leave the dog's side. She trailed behind while Ajax canvased each room. Dante focused more on James than what Grace was doing. His face looked pasty and pale. Grime and abrasions marred his hands. Tired, dark circles eclipsed his eyes as if he could barely keep them open. "Maybe you should lie on the couch for a little while. We'll watch Ajax."

The food helped settle his tremors. And drained his energy at the same time. James stared up at Dante, seeming vulnerable. "Maybe for ten minutes, thirty, tops."

James collapsed onto the sofa with a thud. The frame creaked under the load of all his weight. His arm hung freely. Enough for his hand to lay against the floor. When he went down, he let his entire body sprawl out. His body swallowed the couch like baby furniture. Once he closed his eyes and drifted off, Dante laid a blanket over him.

As he slept, Dante hovered over James. Inspecting every inch of him. His clothes were filthy. Pine needles and debris stuck in his hair, and an untamed, greasy beard. A strong campfire odor oozed from his pores. The evidence sitting before her leaned toward James, living in the woods for a long while.

The cuts in his hands concerned her. The dried blood worried her more than the cuts. Was it his blood? What was he doing with those massive hands of his to make them look that way? Did he get into an argument with Doc? She wondered who this man was sleeping on her couch. On William's couch. James looked innocent enough, but was he? Innocent eyes only skimmed the surface. What lies beneath skin and tissue and a beating heart interested her more. Unseeable dangers. His true nature. Those things matter because he was a hearty man. A powerful man with plenty of muscle to crush Grace and her.

Grace ran up to Dante and tugged at her shirt, wearing distress on her face. "Ajax peed on the floor." With pursed lips.

Dante growled in frustration. "Where?"

Grace got all antsy, as if she had to pee and pointed toward the hallway. "Over there."

Ajax had a collar around his neck, but no leash. His fur was matted and covered in soot. He was in bad shape. Same as James. Initially, when Ajax and James stood at the front door, Dante hadn't noted his poor condition. When she fed him, it clicked in her brain how filthy he was. Not until then.

Dante was at ease knowing James was sleeping. No longer a threat. At least for the moment. She sat on the front steps and watched Ajax run around the yard. Then in certain spots, a shrub, a tree, he anchored nose to grass and sniffed away. Grace trailing after. Glued to Ajax like a natural shadow.

Twilight came and went, and James had not woken. He hardly rustled beneath the blanket. Morning light filtered through the windows. And glided across the floor in the living room as the day moved. Not until evening hours did James eventually wake from a long slumber.

James saw Dante and Grace eating at the kitchen table. Ajax lying on the floor at the foot of Grace's chair. The three seemed to be locked inside a hallmark moment. An American hallmark moment. One where the world hadn't ended.

He stood there for a moment, watching them eat and talk and carry on. His voice sounded hoarse when he said ma'am. Dante stood and smiled warmly. "I made extra. I wasn't sure when you'd wake up."

James coughed and cleared his throat. With a deep tone, he said, "How long did I sleep?"

All eyes were now upon him. Even Ajax. Grace peering at him, quietly observing, still chewing food. Dante tucked her hair behind her ears. "A day."

James sat at the end of the table. Where a place setting had been laid out for him.

Dante spooned a heaping mixture of beans and rice and canned corn onto his plate. "Would you like some bread?"

He started eating and said, "Yes, ma'am."

She handed him a fat slice. "I'm Dante, and this is Grace."

James recognized Grace the first time he had laid eyes on her. He had entered into a business contract with Grace's parents, the Phillips. To repair the water supply and drainage issues at the cabin. A twenty thousand square foot cabin built on the side of a hill. Twenty miles away from town. The cabin sat nestled in a secluded, dense wooded area.

On his first visit, he made measurements and surveyed the hillside, as he did with every job. He saw Grace scale the futuristic jungle gym with devil-may-care abandon. The design soared to ridiculous heights. Equipped with a rock wall, zip line, suspension bridges, a series of intricate netting throughout for scaling. The absence of swings and slides baffled him. He had seen nothing like it. While surveying, he saw Grace tear through the complicated maze with ease.

He smiled and forwent mentioning anything he knew about Grace. "Thank you for opening your home to me."

Dante scrunched her brows. "How did you know we were here? There're so many houses on the block to choose from?"

James set his fork down and made eye contact. "Your porch light, it was still on. I thought it was weird to have a porch light on during the day. If—" He stopped himself and eyed Grace. He peered at Dante again. "You know." He gave her a funny look. His eye moved to Grace, then back again to Dante. "I thought maybe someone was still around. I hoped so anyway."

Dante nodded, as though she understood what he was insinuating without him having to say it out loud, in front of Grace. Dante glanced at Grace's plate. Rice and beans picked over. Half the serving was still ever present. "Why don't you take Ajax into the living room. You guys can play there."

Grace rose from her seat and tried to pick up her plate. "I'll put your plate in the sink."

Dante waited for Grace and Ajax to settle on the couch before she asked James another question. In a low voice, she asked, "Did something happen between you and Doc?"

He moved one seat closer to Dante. He dipped his head low. Edged his face near Dante, as if he was ready to whisper her a secret. James used a soft tone, almost dialed down to a whisper. His campfire odor burned her eyes. "Doc died from SHC. He burned up right in front of me. He went sprite."

Dante scooted closer to James and whispered, "Sprite?"

"Yeah, Sprite." James said. "He started flashing red like lightning in the clouds. Sprite."

Dante immediately understood lighting flash, but not the meaning of sprite. "Why do you have those marks on your hands?"

James scanned his hands and peered at her again. "After Doc died, I tried to call for help. But nobody answered the phone. I couldn't get any help. My cell phone started blowing up. Talking about SHC and such, people dying and such."

He looked over at Grace, making sure she wasn't listening to the conversation. "One news feed said stay in your home. Don't go out, and such. So, that's what I did. I stayed at his place for a while. Maybe four weeks. Maybe longer. Then one day a woman beats on the door."

Dante spoke louder, interrupting him. "What did she look like?"

James raised his palm, signaling her to hold on for a minute. "Some white girl with dyed hair. She tried to kill me. There was a man with her, too. They were going to ambush me. They were going crazy or something." James twirled his finger fast around his ear, making the crazy gesture.

Dante, nose to nose, eye to eye. "Crazy?"

James shrugged. "Yeah, crazy. They probably wanted to steal what I had. Once they started shooting, I took off into the woods."

Dante glared at Grace for a few seconds. Fear clouding those peeps. Then turned her attention back to James. "What if they followed you here?"

James shook his head. "I don't know what happened to the girl, but I killed the dude. I never went back to Doc's place. I got lost in the woods for a few weeks until I came to a clearing and saw houses poking out from the trees."

He didn't elaborate specifics about killing another person. It explained his bloody, battered hands. And somewhere while fending off his attacker, James killed the man. Or did he outright murder before the man could kill him?

After talking with Dante, James showered and put on William's sweatpants and shirt. Those were the only articles that would fit him. Well, not exactly. The pants were highwater on him. And the shirt sleeve stopped above his wrist. James was taller than William and had longer arms, too. William beat James in one area though, he had a bigger waistline.

The next morning, during breakfast, James heard Grace complain about the pancakes not being laced with chocolate chips. As all three sat together at the table and ate, James asked, "Did something happen to the grocery store?"

Dante glared at him. "There's no more on the shelf."

Grace snapped her head in Dante's direction and said, "There's more in the back."

Dante shook her head. "It's too dangerous."

James looked at Dante. Then at Grace. Still chewing, "Is there more in the back?"

Grace started to say something, but Dante drowned her voice out by saying, "We don't know that for sure."

Dante gave Grace an intense glare. "There are several pallets in the rafters. Boxes of stuff."

Grace instantly said, "Yeah, and reindeers."

Dante raised her hand. "Whoa, hold on. I only saw one reindeer. Besides, I already told you, I don't know how to drive a forklift."

James saw the tension rise between Grace and Dante. He smiled and said, "Well, you're both in luck, because I can. Looks like we need to take a brief trip to the grocery store."

Grace's face turned sad, and she said nothing else. James asked, "What's wrong? I thought you'd be happy?"

Dante cleared her throat, nudged her head toward Grace. Eyes all wide. "We can't find the keys." Dante winked at James twice. "Maybe James can help us look. Three pairs of eyes are better than two."

James caught on to Dante's gesture and said, "I think if we look hard enough, we might find the keys."

Grace lit up. "Then can I have the reindeer?"

Grace's hair was wild as a witch. And the state of it had bothered Dante. She always wakes up with a bedhead. Bonkers bed head. Dante began smoothing her hair out. "Yes, you can borrow the reindeer for a little while." She emphasized the borrow part with a deep tone. The way she said it didn't seem to faze Grace. These days, Dante and Grace had their entire way of life on loan, like an imaginary credit line from a bank.

IMPOSTORS GROW WINGS

THEY STOOD as the steel rafters towered, like skyscrapers made of pallets and endless boxes of trinkets. After entering the store, and while Grace was distracted, Dante slipped the forklift keys into James's hand.

Grace locked eyes on the reindeer and started jumping up and down. "Get the reindeer first, James." Dante cleared her throat, giving Grace a scolding eye. "Please, James."

James laughed. And when he laughed, he almost didn't recognize his own voice. When was the last time he laughed at anything? He clapped his hands hard and rubbed them rigorously. "Okay, stand back in case something falls. I haven't operated a forklift since college, and you don't want to know how long that's been."

Grace giggled. Dante bit the edge of her lip. "Be careful."

When he started driving the forklift, his skills were a little rusty. The machine jerked in short sputters, as though the engine was about to conk out. And an ear-splitting squeal when he extended the mast and fork.

After getting used to the controls, he carefully lowered the reindeer crate to the ground. Grace's eyes beamed with utter joy. She screamed and piled her fingers into her mouth, as though reigning in the sheer elation spilling outward.

Dante and Grace unraveled the shrink wrap as James continued to unstack pallet after pallet from the steel rafters. James struggled to locate the chocolate chips. All the boxes displayed a unique alphanumeric code. And lacked a readable description. At least to the untrained eye.

Grocery store employees could read the labels, but James couldn't. So, instead of giving up the search, he had lowered all the inventory and stacked everything onto the floor. Making it easier to go through each box. Three hours had passed when he finally unloaded the last pallet. James went to work by rummaging through each one.

He set the pallet of Christmas decorations to the far back corner of the stockroom, near the employee lounge. Grace and Dante had gone through most decorations. And during the process, they had left a disaster in their wake. By all appearances, the Christmas pallet had gotten sick and barfed all over the floor.

Christmas had arrived months early for this small town right in the stockroom. Plastic reindeers, and Santa Claus lawn ornaments, a large sleigh and wreaths with red bows attached, garland. Things lighting up and bells jingling and toys sounding off like the nutcracker ballet. Miles of lights, ribbons, and festive wrapping paper decorated the area.

James found several useful items during the search. Despite not locating chocolate chips. Once he delivered the bad news about the chocolate chips, Grace couldn't care less. Enthralled over the toys and decorations. In her eyes, Christmas superseded all matters.

Dante's eyes drooped as she sat among loads of glittery stuff that flashed and sang tunes. She hunched and slumped her shoulders as if she had just run a marathon. She flung her arm in the air lethargically. "She'll be fine. We don't need the chocolate, anyway."

Dante ran her eyes all over the mess. Using a whining tone, she said, "She has all this stuff now. It'll take forever to carry this to the car. We need a shopping cart." Dante stared at him and did not try to rise from the floor.

"One or two?"

Grace sprung from the disaster and screamed, "Two!"

Dante mopped her forehead with her wrist and started mumbling to herself and grouping items together.

James saluted. "Two it is."

In the evening, after eating more beans and rice and corn, and bread to sop everything up with, they settled in the living room, wiped out from the venture. Where Grace's spoils littered the floor like Christmas morning. If Grace had her way, the house would teem with holiday trinkets and noise-making gadgets. She wouldn't part with anything her hands touched, and Dante negotiated back and forth. Things became very heated between the two.

The next morning, after pancakes and powder milk flavored water filled their bellies, James made an announcement at the table. "Ever since we got back from the grocery store, I've been thinking."

Dante didn't bother looking up when he spoke. Instead, she looped a rubber utility belt around the waist of a toy robot Grace held in her hands. Grace dictated her wishes on how to tie the accessory. "I think we need to clean house."

Grace handed Dante another toy to embellish while they bickered. "Yeah, okay, clean house?"

Dante trailed off. Still fooling with the toy in her hand. Ajax laid at the base of Grace's chair, gnawing on a stone white rawhide bone. One that had a Christmas ribbon tied to the end.

James scraped the dirt from underneath his nails with a file. "Like I said, we should start now, before it's too late."

Dante lifted her head to meet James's eyes. "I'm sorry? Start what today?"

James didn't make eye contact and continued cleaning his nails. "We must pick this town clean before someone else beats us to the punch. We need guns. Another vehicle, for sure. Gas. Anything that will help us survive longer. The stuff at the grocery will not last. We've got to be proactive and prepare for the worst. No one is going to save us, except ourselves."

"What about Grace? Don't you think I thought about this already? There could be." Dante swiped a forefinger across her neck and made a dead face. "I don't want her exposed anymore. You know what I mean."

Dante or James hadn't realized Grace was listening to the conversation the entire time. Grace softly said, "Dead people." Her eyes quivered and overflowed like clogged gutters during a rainstorm.

Dante seated Grace in her lap and hugged her. "You see, she can't handle it."

James stood and walked over to the refrigerator. His solid built, heavy footsteps caused the table to quake with each step. The sheer size of him gobbled the kitchen more than the average man. A giant living inside a treehouse. His mighty fingers swallowed the entire fridge handle like a child's play set. "I can't do it alone."

"Why not?"

James slammed the fridge door with minimal effort and hadn't meant to in the first place, as if he wasn't aware of his own power. The loud thud startled Dante and Grace. He poured another glass of milky water. "I need a lookout. Someone to be my eyes and ears on the street. Just in case."

Dante stroked Grace's hair. "I won't put Grace through that."

"Listen, this is the only way. Don't you want Grace to live?"

Dante narrowed her eyes, lips pursed. In that movement, James made her feel guilty. Or worse, selfish. As if she had put her needs first. Instead of Grace. When in reality, she worried about Grace's safety every second of the day. Dante didn't need a stranger telling her how to protect a child.

James sat and folded arms on the table and stared at her. "I know you'll make the right choice."

Dante mouthed Fuck You from where she sat. Somewhere deep down, intuition told her he was partly right. They needed to plan for the worst case scenario. Although, how he went about it spoke to his character. Jack taught her that when you meet a person for the first time, they usually present the best version of themselves. The well managed version. Familiarity breeds complacency, revealing their true nature. Dante didn't like James's true nature.

Against better judgment, she went along with the plan. James looted the sheriff's station first. He piled plenty of ammo and shotguns and assault rifles into a patrol car parked in the alleyway. He stumbled upon the first mound of soot and rotting limb, two feet from the door. Another in the sheriff's office. A few sparkled in the holding tank. The smell of death was so bad, he had removed his shirt and tied it around his nose and mouth to mask the smell. Tears blurred his vision after he threw up in the entryway and once in the sheriff's office. Where the smell was more concentrated.

Between ransacking, he walked outside and checked on Dante and Grace. On his last sweep, before he exited the sheriff station for good, he handed Dante a baton and a yellow gun taser.

On the next stop, a small surplus store, on the corner of Grand Avenue and 10th, had more death and more smell. The surplus store hit different from the sheriff's station. Here, the soot piles weren't neat and contained. They spread like black ink stains across the linoleum, as if the people had tried to run. Their final movements were painted in ash across the floor. The smell had changed too. Not just death now, but something electrical, like burning copper wire. Through it all, James moved like a kid in a candy store, pawing through off-brand camo gear and knock-off tactical vests, seemingly blind to the horror show around him.

The surplus store yielded less than James hoped but fed his frenzy all the same. He swept through the aisles like a hurricane, gathering anything that could cut, light, or survive the elements. Dante watched him load camping gear they'd never need, his movements growing more manic with each armful. The dead didn't seem to bother him anymore. They were just obstacles between him and his prizes. The smell that had made him retch at the station now barely registered as he stepped over soot piles to reach a display of waterproof matches. He gathered every item he could imagine, as though preparing for war against the creatures of the forest.

A strange progression unfolded with each conquest. At the sheriff's station, James had stumbled out pale and shaking, barely able to look at them. But by the hardware store, his hands had stopped trembling. At the pharmacy, he'd managed a weak smile. Now, watching him stride out of the surplus store, Dante noticed something different in his walk, a swagger, a lightness, as though each dead body he stepped over made the next one easier. His eyes gleamed with the same wild excitement Grace showed over Christmas decorations, except this wasn't about toys. This was about power.

Sure, Dante stole plenty of food and dire essentials, pads, shampoo, a brush, fingernail clippers, etc. Each time she took something out of necessity, she felt bad, even guilty about it. How long would they survive if they didn't steal? At least that's what she kept telling herself to justify her actions. The mere idea of stealing made her cringe, yet necessary.

James was stealing, just to steal. It thrilled him, too. After a while, he showed little care for the dead. Even immune to the smell. Or too electrified to care. He ransacked shops as though he owned the entire town. Hollering and whistling and celebrating his spoils like he just sacked Rome. It mattered little that he had packed the patrol car and Scout full. The more he took, the more insatiable he became, and greedy. Like a drug he couldn't get enough of.

Dante never clued James in on a little secret. Gunners Firearms was on the corner of 13th and Copper. That place was her first stop, after Sarah stole Jack's Jeep. Watching James now, the way his fingers twitched with each new find, the way his voice rose with every discovery, she knew she'd made the right choice keeping quiet. Gunners had ammo for the Anschütz and plenty of firepower - enough to arm a small militia. The way James was changing, she couldn't trust him with a water gun, let alone the arsenal waiting behind those locked gates. Every time he checked on them, his eyes were a little wilder, his smile a little sharper. The man who'd collapsed on their couch two days ago was disappearing, replaced by someone who seemed to thrive in this new, lawless world.

She found the store keys and lowered the steel gates and locked it up. Now she thinks, why didn't you lock up the sheriff station mijita. Yet, the answer wasn't so simple. Entering the station with Grace was impossible for her. The moment she opened the door six days ago, the dead rested at her feet. The smell was so toxic. She knew more dead lurked about and waited to be discovered.

Dante had entertained Grace as best she could. But as the hours wilted away, Grace tired and got cranky. Grace often got cranky after a long day of play. The second Dante saw James walk out of a shop with more junk in his hands, she said, "We can't fit anything else. The cars are full."

He stopped midstride and looked stunned. "The passenger seat has plenty of room."

Dante shook her head, placed her hands on her hips, in a scolding stance. "You already filled the passenger seat in the sheriff's car. We need nothing else."

She kept saying car instead of SUV, which seemed to annoy James each time she used the word car. James rolled his eyes and mumbled something under his breath and walked over to the Scout. Dante pointed an angry finger at him. "Don't you dare. That's where Grace sits."

James dumped the items in the passenger seat, anyway. "She can sit on your lap."

"Uh," Dante's face turned red hot and her eyes sharp as knives. "No. That's not safe."

James shot his hands straight up as though he were holding up the sky. "That's the most ridiculous thing I have ever heard. Hello. Everyone's dead. The house isn't that far away. Drive slowly. Grace will be fine," he started to head back inside, "In case you haven't noticed, nobody gives a shit about the rules anymore."

Grace sat cross-legged on the ground, her new toys forgotten in her lap. She watched James load the car, careful, studying. But where James moved like someone in a fever, grabbing and stuffing and piling.

Her small fingers twisted the head of her robot back and forth, back and forth, the way she did when thunderstorms got too loud. She had said little since they left the Christmas decorations behind, but her eyes tracked everything and listened to the argument unfold. Turning her attention to James, then Dante. She gasped. Her eyes bulged. "Oh, no, James said a bad word."

PENTAGRAM SHAPED HEART

Autumn light thinned behind the peaks, dissolving into a haunting blue that feathered the mountains like death's crown. Storm clouds muscled in from the east, promising sleet. A wet cold that crawled straight to the marrow, killing anything it touched in minutes.

This was the weather in Glenwood Springs. Wet, snowy mornings where the weight erased pointy roofs and whatever else blocked its path. Where people shoveled their way out to wherever they were going, sometimes freezing to death before reaching their destination. Though those sunny afternoons melted everything away and reached sixty degrees most days.

Dante walked calmly to the Scout's passenger side and tossed James's spoils onto the pavement.

James's attitude shifted like a switch being flipped. Two opposing sides emerged, one humble and appreciative, the other its inverse. He moved between them effortlessly, adapting to fit the moment. *Cold and calculating*, Dante thought.

James held up his hands in surrender. "Okay, okay. Let's cool down. I think it's time to take a break." He turned to Grace. "Have you ever been to a bowling alley?"

Grace jerked her head toward Dante, face scrunched in confusion. "What's a bowling alley, mommy?"

The slip didn't go unnoticed. James caught it, but Dante ignored him and waved Grace over. "Come on. Get your toys. We're going home."

"They have fun games too," James said.

Grace's face lit up. "Games!"

Another false choice wrapped in a pretty bow. His choice alone was the reality. Dante had had enough. "What about the dead? Or did you already forget?"

James smiled and extended his hand like a game show host. "I'll scope it out first. If there's any," He peered at Grace. "Then we'll call it a night. How about that?"

Grace trekked over to Dante, staring up with puppy eyes. "Please."

Dante found it impossible to disappoint Grace. Somewhere inside herself, she loved this little girl who ran her ragged every day. Grace evoked something inexplicable in her, despite her unfamiliarity with children. Maybe Dante needed Grace just as much as Grace needed her. "One hour."

"Two!"

Dante picked her up. "Let's just see how it goes, okay?"

Grace started fluffing Dante's hair, as she always did when being held. She needed to touch some part of Dante's body, a nervous tick or self-soothing mechanism, maybe.

James disappeared into the bowling alley, four blocks east of Grand Avenue, and Dante watched his confident stride. The way he moved through Palmer Street like he'd walked it a thousand times before. His whole spiel seemed rehearsed, each action calculated. Like an actor who'd studied his role too well.

Meager James. Polite James. Lovely James. Humble James. Yes ma'am this and no ma'am that. What a joke. Now he was manipulating Grace. Using her to manipulate Dante. What next?

The Ajax question gnawed at her like a splinter working deeper. A man running for his life didn't stop to rescue a stranger's dog. A man being hunted didn't burden himself with an animal that could give away his position. Yet here James was with Ajax, a dog he barely acknowledged, never fed, hardly looked at. The pieces didn't fit. And that scared her more than the dead.

Ten minutes passed with no sign of James. The clouds hadn't yet eclipsed the sky, the storm still paused in the distance. But she smelled the parking lot cooling as rain dotted the asphalt. Dante clasped Grace's hand. "Okay, let's go home."

Grace peered up with that special face, the one that reeled Dante in every time. "What about James?"

Dante lifted Grace onto her hip. "I think James needs a little time out."

Grace's fingers found Dante's hair again, twisting and smoothing like worry beads. Her eyes fought gravity, but they were losing. "I'm not sleepy." The words slurred together, her small body already betraying the lie.

Dante rubbed her nose against Grace's. "How about we play a game at home? Besides, you look tired."

Grace pressed her hands to Dante's cheeks and yawned. "I'm not sleepy."

Dante giggled. "That's what you say every time, but I know different."

She was walking back to the Scout when James emerged from the bowling alley. "Hey, where are you going?"

Grace's head rested on Dante's shoulder now. Dante didn't turn, just kept walking. "Grace is tired. We're going home."

His massive fingers snapped around her slender arm, pulling her back. "I found something. Something you're gonna want to see."

Dante yanked free, hard. "I don't care."

James blocked her path, locking eyes. He looked almost shell-shocked again. "Listen to me, it's all clear. No dead people. You got to see what I found."

This time he seemed more sincere, urgency eating at him. What if whatever James wanted to show her was truly important? Once again, against her gut instinct, she followed him into the bowling alley.

Her arms strained under Grace's weight. The child's entire body had gone limp, head slumped at an odd angle, bobbing with each step. Dante tried to see if Grace's eyes were closed, but blond hair draped her face. "Grace?" Dante whispered. Grace's soft voice murmured something unintelligible.

The bowling alley swallowed them into darkness, then bloomed with light. Neon rose from the floor like toxic flowers, painting everything in a bioluminescent glow. Each lane shimmered with rainbow light, frozen in eternal cosmic bowling night. A garish memorial to better times. To Friday nights when Dante and her friends would claim lane five, or sometimes six, their laughter echoing under the artificial stars.

She gently laid Grace on her side atop a triple seat high-back on lane five. The child's weight left Dante's arms slowly, reluctantly, like letting go of an anchor in this strange new world. Grace's blond hair caught the black light, transforming into streams of ethereal blue and purple. A haunting reminder of how beautiful things could still be, even now. The neon cast shadows that danced across her peaceful face, and for a moment, she looked like something from before. Before the dead. Before the flame stole everything.

Dante hovered, watching Grace suck on her bottom lip, a new habit. Maybe picked up in dreams. What did she dream about now? Did her mind still remember birthday parties and Christmas mornings, or had it already adapted to this new reality of ash and empty streets?

James led Dante to the front office next to the bar, what she imagined was a supervisor's office. The screen burned her eyes like the sun, making her squint and blink. But the brightness did not steal her breath, it was what was on it. A Google search bar. Links. Colors. The internet, alive and breathing in this dead town.

Her fingers twitched toward the keyboard. How long had it been? Two months since she last checked her email, scrolled through news feeds, searched for answers? The screen felt both familiar and foreign, like running into an old friend who'd changed too much.

"Look," James said, his beer-heavy breath cutting through her wonder. His fingers danced across the keyboard, each click echoing in the hollow bowling alley. "They created a blog for survivors."

The page loaded, revealing a black background with a blood-red pentagram. 'High Priestess,' the header read, and below it, thousands of names. Thousands of stories. Thousands of people like her, searching for someone, anyone, in this broken world.

'Missing Persons Database,' she read. 'Upload Your Loved Ones' Photos Here.'

Her heart stuttered. Mom.

James sprawled in the club chair like a king on a child's throne, his massive frame making the furniture seem toylike. The computer's glow cut across his face at an angle, creating shadows that transformed his features into something almost theatrical, the drunk, the liar, the stranger she never really knew.

Three beers. Just three, and he was already dissolving at the edges, words slurring like wet paint. It didn't add up. Uncle Gerry, built like a beer barrel and half James's size, could down a case before his words started to tangle. But here was James, all muscle and height, coming apart after a few pints.

She watched him take another swig, his movements too precise for someone so supposedly drunk. The condensation on his glass caught the neon light, creating tiny prisms that reminded her of warning signs. Everything about him suddenly felt rehearsed. The slouch, the slurred words, the heavy-lidded eyes. Like an actor who'd studied drunkenness but never quite lived it.

"You go," he waved limply, playing his part. "I'll catch up later."

But would he? And as what version of himself?

"How are people uploading this information?" The question felt important, like picking at a loose thread that might unravel the world.

James lumbered to the back of the computer, movements exaggerated in his supposed stupor. He returned with a blue Ethernet cable, holding it up like a magician revealing his secret. "Hard-wired," he said, too clearly for someone so drunk. "Wi-Fi's dead, but these old connections? They're still alive. They figured it out."

The 'they' hung in the air between them. High Priestess. A name that tasted of rituals and burnt offerings, maybe even human. Dante studied the screen again, noting how the pentagram seemed to pulse in the corner of her vision. Someone had to maintain these servers, keep the power running, create this network of survivors. Someone who knew this was coming.

She scrolled through the missing persons database, each face a story, each name a prayer. Spanish, English, even what looked like Mandarin. Grief needed no translation. But her mother's face wasn't there. Not yet.

JAMES MY GRACE, IS SO LOVELY

DANTE BROUGHT Grace home and curled up next to her in bed, as she did most every night. The house surrounded them with emptiness. The street out front lay silent as a mouse. No traffic noise. No cars puttered down the street at midnight. Their bass no longer vibrated windows with soon-to-be overplayed hits. Gone were the days when one song replaced another, right before skipping back to track one.

Pollution from artificial light had vanished. From the street, the house disappeared into the blackness amid a potter's field that once pulsed. City lights, porch lights, garage lights, even the bedroom light on the second story where a shadowy figure once passed a window at 3 a.m., every day, no longer existed. No more neighbors clinking along as they hauled garbage to dumpsters late at night. No dogs barking and howling in the distance because their owners forgot to let them back inside before sneaking off to bed. Computer screens, cell phones, and televisions no longer ran their endless algorithms. The chaos of the internet had fallen silent. Digital noise. The sound of a thriving city that never slept, even when it needed to, had died. So much noise you couldn't hear yourself think. Or feel anything.

Gone were the latest YouTube sensations and TikTok experts. The ones who told you what to think. What to eat. What to wear. When to sleep, if ever. Who to hate. Who to love. How to live forever if you drank this potion every day of your life, at a hundred bucks a shot. All promising you'd reach the ripe old age of a thousand. If the world didn't implode before then. Because of climate change or pandemic. Alien invasion, maybe. One by sea. One by land. Don't forget outer space.

That same noise you'd been hearing your entire life. Noise for noise's sake. Enough to dilute your entire existence until you're nothing. Or no one. A shell pushing through the day, dropping a coin in every toll passed because that's life. There's a toll to pay every minute of the day. Whether crossing the street or ordering from Starbucks' dollar menu. Or taking an Uber anywhere but home, because your leader told you to. All because you needed to get out more. You were wasting away from TikTok videos. Then, finally, you stopped breathing. And now it was the big one.

Truth was, you never escaped the noise. Even when soaking in the tub, searching for some kind of peace. As forever chemicals tingled the skin and sent chills up the back. Sped the heart. Lights out. A candle twinkling in the corner of a room. Shadows from flame crawling up the walls, like a single star at midnight. And none of it really helped anyway because you finally realized the noise had been transmitting inside your brain the whole time. Inside your soul. Pounding eardrums to death. Because you were the noise.

Noise pollution no longer devoured her. No one else dissolved into the noise either. Now nature collapsed in every direction, seeking to claim what remained.

Dante had difficulty sleeping, not because of James, but because of her mother. Once she rescued Grace, she had forgotten her mission. Mexico City faded into the recesses of her mind, a truth awaiting a future need. She couldn't help thinking most everyone died, so why try in the first place? Priorities changed and evolved. Before it all went to hell, plans were important. She and Jack made plenty of plans, as did the world. But never once did it cross her mind that plans were an illusion. Plans were only powerful if whoever made them lived long enough to see them through. Otherwise, they were pointless, a waste of time. Her new mission, after saving Grace, was to tend to the living. And Grace was plenty.

In the morning, Dante and Grace ate more pancakes and drank milky water. This time, she added peanut butter to their daily course, thanks to James's forklift skills. James hadn't come home. She cared little if he ever came back. She preferred he didn't. But that didn't stop Grace from mentioning his name several times during breakfast. James this and James that. She looked at Dante dead-eye, with dreamy eyes and dreamy face, and said, "James is so lovely."

Dante's face went slack. Her eyes bewildered. "James is lovely all right, real lovely."

What bothered her most was letting a stranger enter their lives. Before SHC, she blindly trusted people. Letting your guard down today could end your life. If she could only see James through Grace's eyes, would her sanity return to its rightful place?

Another thing driving her mad was Ajax. Another gift from James. His massive paws tramped along the house, those monstrous nails clickity-clack, clickity-clack against the wood floor all day long. The upkeep kept piling up in end days, just as it did before SHC. The endless supply to maintain upkeep was exhausted. It would never return. Ajax's grooming needs added to a long list. Dante clipped his nails with toenail clippers. Afterward, Dante and Grace took a shower. They no longer bathed separately. Completing it all at once proved simpler and quicker. She washed her hair first, then Grace's, then onward to toes. Grace liked to sit close to the drain while the water pelted her face. She gazed at Dante, her mouth filling with water. "It's raining." She invariably included a friend, that ghastly little duck or some such thing, to join. Now the robot took its place.

Dante worried about their clothes. Grace had complained a couple times about her shoes hurting her feet. Her jumper fit a little too snug and rested above ankles as clam-diggers. Grace had grown an inch, or maybe a couple, since they first met. Socks were another concern. Dante had developed holes in the heel. The end yielded no fortune. Survivors kept rolling snake eyes.

Yes, their threads were unraveling and needed tending to. The more she washed clothes in the machine, the more brittle the fibers became. Grace's clothes always had dirt and sticky things embedded, which Dante spent hours scrubbing. Her clothes were so velvety at first but soon turned into flannel texture. The closest shopping mall was fifty miles through twisted mountain highways. Might as well be on another planet. No, she wouldn't risk wasting gas and getting stuck in bum fuck dead zone with Grace riding shotgun.

The next rational option would be to go house to house in search of new clothes. The gold standard, gently used. But she'd settle for less. Much less. One big guessing game, though. She and Grace had small frames. Smaller than average. And they had a ton of ground to cover. Was the world smaller than she first thought? Or would it be coincidental they might stumble upon a house with a woman who wore size double zero and a girl who fit size six? Because Grace was six. Not sure size wise. The label on her shirt only showed a designer name in gold cursive on a black background "Made in Italy" and included an illegible size. Shoe size was another mystery. Try them all until one fits sort of deal would be the next approach.

Look for houses with kids' toys sprinkled on lawns like confetti. Or a minivan parked in the driveway. Those weren't hard to spot. Families with small children left an imprint on the neighborhood.

After getting dressed, Dante brushed Grace's hair, while Grace brushed the dog's fur with William's comb. James barreled through the front door helter-skelter like. He startled them. The floor vibrated beneath her bum from James's sheer weight and thunderous feet. His eyes went wild and searched the room as though he was being chased. Hair smashed to one side. Boots unlaced and pant cuffs tucked inside the lip, as if he dressed in a hurry. He looked whacked out.

She didn't notice the smell of alcohol right away. Yet the longer he stood there, the stale beer odor seemed to sweat from every pore, like gasoline vapor. He didn't even make eye contact when he spoke. More like he was talking to himself or the air. He clutched the side of his head, near the temple, as if someone had punched him. "Pack only the important shit, we're leaving in thirty."

Grace gasped all fish-eyed and cupped her mouth with a loud smack like the word shit came from her own lips. Dante, unmoved, continued brushing Grace's hair. "You can leave if you want to, but Grace and I are staying."

He clutched his head and wobbled for a second like an invisible wave had tried to knock him down. His voice boomed and echoed as though he didn't know the power of his own pitch. "We have to stick together, goddamn it!"

Dante stopped grooming Grace, sat for a moment, and appeared deep in thought. The back of Grace's head obstructed Dante's view. She couldn't see the sadness forming on Grace's face. Eyes welling. "I said no. We've made it this long without you."

A sinister cackle ejected. "How long do you think you'll last without a man? You saw it with your own eyes last night. People survived. How long do you think it will take before the town is overrun? They'll come here looking for shit like I did. I know men. They see a young girl with a kid. I'm sure you can figure out the rest."

His knees were shaky as he stood. Another dizzy spell hit, perhaps. Dante rose and glanced at Grace. Her little eyes were now watery and heartbroken. "Grace, take Ajax to the bedroom."

James pointed at the dog right away with that long finger. "Grace stays. This concerns her too. I've got news for you in case you forgot. You are not her mother. You don't get to decide whether Grace lives or dies."

"I've got news for you, I don't—," She stopped herself mid-sentence and looked at Grace, clasping her shoulder. "We don't need a man to protect us."

Dante stopped James with an angry hand on his face as he tried to speak. "We'll die out there. What if we get stuck in the middle of nowhere without gas or food or water? All that shit." Dante looked down at Grace regretfully. "The shit you packed the cars with will not fill your belly. I know how to survive these woods, and you don't."

He glared at her and held his tongue as though his hamster wheel had seized. She brandished a damning finger at him like scolding a child. "You've known Grace for a second and now you think you get to say where she goes. You're a stranger. Go wherever. Do whatever. But we are not going."

He slapped his hands together fast, implying Dante had talked herself into a corner. "Exactly," he sharply said. "You let a complete stranger come into your house on day one. How do you know I didn't make the whole thing up? You know, to gain sympathy. You don't know me. No, no, no. You're the one who's gonna get Grace killed. It only takes one time to let the wrong person in. And when it happens, you won't be able to save her."

Dante couldn't help but agree with his last statement. He was dead right. She thought about all those things the day after she let him in. She had acted foolishly. Although James had a lost-in-the-wilderness-for-weeks appearance about him. Even the best actor in the world couldn't reach that emotional level of despair. Dante had noticed the same look on a hiker's face, who got lost in the woods a year earlier.

She locked eyes on him with a piercing glare. "I've taken on bigger men than you." And she had. At twelve, Dante had attended self-defense classes. Her father's idea. By sixteen, she graduated to kickboxing. Her slight frame was deceiving, and made for an easy target, or so most thought.

The absurdity, his facial expression seemed to say. He etched a patronizing smile. "Oh yeah. I'm sure you can."

Dante picked up Grace and sat her on the couch. Terror gripped Grace. Dante recognized the look. She met Grace's gaze and declared, "Don't be scared. I won't get hurt."

With tears flowing, Grace reached for Dante and said, "mommy."

This was the first time Dante realized Grace had called her mommy. Though this wasn't the first. Grace had been calling her mommy for weeks now, before Dante had caught on like James did in the parking lot. It surprised Dante that Grace had called her mommy instinctually. If only Dante could see the look on James's face. She would see that he was also surprised. He snickered and said, "She's not your mommy, Grace."

Dante lowered Grace's tiny hands and folded them on her lap. "Don't listen to him. I won't get hurt. I promise. Now cover your eyes. Can you do that for me?" Grace nodded and cupped her eyes tightly.

Dante faced James and formed a defensive stance. Feet set apart and rooted to the floor. Elbows bent and arms hiked. Fists raised and stationed breast level. Her body position was reflexive, as though she were a professional boxer. She smiled to antagonize. "I bet you can't even land a punch."

Grace blurted a high-pitched squeak. Her small fingers turned white as she cupped her eyes even tighter. James's body language was sloppy. He flung his hand in the air, warming himself up for the charge. "Hmm. Yeah, right? I can land a punch. Believe me, you don't want any of this."

Dante held her ground. Her entire body was tense and loaded. "What's wrong James? Scared I might kick your ass."

All the alcohol still racing through his veins made those mighty muscles slack and weak. He was so thirsty and queasy from a night of drinking. His slow processing appeared as if his mind had been pickled in beer. He said nothing more, staggered forward, and swung his fist at her.

Dante dodged the incoming blow and sidestepped, still owning that powerful stance, as if she was hungry for more. A look of astonishment gleamed across his face at how quick she moved. Little did he know, Dante was just revving the engine. James swung again, this time faster and harder than before. She deflected his punch with her palm and sidestepped, causing all his weight to shift forward, recklessly. He lost his balance in the process and tripped.

When he grabbed her neck, Dante twisted free with incredible strength. She didn't stop there. A ridge hand shot to the temple paralyzed him. James let out a strange gasp as if he was choking. Dante spun around and knocked his feet out from under him, landing him on his ass and hitting the floor with a clamorous boom.

"Mommy!"

Hearing Grace scream like that made Dante feel guilty right away. In her mind, she told herself, "What have you done?"

"Don't be scared, I'm okay," Dante said.

James went down face first, giving Dante free range over his body. Her training enabled her to exploit pressure points and seek the body's weaknesses. She dug her knee in his back hard enough to pain his kidney. She owned him and twisted his arm at a ridiculous angle. James muffled out, "Fuuuck."

The more he struggled and tried to buck her off, Dante bore down harder with her knee and applied more pressure to his arm. This time, a piercing scream escaped his voice box. He screamed like a mule. At least that's what a girl from school had accused a boy in her class of sounding like. The boy in her class reached the same high-pitched range as James did. She could feel his labored breath beneath her body going up and down fast, as if he couldn't catch his breath. He whimpered, "Stop." Dante wouldn't get off him. Something inside herself just snapped and went elsewhere.

Another blaring howl compelled Grace to shout, "Stop it! Stop! Stop!" Grace's frightened voice seemed to snap Dante back to reality.

She launched herself free and sprang into a defensive stance again. James peeled himself off the floor like his bones and muscles were frail as a ninety-year-old. Still panting and speaking with a hoarse voice. "Ajax is coming with me." He limped to the door. "Ajax."

The dog's ears shot straight up at the sound of his name being called. Ajax swiveled his head in James's direction and lay there with his tail now thumping against the floor. "Ajax, let's go." At first, Ajax jerked forward, appearing to ready himself for lift off, yet rested his snout on the floor lazily.

"You too," James said.

Before James left for good, he said, "You think you're doing the right thing here, but you're not. If you really gave a shit about Grace, then you'd come with me. You're not thinking straight and you're going to get her killed. It's safer in Santa Fe. They have a farm out there, plenty to eat." He wiped the sweat from his brow. His hand was all shaky. "I'll be at the bowling alley if you change your mind. If you don't show up by noon tomorrow, I'm gone. You won't see me again. I suggest you think about coming. You took me down, but that doesn't mean you can defend yourself against a group of men." He placed his forefinger on his temple. "Think about it."

MIJITA

GRACE HARDLY TOUCHED her food that evening. There was nothing quite like watching a six-year-old crack under the weight of end times. The apocalypse rested on her tiny shoulders, and she wouldn't let Dante out of her sight. Most of the night, Grace clutched her hand. Wherever Dante sat, Grace wanted to sit on her lap. She had not played with Ajax either. She asked Dante to be her mommy. She said her mommy wasn't coming for her. Deep down, she knew Grace was right. Her mommy wasn't coming. She knew Grace would never see her mother again. How does one tell a child her mother died? The amount of lies and shame building within Dante weighed on her, too. The apocalypse sparkled in their eyes like life, but resembled death.

In her way of thinking, she was too young to be a mom. But what choice did she have? Grace needed a mommy. Just like she needed a mommy. And when they lay in bed, Grace wrapped her arms around Dante. Twirling her fingers around Dante's dark hair. And never let go. Dante felt her little heart beating against her chest while she stroked Grace's delicate locks. And she smelled like a baby. Her only reference came from little Oscar. Grace had the same scent as Oscar.

The winter night stretched on, everlasting and dreary. Sleep eluded Dante as James's words kept toying with her insides, rash as he was. Was she that naive? And through ignorance, could she somehow get them both killed in the process?

As morning light crept through the sheers, Dante sprang into action. They took two hours in total to eat breakfast, clean up, and load all the important stuff into the Scout. Grace wanted to keep everything and wouldn't part with anything, no matter how insignificant. Some toys she hadn't played with in a while. But they needed to economize the space. Dante spent more time negotiating than carrying out the task. By ten-oh-five, they arrived at the bowling alley.

The sheriff's SUV was missing from its last spot in front. The bowling alley was empty. James was nowhere to be found. He had taped a note on the computer screen: sorry about yesterday. Meet me in Santa Fe. Go to the blog for directions. Be well, James.

Fury took over her at first. It wasn't noon yet, and he had gone against his word. He hadn't waited for them like he said he would. She wondered just how long he had waited before leaving town. That's if he waited. For all she knew, he had left yesterday. After their tussle back at the bungalow.

She sat there for a while, surrounded by a sea of dirty, empty pint glasses. A half-gone bottle of Jack Daniels. James had used one pint glass as a makeshift ashtray. Countless cigarette butts floated to the top of a cloudy amber liquid. Flat beer, she guessed. Cancerous logs drowning is piss water. She couldn't help thinking the new world seemed to carry on without a care. Bonnie had made her plans. Banding with other folks to travel all the way to Aurora. James's next stop was Santa Fe. Her next stop would be Mexico City. Perhaps Santa Fe later. Her plans had stalled because of Grace. The High Priestess used a unique method to lure people in. They were gathering survivors on a farm. Now, those remaining on the planet planned to travel to Santa Fe.

Dante thought about how carefully laid plans fall apart in the everyday world. Before SHC hit. Strangely, no different from today. When she first left the cabin, her plan was to drive to Mexico City and find Lydia. That bombed. How many survivors would complete the journey to Santa Fe? James? What about Bonnie and her group? Aurora anyone. Any takers. No? Yes? Maybe? Cross fingers.

As though plans tethered them to this life, to this world, to these bodies. Feet still rooted to the ash like fallen trees. The will to survive, to move forward whispered promises of meaning, even after the world burned. Once unexpected twists of life destroyed everything, the only reward was wasted time. And while time passed them by, and there was nothing left they could do, except lay in a grave or a tomb for all eternity as the days still ticked away. There was still a sticky note pinned to the refrigerator door. Reminding them to wait in traffic forty-five minutes one way. And an hour back from the other. Or arrive at work an hour early. Then stay three hours past closing time. Then, on your way home, pick up the latest gadget from Walmart, where employees slept on sidewalks next to the store they slaved in, too poor to afford rent in the area they kept running.

In the mind's eye, you were more peeved about the shelves being empty. The items you came to buy. That's how life worked. The employees had it out for you the entire time. They refused to stock the junk that made your life complete. And you thanked your lucky stars that you weren't stocking shelves. Would never be you. Could never be. Because you made better plans. Better choices in life. The world was your oyster. As long as you kept stocking the life-support machine you were hooked to. At least that's how you understood the entire process. The reality as you knew it. Or told. Or taught. Or hoodwinked into trusting. How plans came to fruition. The right way. The hard way. The deserving way. Not through merit. Or education. Or birthright. But through blind obedience. Loyalty and contractual agreement to keep the fire burning white hot. As long as you could. Until there was nothing left to burn, and the fire smoldered out. And someone killed the lights. And the party came to a grinding halt. Like before. Like now. Like tomorrow.

As though you were an angel with wings capable of carrying those plans and flying away to another world. To another life. When birth led to death in a blink of an eye propped up against a universe billions of years in the making, spending most of your time fulfilling plans. And plans kept changing because you once thought the hole you viewed life through was a bottomless hole. A promising one. When the bottom was way closer than the original estimation. So close, that the bottom was on top of you the entire time, crushing the life from you.

Grace crushed Dante's hands. Her fingers felt glasslike in Dante's grip. "I'm scared."

Dante dropped to eye level. "Don't be scared. We are together and that's all that matters, mijita." That's what Jack used to tell Dante when she got scared.

"What's mi... mih."

"Mijita."

"Yeah."

"It means my little daughter." Dante peered at Grace. "My dad used to call me that sometimes."

Grace's eyes were swimming in salty water. Her little face broken. "I'm scared you won't be my mommy."

Until now, they'd been living separate lies. But in that moment, the pretense shattered. No more make-believe about the world righting itself. No more fairy tales about Grace's mother coming to rescue her. No more fucking charade.

"I am your mommy." Dante lifted Grace to her hip and headed for the door. "You are mine Grace, you will always be mine."

CANINE DIPLOMATES

Lush clouds dolloped the peaks like whipped cream. Snow-capped mountains sparkled against the sky from where she stood. Westbound I-70 stretched clear into the Rockies. But eastbound lanes were choked with abandoned cars, a permanent rush hour frozen in time. People had died there on the road, in their cars, on their way to work, Rory guessed.

"There's no going back now." She glanced at Charlie in the passenger seat as they ascended the first mountain pass. His massive pink tongue dangled to the side, quivering as he breathed. "We'll have to find an alternate route if we want to come back this way."

The ride moved forward smoothly until Idaho Springs, where stalled vehicles obstructed the highway. Rory had to get out and push cars to the fog line so they could continue onward. An empty gas station sat right at the exit, but she pressed on. She knew empty gas stations spelled danger these days. The trip continued like this for miles. Some sections of I-70 lay clear while bottlenecks choked other reaches of the journey.

Mountains towered on both sides like an empire of stone. Pockets of waterfalls spilled from the hillside, while pines stood green and rich.

Last year's snow clung stubbornly even in autumn. Below, the Colorado River churned white foam against the rapids.

By the time they reached Glenwood, the fuel needle pointed one notch toward empty. Normally, a trip here would burn half a tank. But she had stopped several times to wheel cars off the road, motor running the whole time if she needed to escape.

Nightfall bled across the mountain peaks. The temperature was already dropping. Mountain nights showed no mercy, especially not since the world changed. Rory had little choice but to stop in Glenwood, her wagon running on fumes and prayers. In the old days, she might have risked pushing on to the next town. But now? Every mile between towns felt like Russian roulette. If she continued, she would stall somewhere in the wilderness. Then what? Then what? she asked herself.

The station wagon crept down Grand Avenue, past the famous hot springs where steam still rose from the abandoned pools. The tourist town's silence pressed against her ears like noise canceling earbuds. Shop windows gaped dark and empty. Their tourist trinkets gathered dust. The first exit's gas station stood abandoned, its prices frozen on the LED board. A relic of the last normal day. The air carried the rotten egg smell of the springs mixed with something else. Now the sweetness of decay seemed to follow her everywhere.

Rory stopped the car at a roadblock. Several vehicles lay parallel, blocked by construction barricades. "I have a bad feeling," she looked at Charlie. "What do you think? Is it safe?" Charlie peered at her with those big brown eyes, as though she held a treat. His tail flopped against the seat.

At the corner of her eye, something darted past the windshield. Rory snatched her gaze from Charlie, scanning the street ahead. "I think we—,"

The crack of a gunshot split the air. Charlie lurched up barking, his usual playful demeanor replaced with nervous whimpers. "Shhh, Charlie," Rory whispered, her own heart hammering against her ribs.

Through the windshield, a little blonde girl materialized, rifle steady in her small hands. She looked like she belonged on a ranch, all wranglers and boots beneath her ball cap. Next to her stood an older girl, beautiful and lethal, with an assault rifle that looked like it belonged in a war zone.

"Get out of the car!" Dante held steady aim, closing in quick on the station wagon. A massive wolf dog landed paws on the passenger window and bellowed. Charlie just sat there submissively, frozen, letting the wolf dog sniff him through the glass. "Now!"

Rory opened the car door and raised her hands. "Okay," her hands trembled like autumn leaves. "I just need gas."

"Shut up!" Dante pointed the assault rifle directly at her head. "Turn around and place your hands on the car." Rory obeyed instantly.

"Shit," Rory whimpered, warmth spreading down her leg as her body betrayed her fear.

"Who's with you?"

"No one."

"Who's with you!" Dante's voice rang like a thunderclap.

"No one."

"Do you have weapons?" Dante roughly frisked Rory, checking every crevice.

"Yes," Rory said without hesitation, tears streaming down her cheeks. Grace kept the rifle trained on Rory as Dante continued searching. "I have a gun in the glove box. It doesn't have any bullets."

"Turn around," Dante motioned to Grace. "If she moves, you know what to do."

Grace nodded, standing her ground, barrel aimed at Rory's chest.

"Will the dog attack?"

Rory shook her head.

"Will it!"

"Yes, I mean no."

When Dante opened the passenger door, Charlie bounded out. He went from cowering passenger to confident explorer. He and Ajax circled each other, tails wagging, sniffs exchanged like diplomatic credentials. They moved together as if they'd always known each other, as if the world hadn't ended, as if humans hadn't forgotten how to greet strangers without guns and fear. Their easy trust opened doors. A reminder of simpler times when strangers could still be friends.

Dante retrieved the revolver and checked it over. Relief washed over her face when she confirmed Rory's truth. The gun had no bullets.

"How bad?"

"Almost empty."

Dante inspected Rory from head to toe, her stance softening as she watched the dogs play. Something flickered across her face, maybe recognition, of another soul just trying to survive. She lowered her rifle slightly. "Listen, I know this is..." she gestured at the weapons, "...extreme. But we have food. Shelter. A safe place. And clearly," she nodded toward the playful dogs, "our troops have already voted you in."

"Mommy," Grace laughed, her earlier fierceness melting away to reveal the child beneath. She lowered her rifle, muscle memory making her flip the safety on first. A gesture that spoke volumes about her life now. "Look at Ajax! He never plays with anyone." She bounced on her toes, momentarily forgetting to be scared. "Can they stay? Please? Ajax needs a friend too."

"No," Rory shook her head, pants still soaked. "I just want to go. Please, just let us go."

Dante's expression softened as she shouldered her weapon. "You won't make it far. I'm sorry about the introduction, but you can never be too careful. I'm Dante," she gestured toward Grace. "That's my daughter, Grace. We're the only ones left. It's better if you come with us."

"Please," Rory's tears kept flowing. "We just need gas. I can pay." She pulled out her credit card, hands still shaking.

"The gas pumps aren't working." Dante's eyes scanned the darkening street as she spoke. "Electricity's like a ghost now. It comes and goes as it pleases. Sometimes we get an hour, enough to pump gas, charge batteries, to remind us of what we lost." She checked her watch. "It's been three days. Last time this happened..." She didn't finish the sentence, but her tightening grip on the rifle spoke volumes. "Look, night's coming. You really don't want to be out here when the sun sets. Not anymore."

NUCLEAR FAMILY

D AY TWENTY-ONE IN GLENWOOD, Rory still caught herself checking the rearview mirror for bad people. The town had become home. A thought that terrified her as much as it comforted. Dante had moved Tala's station wagon behind the Scout weeks ago, both vehicles now permanent fixtures outside William's bungalow. Like everything else in their new life, even parking had become strategic.

The electricity's return had been their first real victory. Grace spotted it, the way kids notice everything. Even the tiniest details. "Look!" she'd shouted during their afternoon sweep, pointing at the Humble Traveler's neon signs dancing in the twilight. For a moment, they'd all stood there, mesmerized by the ghost of the past.

They worked like landscapers that day, knowing the power might fail any second. Dante coordinated their gas-gathering operation with military precision. Grace watching the street, Rory filling containers, Dante running them back to William's garage. The sharp smell of gasoline poisoning every morsel, down to their hair follicles. Still, every splash precious as gold. Hours passed in a blur of heavy lifting and burning muscles.

"More coming," Grace would whisper from her lookout position, and they'd scatter like shadows, only to resume once the threat passed.

By nightfall, William's garage looked like a prepper's dream, or a bomb waiting to happen. Gas cans covered every inch of epoxy flooring, forcing the Scout onto the street. James would have approved, Dante thought, remembering his lectures about preparation. The man might have been paranoid, but paranoid people had survived the longest.

"It's too obvious," Rory said one morning, staring at their vehicles. "We might as well paint a target on the house." She hadn't meant to criticize, but survival instincts died hard.

Instead of arguing, Dante disappeared for hours. When she returned, she was driving different cars, positioning them carefully in front of neighboring houses. "Now we're just another block having a neighborhood party," she said, pride mixing with exhaustion in her voice. "One that's been going on since the world ended."

The deception worked. Their street became a museum of abandoned vehicles. Their house was one more dark window among many. At night, they transformed William's bungalow into a fortress. Blackout blinds Rory had salvaged from the crawl space. Curtains drawn tight against any betraying light. They'd turned his tomb into their sanctuary, though none said it aloud.

Charlie and Ajax wrote their own love story in the margins of survival. Some days they were inseparable, sharing food and warmth, teaching each other their grooming secrets. Other days they squabbled like siblings, especially over the holiday bone Dante had found at the grocery store, in the pet supplies. Their relationship defied the darkness around them. Half wild, half domestic. Still, wholly devoted to the way of the canine.

"Look at them," Rory whispered to Dante one evening, watching the dogs patrol their territory together. "They figured it out faster than we did." The words slipped out before she could catch them, hanging in the air between them like a question neither dared to answer.

By month end, glances lingered. Hands brushed accidentally-on-purpose during supply runs. Each moment of contact sparked with possibility and terror. They'd both seen what happened to love in this new world. How SHC turned passion to ash. How it seemed to hunt people who dared to care. A billion hearts had already burned.

Still, something grew between them, stubborn as hope. They found excuses to work together. To talk late into the night after Grace slept. Their orbit tightened day by day, even as they tried to keep their distance. Some forces were stronger than the fear that tranced the shadows along the walls.

Grace noticed everything. "You smile different now," she told Rory one morning while they sorted supplies. "Like Mommy does."

The observation caught Rory off guard. "Different how?"

"Like you belong here," Grace said, with that devastating childhood honesty. "Like you're not scared anymore."

But they were all scared, just differently now. Not of each other, but for each other. Their daily routines became rituals of protection. Sweeping the streets for threats, reinforcing barriers, watching the horizon. They moved together like planets in a private solar system, each rotation bringing them closer to something that felt dangerously like home.

BEDHEAD

On the corner of 10th and Minter, Rory found a home where a girl Grace's age had lived. A dark-haired girl's portrait sat on the mantel, nestled in a frame made of red-painted twigs and leaves, a school project, Rory guessed, remembering her own childhood crafts.

The girl beamed from the photo, positioned next to another frame where a couple draped their arms around each other, faces bright with joy. Rory lingered, studying each image. The happiness radiating from their faces felt like a gut punch. Goodness glinted in their eyes, a reminder of everything lost.

Then she entered the galley kitchen, and the house's warmth evaporated. The smell hit her first. Sharp and sweet and wrong. She barely made it to the sink before retching.

At the galley's end stood a table with three chairs, each bearing dark burn marks on their seats. Between one chair's stretchers, Rory swore she could see the ghost of a little girl's leg, trapped there, when spontaneous human combustion claimed her life. All three, gone in an instant. Part of her envied their swift end. Then she thought about her own circle of three, Dante, Grace, and herself. What fate awaited them?

Once she steadied herself, Rory pressed a dish towel to her nose and forced herself to search the cupboards. The last one near the stove yielded unexpected treasures, three bags of gourmet chocolate chips, unbleached flour, and real Madagascar vanilla extract, not the imitation kind. Even kosher salt. Small luxuries from a world that no longer existed.

The little girl's bedroom called to her next. Grace needed more than just supplies. She needed pieces of childhood to hold onto. A bird-themed bookshelf lined one wall, its shelves still holding stories waiting to be read. Rory's fingers trailed along the spines until they found "My Powerful Hair" and several others she knew would make Grace's eyes light up.

Winter gear came next. Practical things were the new couture. The family's portraits showed they'd owned good equipment. Sorel boots and thick winter parkas. She packed those first. Then came the little girl's Zara collection. Knit tops, safari-inspired jumpsuits, and vibrant prints that made Rory's heart ache with their normalcy. She'd never heard of Zara before, found herself wishing these trendy pieces came in her size. That print jumper especially. She folded a few choice items for Grace and headed back to William's bungalow, eager to share her finds.

"You won't believe what I found," Rory burst into the bungalow, dumping bags onto the table where Dante and Grace sat eating lunch. Grace's eyes widened at the interruption, sandwich forgotten.

"What is it, Rory?" Grace leaned forward as Rory began unpacking.

"Will you look at this?" Rory held up the print jumper like a prize. "Isn't it gorgeous?" She turned to Grace, waiting for the excitement to catch.

But something shifted in the room. Dante's smile faded, a shadow crossing her face as she gave a subtle head shake. Rory, caught up in her enthusiasm, missed the warning.

"Try it on," she urged, holding the jumper out to Grace. "Let's see how it fits."

Grace took the fabric with trembling fingers, her eyes seeking Dante's face. "Mommy?" Her voice wavered.

The tears gathering in Grace's eyes finally broke through Rory's excitement. "Did I... did I do something wrong?"

Dante gently took the jumper from Grace's hands, setting it aside. "Grace doesn't like pink," she said softly, trying to cushion the moment.

"Oh." Rory dug through her bag again, determined to salvage the situation. "What about this one? The pattern's different..." She held up a knitted blouse in bright prints.

Dante shook her head again, her eyes kind but firm. "Grace prefers different kinds of clothes." She paused, choosing her words carefully. "More practical things. Wranglers, boots, shirts that can take a beating. She's never been one for frills."

That night, shadows danced on the walls as Dante and Rory took turns reading to Grace. The books from Minter house spread across the quilted bedspread, their spines cracked with love from another child's hands. "My Powerful Hair" became an instant favorite. Grace insisted on hearing it three times. Her eyes grew heavier with each reading but her attention never wavering.

"Mommy?" Grace's voice came soft and serious in the lamplight. She gathered her blond hair in one hand, holding it like something precious and strange. "Can you cut my hair like the girl in the story? I want to send it to the spirits..." The words faltered on her tongue, but her eyes held determination.

Dante studied her daughter's face, searching for the thoughts behind the request. The silence stretched between them, heavy with meaning. "If you really want me to," she finally said.

"Right now?" Grace sat up straighter, suddenly alert.

"How about tomorrow?" Dante eased her back down, tucking the quilts around her small frame. Grace's protest dissolved into a yawn wide enough to click her jaw. "It's bedtime. I can see dreamland calling your name."

"'Mmm not tired," Grace mumbled, even as her eyelids drooped.

"Yes," Dante kissed her forehead, breathing in the sweet smell of her daughter's hair, hair that might be gone tomorrow. "You always say that, too. But I know different."

Rory watched from the doorway, struck by the tenderness between them. In this moment, the world outside couldn't touch them. They were just a family saying goodnight, and somehow that felt like the most powerful magic of all.

MY SPIRIT

Morning light felt timeless, yet fragile in William's bungalow. The chocolate chip pancakes they shared tasted of borrowed time. A bittersweet moment against the knowledge that their supplies dwindled. No more milky water. Just clear liquid from taps that might run dry any day. Dante watched each drop fall, wondering how many remained. Change had found them, patient as winter, waiting to collect its due.

The kitchen smelled of imitation maple and worry. Grace bounced by the door, dogs' leashes tangled in her small fists, while Dante performed their daily safety ritual. It was a dance they'd perfected, each step vital as breathing.

"Body alarm?"

A black device flashed from Grace's pocket.

"Whistle?"

Silver glinted at her throat.

"Watch?"

The timepiece caught the morning light.

Each item a tether, each check a prayer.

"Fifteen minutes, that's all you get, so don't ask."

Grace growled. Though her eyes looked tempted to barter more time. "Ok."

"If you're not back in fifteen—,"

"Oook."

The forest had teeth. They knew that well. Rory felt them as she crossed into shadow, where boot steps cracked like gunshots against fallen branches. Pine sap sweetened the air but underneath lay something ancient, something that remembered when humans were prey. Death was more cunning than them.

"Grace!" Her voice scattered like startled birds. The forest drank her sound and gave nothing back. She tried again, harder this time, until her throat burned. "Grace! Ajax! Charlie!"

The silence that followed wasn't empty, it was waiting.

Then came the scream. Distance warped it. Stretched it wrong, like sound traveling underwater. A dog's bark followed, but the forest played tricks with direction, spinning sound into echoes that came from everywhere and nowhere.

Her heart clobbered those burning ribs. The woods weren't closing in like her neighborhood had during her panic attacks. No, this was worse. The forest was expanding, pulling away like a tide, taking Grace with it. Trees multiplied in every direction, each the same as the last, hiding whatever secrets they held in their shadows.

Dante materialized from the trees like an apparition, the assault rifle across her back both promise and threat. "Stay here." The air horn she pressed into Rory's hands was cold. "If she makes it back, use this. I'll follow the sound."

Rory caught Dante's wrist, fingers finding warmth and a pulse. All their unspoken words crowded the space between them. Possibilities, fears, and that almost-kiss neither had mentioned. "What if—" The words stuck like a knife to the heart.

"Don't." Dante's voice held steel, but her eyes betrayed her. "Just don't."

The body alarm's shriek shattered their moment. High and desperate as a wounded animal. Rory watched terror reshape Dante's face, watched love transform it into something fierce, animalistic.

"Grace!" When Dante screamed her daughter's name, it carried every ounce of her heart. Biology had nothing to do with motherhood. Not anymore. Not here.

Then she was gone, swallowed by green shadows, leaving Rory to count boot falls, and cracking twigs, heartbeats bleeding into the silence.

Time liquefied at the orange line. Rory paced its length, each turn marking moments she couldn't measure. No watch. No sun visible through the canopy. Just the space between breaths, between heartbeats, between hoping and knowing.

The forest kept growing. With every passing minute, the trees stretched further, taking her family deeper into the maze. Family. The word caught her off guard, true as marrow. When did these two become her whole world? Somewhere between chocolate chip pancakes and bedtime stories. Between morning coffee and evening watches, they'd rebuilt her heart.

Now Glenwood yawned around her, too vast for three and impossible for one. She thought of the almost-kiss, of how Dante's eyes had met hers over Grace's sleeping form. That same electric recognition she'd felt with Chloe in the basement. But different, deeper, somehow. More real. Like coming home instead of running away.

The forest wept with her. Pine sap bled from wounded bark. Leaves trickled like tears. Birds called, but no one answered. This green universe mourned what might be lost, while Rory stood at its edge, a sentinel at the border between safety and love, praying to whatever gods survived the apocalypse to bring her family home.

"She went past the markers once," Dante said, stacking dishes with military precision. "Mistakes were made." Her eyes caught Rory's, heavy with memory. "She used her body alarm like we practiced. Like I taught her."

The words carried weight, stories beneath stories. How long had Dante spent teaching Grace to survive? How many sleepless nights had she laid awake, planning for every possible disaster? Love, Rory was learning, looked different after the world ended. Sometimes it looked like rules. Sometimes it looked like letting go.

"She's so young," Rory whispered, but she already knew the answer.

"Young enough to learn. Young enough to adapt." Dante's hands stilled on a plate, knuckles white against porcelain. "What if something happens to me, Rory? Then what?" The question hung between them, sharp as broken glass. "Every time she walks out that door, I die a little. But keeping her helpless, that's not love. That's fear."

FLAME THE BEAST

THE WORLD DIDN'T END with a whimper. It didn't end when the sprites came. Not when everything turned to ash. It ended with Grace's horror-struck scream. It ended in a child's bedroom, with blood soaked sheets and a mother's broken promises shattered like glass.

Dante stood there, holding up what remained of her universe with trembling hands. She'd spent so long fighting against sprites, against James's warnings, against the dying world itself. But death had found them anyway, patient as winter, quiet as sleep. It had crept in through the forest's shadows and stolen her whole world in one savage afternoon.

What a goddamn fool she'd been, thinking love could outrun the apocalypse. That she could build something lasting in a world that only knew how to burn everything to the ground.

Charlie died where he fell, defending Grace until his last breath. But Ajax—God, Ajax made it home to die. She dragged herself back through miles of forest, ribs gleaming white through shredded flesh, back leg hanging by threads of tendon and hope. Her beautiful salt-and-pepper coat had been painted burgundy, each step leaving bloody footprints like accusations.

Rory watched Ajax refuse food, refuse water, refuse everything except the dignity of dying on their back porch. She stroked that ruined fur until the shallow pants grew quiet, until her loyal heart finally stopped. Blood tears dried on the wooden steps, marking another ending in a world that had nothing left but endings.

Later, Rory would remember this moment. How death came in stages, taking the dogs first like some terrible dress rehearsal for what was coming.

"Mommy." Grace's voice barely stirred the air, soft as secrets.

Dante's hand found her daughter's, burning with fever. Each small finger was a miracle she couldn't keep. "I'm right here, Grace. Right here."

"I'm scared." Tears cut clean trails through the sweat on Grace's face, and for a moment she looked so young, too young for this world, too young for its savage rules.

Dante turned away, choking on her own terror. Without Grace, there would be no after. No tomorrow. Just an endless string of empty days stretching toward nothing. "It's okay to be scared." She forced the words past the grief already crystallizing in her throat.

"I don't want to die." Grace's eyes found Dante's with terrible clarity, as if death had burned away everything except truth.

Dante shattered then, a sound like the world ending twice. "You're not going to die. I promise." The lie tasted like ashes and shame.

Grace's focus sharpened suddenly, burning through a fever's haze. "Cut my hair."

"What?" The word fell from Dante's lips like a stone.

"My hair." Grace's fingers twitched toward her blood-matted blond strands. "My spirit."

In native traditions, hair carried the spirit's weight. Grace knew this. Dante had taught her, never thinking she'd use the knowledge like this. Never imagining her daughter would ask for this final ceremony, this letting go.

When Dante returned with the scissors, the universe had already shifted on its axis. Grace's eyes stared at nothing. All that fierce energy fled to somewhere mothers couldn't follow. The scissors clattered to the floor, ringing like a bell that tolled for endings.

Time folded strangely. Rory stood with her hands pressed against her mouth, tears sliding between her fingers, watching history repeat itself with cruel precision. She was back in that hospital room with Tala, only now she wasn't alone. She had Dante. But life's darkest joke was that Dante no longer had Grace.

The silence that followed wasn't empty. It was alive with all the words they'd never say, all the futures that would never happen. Morning pancakes that would never be made. Bedtime stories left unfinished. A child interrupted mid-sentence. Forever.

"It's not your fault." Dante's voice came wet against Rory's neck, each word heavy with self-loathing. "James was right. I had no business raising a kid. What gives me the fucking right?" She pulled away, hands rising like surrender to an unseen enemy. "What was I thinking, Rory? Playing house at the end of the fucking world?"

The calm in Dante's voice terrified Rory more than screaming would have. It was the calm of someone who had nothing left to lose, someone who had already decided something terrible.

Dante lay beside Grace's broken body, gathering her close one last time. Blood soaked through her clothes, but she didn't seem to notice. "Please," she said, voice distant as starlight. "I need to be with Grace."

Rory backed away, her own grief tangling with fear for what came next. "Okay." The word felt inadequate, microscopic against the vastness of their loss. "I'll be in the living room if you need anything."

But some needs were beyond meeting. Some wounds beyond healing. Some spirits, once broken, stayed that way. And sometimes, Rory realized, watching Dante cradle her dead child, love wasn't enough to save anyone.

Dante didn't reply. She just stared at Grace, cataloging every detail like an archaeologist at a dig site. The tiny whorl in her hair that never lay flat. The chicken pox scar behind her ear. The callus on her thumb from holding pencils too tight. All these pieces of a life cut too short, artifacts of a future that would never come.

Something violent thrashed behind her ribs, a creature made of rage and grief. She held it back until Rory's footsteps faded down the hall. Until the house settled into the silence of all those dying spaces.

Then she let it out.

Her scream split the air like lightning, raw, electric, and devastating.

The sound a mountain might make if it tore in half. The sound of a heart learning it can break more than once.

"It's my fault." The words fell like stones from her lips, each one heavier than the last. "It's my fault. It's my fault."

The guilt came not in waves but in flames. Jack burned while she watched, helpless as a foolish girl. His flesh melted away like wax. His silent screams echoing in the chambers of her heart. James warned her she was playing Russian roulette with Grace's life. "You can't protect anyone in this world," he'd said. And now his words tasted like a deadly prophecy.

She pulled Grace closer. Her daughter's body was already growing unfamiliar in death. "I killed you," she whispered against the cooling skin. "Just like I killed Jack. Just like James knew I would."

Two deaths. Two failures. Two infernos of guilt, each burning hotter than the last until there was nothing left but ash where her soul used to be.

Dante made a promise then, to the ghosts that would haunt her. I will not lend my heart to another. Love was a con game, a loaded gun, a poison masquerading as medicine. It follows no rules, respects no boundaries. It took and took until nothing remained but bone and regret.

She would carry these deaths like bullet fragments in her chest. Jack's charred remains, Grace's shredded body. Their deaths would remind her that some hearts weren't meant to survive their own beating. Some loves were too sharp to hold.

As darkness crept across the room and Grace's skin grew cold beneath her touch, Dante felt something fundamental shift inside her. The part that had dared to hope, dared to love in this broken world, it died with Grace, there in that blood soaked bed, under a sky that no longer held any stars.

The beast of fire settled in her chest, satisfied with its destruction. In its wake, it left only silence and a truth as old as pain itself. In a world of sprites and ash, love was the cruelest monster of all.

THE WHITE ROOM

SHC BEGAN ON FRIDAY MORNING. Astronomical half-light. Around midnight in Sydney, on the thirteenth day. Different times in other cities, but the same horror unfolding like a dark flower. Two significant events collided, one religious, one numerological, as if God and mathematics had finally found their intersection point.

Fridays had always carried disaster's weight in biblical tales. Eve's fingers wrapping around forbidden fruit, the first sin's sweet poison. Cain's stone cracking Abel's skull, his brother's blood soaking holy ground. And most significantly, nails piercing Christ's flesh on Calvary while his mother wept below. Judas, the thirteenth guest, had sealed these patterns with his traitor's kiss, thirty pieces of silver jingling in his purse like Satan's wind chimes.

Yet Fridays also birthed discovery, particularly on the thirteenth day. Water—Earth's lifeblood, our bodies' primary part, revealed its cosmic dance. November 13, 2009: NASA's telescopes found lunar ice in shadows where sunlight never reaches. Water, defying vacuum's hungry mouth, surviving where nothing should survive. Like faith in darkness. Like hope in the apocalypse.

Like Mary Magdalene seeing resurrection through tear-blurred eyes, Sister Gomer, now Messenger of Light, had seen extinction bloom. She

225

watched as people froze mid-praise, their skin turning translucent before the flames took them. A jogger caught between strides, headphones still pumping music into deaf ears. A mother reaching for her child, fingers inches from salvation. A businessperson checking his watch one final time, as if death might wait for a more convenient hour.

She had seen what others couldn't comprehend, civilization's death rattle echoing through empty streets. The phenomena stripped humanity bare, left nothing but ash-statues and questions. Billions frozen as flame devoured their flesh, their screams trapped inside throats that could no longer voice them. Time itself seemed to stutter, skip, then resume its merciless march without most of its passengers.

Now she dwelled in solitude, in an abandoned town where empty swings still creaked in end days winds. Her vow of silence matched the world's new quietude. No birds sang, no dogs barked, no children laughed. Dawn to dusk, she transcribed visions onto parchment with trembling hands, certain that future eyes would understand what she could barely comprehend herself.

The white room rose like a tumor in the abandoned church's heart. Soundproof walls thick enough to muffle God's voice. White walls scrubbed until they gleamed like bone. White door sealed tight as a tomb. White floor tiles reflecting infinity back at itself. White ceiling smooth as heaven's floor. Windows painted thick with white, layer after layer until natural light admitted defeat.

No shadow dared cast its dark truth here. Halogens burned brighter than the desert sun, transforming the temple into a white void. Every inch identical to nothingness. Frightening. Soundless. Empty. A portal to white hell where even darkness feared to tread.

The paint they used came from a factory three towns over. Brother Matthew had driven there himself, past stalled cars and frozen corpses still standing like macabre street art. The paint needed to be pure, no tint, no shade, no compromise. They mixed it with turpentine until it flowed like milk. Until its fumes made the mixing room feel like a gateway to another dimension.

The Messenger of Light approached the white room like a bride approaching an altar. They stripped her at dawn. Not just clothes, but every vestige of the world she'd known. Her hair, once flowing past her shoulders, fell to the floor in chunks. They shaved her until she was smooth as an egg, hairless as a newborn. Every follicle, every stray strand that might cast a shadow, every trace of humanity's darkness gone.

She stood naked before the congregation, trembling not from cold but from holy burden. Brother Thomas approached with the paint bucket, its contents thinned with turpentine until it moved like liquid moonlight. The first brush stroke across her shoulder made her gasp, cold as judgment, wet as baptism. They painted every inch of her. The hollow of her throat. The spaces between her fingers. The delicate skin behind her ears. Every crevice, every fold, every scar transformed into a blank canvas.

The turpentine fumes rose like invisible prayers, burning eyes and throats. The congregation wept, though whether from chemicals or religious ecstasy, none could say. Their tears cut tracks down cheeks as white as their prophet's newly painted skin. Even the children, usually fidgeting during ceremonies, stood stone-still, hypnotized by this transformation of flesh into pure light.

Brother Matthew, head shaved mirror-smooth, feet bare against the concrete, would be her only connection to the outside world. Each day at noon, precise as death, he would bring her sustenance. White rice like fallen angels. Bread with crusts removed, for even golden-brown might taint the sacred space. All served in bowls so white they hurt the eyes. No water would pass the threshold. They believed color lived in water's memory. Even clear water held rainbows when the light struck right. And this room could tolerate no spectrum, no shade, no suggestion that the world contained anything but white.

She entered backward, not daring to face the void that would become her universe. The paint was still wet on her skin, dripping onto the white threshold like snow melting into snow. The door sealed behind her with a sound like thunder.

In that moment, as white embraced white, as paint-flesh met paint-wall, the Messenger of Light understood, this was how angels rose, creatures of pure light, unburdened by the weight of shadow. This was how God felt, before He spoke darkness into being.

Day One: Silence pressed against her eardrums like wool soaked in eternity.

Day Two: Whispers crept in through invisible cracks. Children's laughter echoing down memory's halls. A game of tag played by ghosts. "Can't catch me!" they seemed to giggle, their phantom feet pattering on white tiles that never showed footprints.

Day Three: Turpentine's chemical bite faded, replaced by stranger scents. Myrrh, like Christ's burial gift. Seawater, though they were hundreds of miles inland. Paint that smelled like communion wine.

Day Four: The walls began to breathe. In and out, subtle as a sleeping infant. The ceiling rose and fell like a great white lung. She pressed her paint-covered hand against the wall and felt a pulse.

Day Five: Oceans crashed against her consciousness. Seagulls wheeled overhead in a sky she couldn't see. Ship horns moaned like dying leviathans. Through it all, pleasure-moans woke her from nightmares where people still burned, their faces melting like wax offerings.

Day Six: Reality cracked. A vibration started in her bones and worked outward, turning stomach to water, thoughts to static. The feminine chord struck—not sound but pure energy, splitting her skull like an overripe melon. God's voice, perhaps, or madness wearing God's face.

Brother Matthew found her sprawled in her own vomit, white on white, a Rorschach test of human frailty. Her eyes had rolled back, showing only whites to match the room. Her tongue, thick with dehydration, pushed out broken syllables like dying prophecies.

They carried her down three steps that might as well have been three thousand. Her painted-white feet left tracks on concrete that had witnessed the world's end. When natural light touched her for the first time in six days, her painted skin cracked like old porcelain.

She saw, in that moment of collapse, what the white room had been hiding. Colors rushed back. Blue sky, green leaves, fresh blood still staining the sidewalk from when the phenomena came. Her mind couldn't handle the transition from divine void to earthly chaos. She fell, and as consciousness fled, she understood finally what the feminine chord had been trying to tell her. Even God needs darkness to create light.

BEAR FRUIT

THREE DAYS AFTER HER COLLAPSE, sanity trickled back into the Messenger of Light's mind like water to spoiled land. Her voice, when it finally returned, carried new authority. They gathered twelve men, not counting Brother Dan with his melted face, and seven women for the Tribe of Judah. The Bible, she claimed, had whispered secrets to her in the white room. A new Messiah would rise, born from the ashes of the old world. The Tribe of Judah would build God's army, and she, Messenger of Light, would birth this promised child.

Seven days remained the benchmark for surviving the white room. Out of nineteen, only one succeeded. The others produced a grotesque spectrum of failure, blackouts, hallucinations, madness wearing different masks. Most lasted five days before their minds cracked like thin ice. At least two men, maybe more, faked unconsciousness to escape. Few spoke of their experiences afterward, fear sealing their lips tighter than any vow of silence.

Isolation proved their greatest enemy. A soundless white void with only imagination for company. Their sole anchor to reality, Brother Matthew's noon appearance with white food on white plates. Sister Lindsay lasted the full seven days before collapse, but the room had taken something from her that a week of recovery couldn't return.

When the Tribe of Judah forced testimonies, consensus emerged from trembling lips. No one heard God's voice. No saint visited their dreams. No phantom children played in white corners. No oceanic symphonies. Only Brother James spoke of something different, plastic burning somewhere in the room. A smell that haunted him for three days straight. He searched until his fingernails bled but found nothing.

Sister Francis broke first. "The walls," she'd gasped between hyperventilated breaths, "they were stealing my soul." Two nights later, she vanished into darkness, leaving only white footprints in morning dew.

Now six women remain. An ominous number that the Messenger of Light transformed into prophecy. Six women, six days, twelve men, twelve tribes. Divine mathematics, she called it. Her eyes were fever-bright with certainty.

They emerged from the white changed. Humbled, shaken, disturbed. Yet none carried the divine light they'd sought, except their leader. Four women had husbands among the Tribe of Judah before SHC came. Two couples bore wounds no white room could heal. Jody, eleven, and Gabriel, eight, taken by the phenomena's hungry flames.

The abandoned town had started peacefully enough. Each survivor filled roles eerily similar to their lost lives, as if playing parts in a post-apocalyptic theater. They maintained modern conveniences with medieval manpower. Scattered across separate dwellings but bound by necessity.

Their church stood sentinel in a flowery meadow. Steep triangular roof. Twin oak doors. Circular stained glass windows near the peak. A wrought iron sign post proclaimed "FOUNDED 1889" to a world that no longer cared for dates. Brother Dan's sermons ended with his stroke. Brother Dillon, former paramedic, inherited the pulpit.

Attendance grew like a slow cancer. First the grieving parents. Then converted atheists. And finally single women—one atheist, one agnostic. After Brother Dan's collapse, all nineteen gathered weekly. Half still doubting the God whose house they occupied.

When testimonials concluded, the Messenger of Light revealed God's new commandment. All six women must share their beds with the Tribe of Judah's twelve men. The church's air thickened like cooling sterilization from the flame.

Sister Jennifer, twenty-four, erupted from her pew. "Just because you'll sleep with twelve men doesn't make it a prophecy. We all hallucinated. Who's to say your vision wasn't madness wearing God's face?"

The Messenger of Light's hand rose and fell like an executioner's blade. "Look around you. We have few children. How does society grow from barren soil?" Her gaze found the childless couples. "Love these men as yourselves, that we might birth a better world."

The two couples who had lost children sat in heavy silence. Their nods mechanical, like puppets dangling to grief's strings. Each motion seemed to cost them something important. Something already stretched paper-thin by loss.

Zach rose slowly, his frame casting a trembling shadow across the pews. "I..." His voice cracked. He swallowed hard and tried again. "I respectfully request exclusion from this list." The words tumbled out quick and desperate before he sank back down, as if the very air had grown too heavy to stand in.

Messenger of Light's eyes fixed on him like spotlights. "May I ask why?"

He forced himself up again, knuckles white against the pew in front of him. "Before SHC, I was engaged—,"

"Go on." Messenger of Light's hand slashed through the air, impatience crackling like static around her.

His voice dropped to barely a whisper. Each word seemed to scrape his throat raw. "I can't father a child." Color flooded his face, bright as a fever. "Testicular cancer saw to that." The last words hung in the air like white smoke, while whispers rippled through the congregation like snakes through dry grass.

Brother Henry struggled to his feet, his weathered hand still locked with Sister Becky's as if they were crossing rushing water together. "I'm sixty," he announced, voice rough with age and something like shame. He glanced down at his wife, love and apology mixing in his eyes. "Sister Becky had a hysterectomy five years ago. And..." He attempted a weak smile that looked more like a grimace. "Well, my troops aren't as young as they used to be. Don't reckon I'll be of much use to anyone." He eased back down, arm circling his wife's shoulders like a shield.

The silence that followed shattered when a man leaped up, his enthusiasm obscene against the room's somber mood. His wife's face streaked with tears beside him, but his voice rang out with horrible eagerness: "I'm thirty-two and I'll be of service!"

Messenger of Light's response came like a serpent's strike. Her words dripped venom. "Let this serve as a warning." Her voice dropped to a hiss that somehow filled the entire church. "We will not tolerate rape here." Her eyes burned into the man until he wilted back into his seat. "This is a holy matter. Not your playground for pleasure."

The man's enthusiasm drained away, leaving him pale and small beside his weeping wife. In that moment, the thin line between divine mandate and human horror became razor-sharp, cutting through any illusion that this new world would be kinder than the old.

Sister Elizabeth's muscles tensed, her body rising in protest, but the Messenger of Light's hand shot out like a prophet's staff, freezing her in place. The air grew thick with holy terror.

"God chose each of you for a reason." Messenger of Light's voice filled the church like winter frost, choking out doubt. Her finger traced an arc through the air, landing on the couple who had lost their child. A gesture both blessing and curse. "He will bless you with children again."

She stepped away from the pulpit, her bare feet silent against worn wood. "Remember Sarah, how she laughed when God promised her a child." Her lips curved into something between smile and snarl. "Ninety years old, her womb dry as desert sand. Yet she conceived. She bore Abraham a son."

The words hung in the air like suspended daggers as she moved between the pews. Her white garment brushed against knees, shoulders, bowed heads. "Those who reject this divine calling must leave." Each word fell heavy as judgment. "You have seven days to decide." She paused, letting silence build like pressure. "But ask yourselves this, what waits beyond our walls?"

Her gaze raked across the congregation, cold as a winter night. Tears carved silent paths down some faces. While others wore masks of unholy excitement. Wolves scenting prey. Horror had transformed the rest into living statues. Faces frozen in eternal scream.

"Out there," she whispered, her voice dropping to a serpent's hiss, "it's the tumble effect." Her hands spread wide, mimicking collapse. "When one goes..." She let the words trail off, leaving imagination to fill the void. Then, softer still, as if sharing a lover's secret. "They all go."

She returned to the pulpit, each step deliberate as execution. Standing there, bathed in light from the stained-glass window above, she delivered her final judgment. "Only God can save us now."

The words settled over the congregation like ash after fire, burning away the last traces of the world they'd known. In its place stood this new reality. Salvation wrapped in barbed wire. A heaven built on human wreckage.

The moment church doors creaked shut behind them, Brother Zack's feet carried him to the internet café like a man possessed. His hands trembled as he jabbed at keyboard keys, printer humming to life. Each printed page felt like contraband— directions to salvation inked in black and white. Brother Zach's flyer promised: ALL ARE WELCOMED, ALL BELIEFS RESPECTED AND PROTECTED. An inverted pentagram marked their salvation.

Monday dawned gray and tentative. Brother Zack moved through town like a ghost, slipping flyers under doors, pressing them into trembling hands. His whispered explanations carried the weight of rebellion. "There's a place, a farm. Where they don't force themselves into your bed. Where God doesn't demand your body as tithe."

The paper rustled like autumn leaves as it passed from hand to hand. Each recipient's eyes grow wider with desperate hope. Some doors slammed in his face. Others opened just enough for shaking fingers to snatch the offering, fear of being seen warring with the need to escape.

By Wednesday, they were eight strong—eight souls choosing uncertain freedom over certain violations. They gathered in shadows, planning in whispers, packing only what wouldn't slow them down. Their fear tasted like copper pennies, their hope like morning dew.

Thursday broke cold and clear. The exodus began quietly. Without ceremony or goodbye, they hit the fucking road. Their caravan of mismatched vehicles pulled away from the town's suffocating embrace, engines growling defiance against Messenger of Light's divine order. In rearview mirrors, the church spire grew smaller and smaller until it was just another scar on the horizon.

Eight people choosing their own damnation over someone else's salvation. Eight people who'd rather risk death on open roads than suffer rape disguised as holy duty. They drove toward Santa Fe like souls fleeing hell. Each mile between them and the white room a victory, and each passing hour a rebirth.

Behind them, the town grew quiet with their absence, like a wound beginning to fester.

By Sunday, Messenger of Light surveyed her reduced flock beneath somber skies. The volunteer sat alone, wife fled three days before. Only the bereaved parents remained, clutching hands like lifelines. Brother Dale, massive as judgment, watched from the back pew.

"Rise," the Messenger of Light commanded, voice climbing toward heaven, "and remove your clothes. May God deliver us children."

Every new civilization learns the blood-price of tyranny. Eight chose freedom's uncertain path over prescribed salvation. Better to die seeking choice than live without it. Messenger of Light saw her error too late, the rats know their maze. The trick isn't bars but invisible chains. Normalizing horror until it feels like grace.

Sometimes, she decided, watching her flock disrobe, salvation requires force. Apply enough pressure, and even the hardest heart cracks open to let God in. They'll understand eventually. They must.

BEHIND THE CURTAINS OF THE HIGH PRIESTESS

THE INFIRMARY'S SWAYING FLUORESCENT lights buzzed overhead, casting everything in a sickly green tinge. Through the cracked window, dawn was climbing over the compound's walls, bringing with it the smell of wood smoke and morning dew. The contrast between the sterile interior and the backcountry outside made the infirmary seem like a time capsule from the civil war. One of the last places where modern medicine still clung to existence.

Dante came to, in the infirmary. Her vision swimming into focus. Rory dozed in the chair beside her. Fingers still curled around a weathered copy of THEY BOTH DIE AT THE END. The book's spine had warped. Its pages mottled with black spores, a remnant of better days.

When Dante tried to prop herself up, a horrendous moan tore from her throat. The sound yanked Rory from an unintended slumber. She'd only meant to rest her eyes for a moment, but exhaustion had won again. Days and nights had blurred together in this metal torture contraption of a chair. Her back and tailbone protested every hour she kept watch at Dante's bedside.

Rory gently eased Dante back against the pillows. Dante's eyes, dilated and unblinking, gleamed against her ashen face. Her pale skin and matted hair sent chills through Rory. Dante's chest quivered with each breath. Her body trembled with the effort to stay conscious.

"Don't move," Rory whispered, trying to keep her voice calm. "You need to rest."

Dante stared at Rory in disbelief, as if seeing a ghost. Was this heaven? Or another cruel dream? The world swam before her. Everything tinged with a cloudy haze. Her mouth tasted of metal and medicine, making her stomach queasy. The harsh halogen swaying above stabbed at her eyes, forcing them closed. While the sharp tang of disinfectant filled her senses. The same antiseptic smell that had surrounded Grace during that desperate rescue at the pharmacy.

Wires snaked from her chest and arms that traced back to humming medical equipment. Somewhere nearby, a monitor tracked her heartbeat with steady, rhythmic beeps. A mechanical lullaby marking each moment she remained alive.

Her trembling fingers traced Rory's lips as if touching fine crystal, afraid she might shatter this beautiful illusion. "I saw you die," she whispered, voice cracking. "I watched the waterfall take you."

Rory caught Dante's quivering hand in hers, managing a gentle smile. "They found me downstream. They saved me."

Ice-cold medication seeped through Dante's IV line, making her shiver. The starched sheets pinned her legs, and her hand lay limp in Rory's grip like dead weight. Unresponsive flesh that reminded her too much of the corpses she stumbled upon at Minter house.

Through a puddle of tears, Dante met Rory's eyes. "Don't leave me," she breathed, barely above a whisper.

Rory bent down and kissed Dante's lips. Her lips prickly as autumn leaves. "I'm right here," she murmured against Dante's mouth. "I'm not going anywhere." Those words held the promise of the universe in them.

Watching Dante suffer tore at Rory's heart, threatening to unleash a flood of tears she'd been holding back for some time. But she couldn't break. Not just yet. She'd walked this path before. Knew the carnage of grief intimately. There would be time for tears later, when Dante was stronger.

Strength wasn't optional anymore, it was survival. Rory swallowed the fear climbing from her throat and locked away the grief. The tears could wait until Dante was healed. Until they were back on the road again. If there was still a road to follow. That was the question that haunted her now. Where could they go in this broken world? Every direction led to the same wasteland, the same twisted civilization.

Part of her wanted to fetch Dr. Kelsey, their recently promoted doctor who'd spent her career treating livestock before the SHC forced everyone to adapt. The previous doctor, Rebecca, had been fresh out of pediatric rotation when the crisis hit. Now she lay recovering from delivering her own baby, helped only by Rose, a former CNA who'd worked alongside her in the old world.

Though Rose had twenty-five years of medical knowledge under belt. Rebecca was bedridden because of a very large perineal tear while giving birth. Almost reaching her bottom. They upgraded Rose to head nurse status shortly after that.

Rory didn't want to alarm Dante by getting the medical staff involved. She didn't look well enough to handle the news. Truth is, she hadn't looked well in days. In Rory's mind. She hoped keeping things calm and quiet would put Dante back to sleep. Which she needed. To abandon her by getting a doctor would only make things worse. She was familiar with Dante's idiosyncrasies.

So Rory stayed. And threaded fingers through Dante's tangled hair, massaging her feet with practiced hands. The same soothing rhythms she'd once used to comfort Tala. The parallel wasn't lost on her. Here she was again, another sterile room, another hospital bed, another woman she loved fighting for survival. SHC had dragged her full circle, forcing her to relive her worst nightmare.

Watching Dante's chest rise and fall, Rory remembered the last time she'd sat this vigil. Her mother, Tala, had taught her how to read vital signs between chemotherapy sessions, showing her how to spot the subtle changes that meant trouble. "Medicine isn't just about knowing the body," she'd said. "It's about knowing the person." Now, years later, Rory understood what she'd meant. Every tiny shift in Dante's breathing told a story. One she was desperate to understand.

Dante's eyes followed Rory's every movement, heavy with exhaustion but refusing to close, as if afraid Rory might vanish the moment she surrendered to sleep. Only after long minutes of gentle touches did her eyelids finally flutter shut, her breathing settling into a steady rhythm.

———

The farming community did not operate in the old ways. Men and women were equal inside the massive compound. Though women outnumbered men. And held critical roles within the community.

SHC had erased the old hierarchies, replacing degrees and certifications with raw skill and adaptability. In this new world, experience trumped credentials, like Kassie. The mechanic who now served as the community's chief engineer. Her practical knowledge was worth more than any university diploma.

Their farming community had abandoned pre-collapse social structures, establishing something both primitive and progressive. Women dominated leadership positions. Their practical authority grew naturally from both their numerical majority and their critical roles in everything from governance to reproduction. The old power dynamics had crumbled along with the old world, leaving something harder but maybe more honest in their place.

Not everyone adapted easily to this new reality. Men who couldn't accept women's leadership found themselves exiled. Though many eventually returned, humbled by the harsh realities of isolation. They'd learned that survival meant trading their pride for access to the community's resources, especially its medical care. The compound's healthcare had prevented countless deaths. Treating everything from infected wounds to gunshot trauma. Their makeshift hospital felt like something from a civil war battlefield, where medicine and frontier justice walked hand in hand.

People who remained within the compound walls found their roles based on ability rather than gender. Men discovered talents in childcare and domestic duties, while women excelled in hunting and security. Traditional gender roles dissolved in the face of practical necessity. Some of their best scouts were new mothers who returned to scavenging just days after giving birth. Entrusting their infants to partners who showed more aptitude for nurturing than warfare.

The community operated on social currency, guided by three unshakable principles. Service to the collective, absolute honesty, and moral integrity. When traditional wealth meant nothing, character had become the only reliable measure of worth.

Their makeshift blood pressure cuff had been salvaged from a pediatrician's office. The numbers were barely visible through its scared face. Dr. Kelsey had jury-rigged the IV stand from an old coat rack, but it worked, like everything else in this patchwork hospital. They'd learned to make do. To heal with whatever tools survived the collapse.

Dr. Kelsey moved methodically through Dante's physical examination, testing reflexes while her patient slept. Rory hovered nearby, questions spilling out in an anxious stream: "Why are you checking that?" "What does that response mean?" "Will she recover?" Through it all, Dante remained unnaturally still. Her usual restless energy was conspicuously absent.

The stillness terrified Rory more than any symptom. She knew Dante's sleeping habits intimately. The constant tossing and turning. The way she fought her dreams until dawn. This unnatural peace felt like surrender, feeding Rory's growing certainty that Dante's condition was deteriorating rather than improving.

Dr. Kelsey tucked her glasses into her breast pocket, a gesture Rory recognized as a prelude to difficult conversations. The doctor's maternal instincts always seemed to surface around Rory. Maybe because she was the same age as her daughter would have been, had SHC not claimed her.

Sometimes, when Dr. Kelsey looked at her, Rory caught a flash of raw grief in the older woman's eyes, as if she were seeing a ghost. Rory imagined the doctor kept a photograph of her daughter somewhere private. Maybe in a tarnished locket or in a gold frame sitting on a nightstand. A sacred image you say goodnight to and good morning, even when it breaks your heart every time.

Dr. Kelsey guided Rory to the chair beside Dante's bed. Her touch was gentle but insistent. "I need you to understand something," she began, gesturing at the primitive medical setup around them. "Dante's lost a significant amount of blood, and our resources are limited. We tried to salvage supplies from Grandview Hospital's blood bank, but the failed refrigeration system rendered everything unusable." She squeezed Rory's shoulder. "But focus on this, she's fighting. She's out of the coma."

"Look at her," Rory choked out. "She's so pale, she's—,"

Dr. Kelsey crouched down, meeting Rory's gaze. "I know she looks fragile right now but let me show you what I see." She ticked off points with quiet confidence. "Blood pressure better than mine. Heart rate steady and strong. Oxygen levels exactly where we want them. The antibiotics are doing their job. No fever. Normal pupil response." She tapped her temple with a knowing smile. "That means minimal risk of brain damage. What she needs now, more than anything, is time and rest. And you, taking care of yourself while she heals."

Rory couldn't quite shake her doubts about Dante's care. Yesterday's slip, when Dr. Kelsey had described Dante's "healthy coat" instead of her "complexion", had sparked a fresh wave of anxiety about their makeshift medical setup. The veterinarian-turned-doctor was trying, but those old habits crept through.

Before Rory could voice her concerns, Dr. Kelsey raised a hand, her expression softening into something almost maternal. "I know what you're thinking," she said quietly. "And yes, I sometimes use the wrong terminology. But trust my experience, if not my vocabulary. Dante will pull through." She leaned forward, her voice gentle but firm. "What won't help is you running yourself into the ground. You've been here day and night, and it's taking its toll. Whether or not you decide to make this community your home, there are better ways to spend your energy while she heals. Time and rest that's what she needs. And that's what I promise to give her."

Dr. Kelsey pulled Rory into an unexpected hug, then drew back to study her face. "You know, I've been watching you. The way you read those monitors, how you helped Rose with that IV setup the other day, you have an instinct for this work. Where did you learn it?"

"My mother," Rory said softly, meeting the doctor's eyes. "She was a nurse."

"Did she—during SHC?"

"Cancer." The words hung between them, heavy with shared

understanding. They'd all lost someone. Dr. Kelsey's daughter, Grace, Dante's father, her mother. Different wounds, same scar tissue.

After a moment, Dr. Kelsey squeezed Rory's shoulder. "I have a proposition for you," she said, her voice taking on a purposeful tone. "We're stretched super thin here. Only the critical cases get beds. The rest, we handle through house calls, rotating staff weekly." She paused, letting the idea take root. "You could train with us. Learn proper technique to go with those instincts of yours. You'd be helping others, and you'd never be far from Dante. What do you say?"

Dr. Kelsey's offer made sense, almost too much sense. But beneath her logical consideration, Rory's heart raced with familiar dread. Her life had taught her harsh lessons about hope. Every time she dared to care, to build something new, fate had torn it away. The people she loved usually died, leaving her alone with another scar. Another reason to keep building these walls higher and higher. Not to tether, but to insulate.

She could predict bad things creeping on her. It usually started with a slight flutter of the heart or a chill exploding inside. And in her gut, she knew something bad was quietly rising somewhere out there. The flutter in her chest. The cold spike of fear in her gut. Somewhere in the shadows of tomorrow, she sensed tragedy waiting to claim whatever happiness she might build here. But as she wiped tears from her cheeks, Rory realized something. Maybe helping others was the only way to fight back against that darkness.

And she could predict bad things creeping on her. It usually started with a slight flutter of the heart or a chill exploding inside. And in her gut, she knew something bad was quietly rising somewhere out there.

As the morning shift change approached, bringing with it the sounds of the farming community's awakening, Rory made her decision. She couldn't fight fate, but she could arm herself against it. If death was determined to stalk her loved ones, she'd learn every possible way to push back.

"When do we start?" she asked Dr. Kelsey, her voice steady despite her exhaustion.

The doctor's face brightened. "Rose begins her rounds at sunrise. Get some sleep and meet us at the dispensary in four hours. We'll start with inventory. You'd be amazed how much medicine is hiding in plain sight, if you know where to look."

Through the window, Rory watched the first rays of sun paint the compound's walls gold. Somewhere in the distance, a rooster crowed. Another remnant of the old world welcoming the new. Behind her, Dante slept peacefully, her breathing finally strong and regular. Maybe this time, Rory thought, she could be more than just a witness to loss. Maybe this time, she could be part of the healing.

GOD'S LITTLE HELPER

Four hours later, Rory was already second-guessing her decision. The infirmary's morning shift brought new sounds, new smells. Antiseptic mixed with coffee and whatever passed for breakfast these days. She paused at Dante's bed, pressed a gentle kiss to her cheek, then forced herself to walk away. Time to earn her keep.

Rose waited at the nursing station. All efficiency and sharp edges. Middle-aged with a military-precise crew cut. She moved like someone who'd learned to make every second count. Her kind face carried a perpetual eagle-eyed expression that suggested little escaped her notice.

Rose had laid out Rory's day like a battlefield strategy. Complete with detailed instructions and precisely measured medications. She was getting heavy Tala vibes for a second. The medical table between them looked like a game board. Each item represents another test of Rory's abilities and memory to recall patient rotation schedules.

"Start here," Rose's rapid-fired finger, pointing to the top left of her diagram. "Rebecca needs witch hazel pads for hemorrhoids and fresh dressing for a vaginal tear. Her sleeping quarters are at the top of the hill. Big house, can't miss it." She caught Rory's slight flinch and grabbed her arm. "Listen. I've watched you with Dante. You have good instincts. Use them. Treat every patient like they're her."

The words hit home. Rory had spent enough time in hospital rooms during her mother's cancer battle to recognize competent care. The smells might still turn her stomach, the sights might still haunt her, but she knew what it meant to be someone's lifeline.

The mansion loomed ahead, a relic of pre-collapse luxury now transformed into something between a fortress and military headquarters. Armed guards patrolled with alertness that suggested recent threats, not just theoretical ones.

The guard who stopped her moved with practiced efficiency. Her assault rifle never pointed at Rory but never far from ready. "New nurse, right? Arms up, legs apart." Her hands were professional but thorough. Checking places Rory hadn't even considered as hiding spots. "Nothing personal. Last year, the Tribe of Judah's people nearly got to Rebecca. We don't make mistakes twice."

The name meant nothing to Rory, and her blank expression triggered something between disgust and pity in the guard's face. "The Tribe of Judah? The breeders?" Each question landed like an accusation. "Girl, your ignorance might get you killed out here."

Rory's silence and eyes filled in the blanks. The guard gave another concerned look, then said, "Upstairs, hard right."

As soon as she reached the second floor, she saw a female guard dressed in the first room. The wrong turn led her straight into the guards' quarters. A redhead with a crew cut. Her entire body shaved baby smooth. Seemed like everyone in the compound favored military precision these days. The woman barely acknowledged Rory's presence, continuing to pull on her black socks with practiced efficiency. Her casualness about being naked spoke volumes about life in the compound. Modesty had given way to practicality.

Rory started to retreat, remembering the guard's directions, "hard right," not left. But something about the scene held her attention. Not just the woman's confident nudity, but what it represented. A community so focused on survival that traditional social norms had become irrelevant.

The guard's well-maintained appearance sparked an unexpected wave of self-consciousness in Rory. Her own body told the story of survival. Calloused hands. Stained teeth. Hair that perpetually smelled of campfire smoke. The last time she'd felt truly clean, let alone smooth-skinned or silky, was a distant memory. Dante had embraced their wilderness existence, wearing her unshaved state like a badge of freedom. But Rory still yearned for small comforts from the old world.

The guard, who couldn't have been much older than twenty-five, fixed her eyes on Rory. "Rebecca's room," she said, nodding at Rory's medical caddy. "Other hallway." Her tone suggested both dismissal and a hint of curiosity about the newcomer who'd wandered into their domain.

The walk to Rebecca's room gave Rory time to process what she'd seen. The guards' quarters spoke of military discipline. Perfectly made beds. Weapons maintained with religious devotion. That underlying readiness for violence. Whatever threats existed beyond the compound's walls, these people took them seriously.

More crew cuts passed her in the hallway. Each person carrying themselves with the same alert purpose. Even the air felt different here, charged with an energy that made her pulse quicken. This wasn't just a community, it was the unofficial ground zero for SHC. And somewhere in this maze of corridors, the High Priestess waited for her medical attention.

Rory adjusted her grip on the caddy, mentally reviewing Rose's instructions. Focused on the immediate task. Witch hazel pads, fresh dressing, check for infection. She could unravel the mysteries of this place, the guards, the threats, this Tribe of Judah, later. For now, she had a patient to tend to.

Standing before Rebecca's door, Rory took a steadying breath. The morning had already challenged her assumptions about this new world. About privacy and security. About what passed for normal now. She thought of Dante, peaceful in her infirmary bed, and felt a sudden ache for simpler times. When did survival become so complicated? When had they stopped being lovers and become merely fellow travelers?

But Rose's words rang in her ears. "Treat each patient like you'd treat Dante." Maybe that was the key to navigating this strange new existence. Care enough to do the job right but maintain enough distance to keep functioning. Love and duty, balanced on a sharp blade.

Rory squared her shoulders and knocked. Whatever lay beyond this door, High Priestess or simply another woman in need, she would face it with the same determination that had kept her alive so far. In this post-collapse world, that might be the only thing that truly mattered.

Rebecca sat like military royalty in her massive bed. Dark skin luminous against white linens. Head smooth as polished obsidian. The newborn at her breast seemed impossibly delicate, pale skin and caterpillar movements. The infant's diaper sagged like an afterthought around cucumber legs. Too small even for the smallest size they had.

"Rory," Rebecca's voice carried the same rich timbre as Tala's, making something in Rory's chest ache. "Would you bring the bassinet closer? This little one needs his rest." She spoke as if they'd done this dance a hundred times before, as if Rory belonged here.

The sound of her own name startled her. How did Rebecca know? But of course she would. Nothing happened in this compound without the High Priestess knowing. Rory's hands trembled as she approached the ornate bassinet. What if she knocked it over? What if her sweaty palms slipped at the wrong moment? The thought of dropping either the bassinet or, God forbid, the baby later made her throat close.

She dragged the bassinet close, then retreated like it might explode. Rebecca's eyes held amusement, but also understanding. She settled the infant with practiced ease. Her breast was still exposed, unbothered by nudity in the way everyone here seemed to be.

When Rebecca shifted, pushing back the bedding, Rory caught sight of the mesh underwear. More medical device than garment, heavily padded. Pain flickered across the High Priestess's face, a reminder that even leaders weren't immune to the basic brutalities of survival.

"Perhaps we should move to the bathroom," Rebecca suggested, wincing. "The tub might make this easier. What do you think?"

Rory's mind raced back to Rose's instructions. She needed to ask about bowel movements, of all things. How did you broach that subject with someone who almost radiated authority? Someone you'd just met.

"Um, Rebecca, have you...?" The question died in her throat.

A knowing smile crossed Rebecca's face. "That's all I seem to do these days. That, and feed and change diapers. Both kinds." Their eyes met, and suddenly they were just two women, sharing the absurdity of bodies and their demands. Their laughter felt like breaking ice.

Something shifted in Rory then. She saw Tala in Rebecca's eyes for just a moment. Not a ghost, but a reminder. What would her mother do? The answer came with surprising clarity. Rory stepped forward, offering her arm. "Yes, the tub would be better."

Rebecca took it, stronger than she looked but accepting the help. As they made their slow way to the bathroom, she paused, breathing hard through her teeth. "You think this is bad? I tried blowing my nose yesterday. Thought I'd torn everything open again. Couldn't even see straight. Nobody warns you about sneezing after birth."

In the bathroom's harsh light, Rebecca lowered her mesh underwear, revealing skin as hairless as the guard's had been. Another surprise in a morning full of them.

"Everyone here is shaved," Rory observed, trying to sound professional rather than curious. When razors had become precious as gold, the smoothness seemed impossible.

Rebecca's eyes flickered with something darker. "There's a story there. One I don't want to scare you with just yet." She caught Rory's questioning look. "Let's just say we had an outbreak, crabs, lice, scabies. All three. Spread faster than wildfire. We didn't have enough medicine, so..." She gestured at herself. "Now we screen newcomers better. Technically, pubic hair is healthier. Less risk of infection. But old habits die hard."

She spoke about bodies and illness with Tala's matter-of-fact confidence. Another reminder of how the compound had reshaped itself. Women's bodies weren't secrets here, just reality. Like everything else, they'd stripped away old taboos for survival.

The medical exam itself felt less daunting now. Rory checked the tear, pink and healthy, thank God, while Rebecca talked about wine. Sauvignon Blanc, specifically, a longing in her voice with nothing to do with alcohol and everything to do with the world they'd lost.

"Stay a while," Rebecca said when they'd finished, once she was settled back in bed. "There are things we should discuss." She patted the edge of the mattress. "You haven't decided yet about staying. What's holding you back?"

The question hit harder than it should have. Rory's eyes drifted to the inverted pentagrams she'd noticed around the compound. "It's not the religious thing, if that's what you're thinking. I don't even know if there's a heaven anymore. If my mom..." She swallowed hard. "If there is a God, where was He when cancer ate her alive?"

"I know that feeling." Rebecca shifted, finding a more comfortable position. "But maybe SHC is just evolution doing its work. Maybe God's letting us figure it out ourselves. We learn through failure, after all." The baby stirred, and she glanced at the bassinet before continuing. "Before all this, people couldn't care less about each other. Now, we need each other more than ever. Maybe that's the point."

It made a certain sense. But then Rory thought of Dante, of promises made. "We're heading to Mexico City," she said, the words feeling both true and false somehow.

Rebecca's eyes carried the weight of a commander, but something else too. A kindness Rory hadn't expected. "Mexico City," she repeated, testing the words. "That's a long way to carry hope."

The truth of it stung. They'd been carrying that hope across broken highways and through dead cities, past horrors that still visited Rory's dreams. Each mile marked by Dante's quiet insistence, "my mother is alive. She has to be."

"Sometimes," Rory said carefully, "hope is all you have left to carry."

Rebecca's hand drifted to her sleeping infant. "And sometimes," she answered, "you find something worth putting that burden down for."

Rory kept her silence, though her eyes seemed to agree with Rebecca.

"I've heard stories from the south. Survivors who made it here. They say the cartels didn't die with civilization. They evolved."

Rory's fingers traced the edge of her medical caddy, remembering the bruises on Dante's body when they had found her by the river. "We've handled worse."

"Have you?" Rebecca's eyes held something between compassion and challenge. "The Tribe of Judah is just one faction in this new world. At least here, we have walls. Numbers. A chance to build something more than just survival." She paused, letting the words sink in. "Out there? The strong don't protect the weak anymore. They collect them."

The morning sun caught Rebecca's smooth head, creating a momentary halo. For a second, she looked almost like the religious figure her title suggested. But there was nothing divine in her next words, only hard-earned wisdom.

"You know what I see when I look at you, Rory? A woman fighting two wars. One for someone else's dream, and one with herself." She lifted the baby to her shoulder, the movement practiced and gentle. "The question is, which one will cost you more?"

The truth of it stung like antiseptic on an open wound. Rory thought of Dante's determination, burning bright as fever. The endless talk of Mexico City, of reunion, of happy endings in a world that had forgotten how to write them.

"I made a promise," Rory said, but the words sounded hollow even to her.

"We all made promises before SHC. To love. To cherish. To be there until death did us part." Rebecca's laugh held no humor. "Death came for everyone, Rory. The promises that matter now are the ones we make to the living. To ourselves."

The baby stirred, making those tiny mewling sounds that somehow survived the apocalypse unchanged. Rebecca soothed him with a touch, her authority momentarily softened by motherhood.

"When we found Dante on that hill near death," she said carefully, "you made a choice. To save her. To heal her. But healing isn't just about keeping someone alive. Sometimes it's about helping them let go of what's already dead."

Rory stood abruptly, her medical caddy clutched like a shield. The room suddenly felt too small, too intimate, too full of truths she wasn't ready to face.

"Rose will be wondering," she managed to say.

"Of course." Rebecca's smile held understanding. "But Rory? When the time comes, and it will come, remember something, Mexico City is a dream. What we're building here is real. As real as that medical training you're running from right now."

At the door, Rory paused. "I'm not running."

"No?" Rebecca's voice carried that same mixture of judge and mother. "Then why are your hands shaking?"

The question followed Rory into the hallway, echoing like gunfire. Behind her, she could hear the baby beginning to fuss, and Rebecca's soft singing, some pre-collapse lullaby about sunshine and gray skies clearing up.

But it was another sound that made her steps falter. The distant pop of gunfire, so faint she might have imagined it. Except in this new world, imagination was a luxury none of them could afford.

The war Rebecca spoke of wasn't just metaphorical. It was coming. The only question was whether Rory would be here to fight it, or somewhere on the long road to Mexico City, chasing ghosts with the woman she loved.

Love. When had that word become so complicated? When had it transformed from something that filled her chest with light into this heavy thing that felt more like duty than desire?

She thought of Dante, waiting in the infirmary. Of promises made and kept and broken. Of Rebecca's words about letting go of what was already dead.

The medical caddy grew heavier with each step, like it was filling with all the choices she didn't want to make.

BOX OF LIES

THE MOOD at the mansion's entrance had transformed. Where the squat guard with the ponytail had stood alone earlier, now a cluster of armed women gathered. Their bodies taut with nervous energy. The flawless woman from the barracks commanded the space, her earlier casual nakedness replaced by tactical gear and focused intensity.

Her eyes found Rory's, carrying the weight of urgency. "Infirmary. Now."

Around them, guards whispered in tense clusters. Their fear a real thing. A teenager among them, who couldn't have been over sixteen, clutched her rifle with white-knuckled hands, eyes wide with barely contained panic.

The flawless woman's whistle cut through the chaos like a blade. "Everyone shut up!" Her voice carried drill sergeant command as she jabbed fingers at specific guards. "You two, back entrance. You, north side. You take the south side. I want coverage now. The rest hold the front line. Move!"

Rory's heart hammered against her ribs. Something was wrong, deeply wrong. "Dante," she managed. "Is she—,"

"The Tribe of Judah is at our gates." The woman's face hardened. "I don't know about your partner, but right now, we've got bigger problems. Get to the infirmary. You'll be safer there."

The Tribe of Judah. That name again. First the warning about assassins targeting Rebecca, and now this. The fear in these hardened warriors' eyes told Rory everything she needed to know. These weren't ordinary raiders or desperate survivors. Was this the same group that had attacked Dante? The thought sent ice through her veins.

The compound's relative safety. Their medical training. Rebecca's offer of belonging. It all suddenly felt like a cruel illusion. The world beyond these walls had finally caught up with them. And somewhere in the infirmary, Dante lay vulnerable, possibly unaware of the approaching threat.

The compound's routine had fooled her. Meals served at regular hours. Guards rotating shifts. Rose's meticulous medical schedules. It all felt so normal. Almost pre-collapse normal. She'd started to believe in it, this pocket of order in a chaos-drunk world.

But order was just another lie. The guards' sharp eyes. The weapons were cleaned daily. The evacuation drills that nobody questioned. They knew. They'd always known. Safety wasn't a place you found, it was a war you fought every day, hoping tonight wouldn't be the night you lost.

Rory clutched her medical caddy, such a mundane thing now, in the face of violence, and ran. Behind her, she could hear the flawless woman barking more orders, positioning her people for what was coming. The morning's lesson in healing felt like a lifetime ago.

She thought of Rebecca, newly delivered and nursing her infant. Of Rose's careful instructions about witch hazel pads and vaginal tears. Such intimate, human concerns. And now, at the gates, waited something that threatened to tear it all down.

The compound had survived an assassination attempt. But as Rory raced toward the infirmary, toward Dante, she couldn't shake the feeling that this time would be different. This time, the Tribe of Judah hadn't sent a single killer. They'd brought an army.

The gravel path to the infirmary seemed longer now. Each step echoing with urgency. Other community members rushed past, some toward the mansion. Others flee to their homes. The crew cuts and military precision that had impressed Rory earlier now made terrible sense. This wasn't just a community, it was an army in waiting.

Through the infirmary windows, she caught glimpses of frantic movement. Rose's voice carried through the open door, sharp with authority: "Move the critical patients to the basement. Now!"

Rory burst through the entrance, her medical caddy still clutched tight. The morning's careful organization had dissolved into controlled chaos. Staff members wheeled beds toward the stairs, their faces grim with purpose. In the corner, Dr. Kelsey prepared syringes with mechanical efficiency, her glasses forgotten in her breast pocket.

"Where's Dante?" Rory's voice cracked.

THE MARTYR AND THREE DAYS' TIME

THE infirmary's air had changed, thickened with something worse than antiseptic and injuries. Rose's face told Rory everything before a single word was spoken. The older woman crossed the space between them in three quick steps, pulling Rory into an embrace that felt more like desperation than relief.

"Thank heavens you're okay."

But Rory's mind was already racing ahead, focused on the one thing that mattered. "Dante. Where is she? Is she—,"

"We had to move her." Rose's hands found Rory's shoulders, grip tight enough to bruise. "Somewhere safe."

"Is she okay?" The question came out sharp.

"She's alive." Rose guided her to an empty bed, and the gentleness of the gesture sent chills. "But I need to know something first. The Tribe of Judah, have you encountered them before?"

Frustration burst through Rory's fear. "What is it with everyone and the Tribe of Judah? First the guards, now you."

"Have you?" Rose's voice carried an urgency Rory had never heard before.

"No!"

Rose's fingers dug deeper into Rory's shoulders, as if trying to anchor them both against a coming storm. "What about Dante? How long have you known her? Has she ever mentioned...?"

Rory twisted free from Rose's grip. "No. She's never." But something clicked then. The hill. The bruises on Dante's body. The way she'd never fully explained what happened before the community found her.

Horror crawled across Rose's face, settling into the lines around her eyes. She opened her mouth, closed it, opened it again.

"Just tell me," Rory demanded. "I'm not a child."

"The Messenger of Light is at our gates." Each word fell like a stone. "She's demanding we hand Dante over. And she..." Rose's attempt at a smile looked more like a grimace. "She usually gets what she wants."

The world tilted sideways. "Where is she? Where's Dante?"

"James has her. Yellow adobe with the red door, down the hill." Rose's voice followed her as she moved toward the door. "Rory, wait—"

But Rory was already running. Her feet carried her through a compound that suddenly felt like a maze designed to keep her from the one person she couldn't lose. Not again. Not ever.

Behind her, she could hear the first sounds of gathering crowds, of weapons being checked and orders being given. The war had finally found them, wrapped in white paint and religious fervor. And Dante, somehow, was at the center of it all.

The yellow adobe's red door gave way under Rory's desperate push, releasing a cloud of pine smoke and darkness. Her entrance startled movement from shadowed corners, then the unmistakable sound of a shotgun being cocked.

"James, wait!" Dante's voice, weak but urgent. "It's Rory."

The darkness felt alive, thick with wood smoke and tension. Rory's eyes struggled against it, catching only the orange dance of firelight on clay walls. Her hands found air, waving uselessly against the smoke. "Dante?"

A pained sound from the shadows. "I'm here."

Strong fingers gripped Rory's arm. James, guiding her through the murk. "Easy now," his voice rumbled, somehow both gentle and fierce. The man who'd left Glenwood in the rearview mirror, now standing between Dante and whatever storm was coming.

The sofa materialized from the gloom. Dante lay there, pale as morning frost, but alive. Rory fell to her knees beside Dante, gathering what she could of her love into her arms. "We have to run."

James's voice filled the small space like thunder. "You're not going anywhere." The shotgun's barrel caught firelight as he turned toward the door. "They'll have to go through me first."

But the world had other plans. The door burst open again, admitting two guards. One built like a wall, the other barely more than a girl. But both carry the weight of terrible news.

"The Messenger of Light demands the girl." The larger guard's words landed like stones in still water. "Says her peers need to judge her. Crazy fucking cult."

James seemed to grow taller, broader, his shadow stretching across the adobe's walls. "You're not taking her."

The younger guard's voice carried surprising steel. "Community law, James. Rebecca decides."

"Fuck around and find out." James's hands spread wide, an invitation to violence.

"James, don't." Dante's whisper carried more power than any shout.

Rory pressed closer, breathing in the impossible scent of blossoms that somehow still clung to Dante's hair. Even now, even here, that smell remains. A miracle in a world that had forgotten how to make them. But Dante's skin was cold, too cold. Blood loss? Shock? The questions crowded Rory's throat, choking back everything except three words, "I love you."

The kiss that followed tasted of smoke and tears and promises about to be broken.

Dante's weak hand pushed against her chest. "Don't."

Rory forced a smile so bright it hurt, stuffing down the terror that threatened to crack her soul. "It's going to be okay. I promise." The lie felt holy in her mouth, a sacrifice to whatever gods still listened.

She turned to James, met his eyes in the firelight. "Don't let anyone take her." Then, to the guards: "I'll take her place."

"No!" Dante's protest barely carried, but its desperation filled the room.

The guards exchanged glances, uncertainty crossing their faces like shadows. No one had ever volunteered for judgment before. The younger guard recovered first, voice sharp with false confidence, "Well? Take her."

The larger guard reached for Rory's arm, but she twisted away. "I'll go peacefully."

Outside, the world had transformed. The entire community lined the road like mourners at a funeral procession. Their whispers rise and fall like wind through dead leaves. Dust devils danced between them, carrying clouds of silt skyward.

Rory had forgotten there could be so many people in one place. Not since before SHC had she seen humanity gathered like this. If God was watching, she thought, let's make a deal. *You took everything from me, my mother, Bruce, and Grace. I will forgive those things, just leave me Dante.*

Dirt stung her eye, bringing unwanted tears. Through the blur, she could see the gate standing open, a wound in the compound's defenses. Beyond it, figures in white swarmed like maggots on a corpse. Their weapons caught sunlight, winking like stars.

The woman at their center might have been beautiful once, before the white paint and black symbols transformed her into something ancient and evil. Her finger rose, pointing at Rory with the certainty of an executioner.

"This is not the girl who has killed six of my tribe." The words fell like judgment, and chaos erupted in their wake.

The Messenger's white-painted face caught sunlight like bleached bone, black symbols withering across her skin with each movement. Her accusations poisoned the cool morning air.

"Your God is the prince of deceivers," she hissed at Rebecca, blue eyes burning with zealot's fire. "These walls reek of Satan's influence."

The Tribe of Judah moved as one organism. White robes rippled in the dust-heavy wind. Their weapons caught light like teeth in a predator's mouth. "Praise the high God!" The cry echoed off adobe walls, multiplying until it seemed to come from everywhere at once.

The Messenger of Light's painted face twisted with disgust as her eyes found the inverted pentagrams. "We cannot trust your words, devil woman."

"Praise the high God!" The cry rippled through the white-clad crowd.

Her crooked finger jabbed toward the gate guard. "That woman has identified the girl. She remains within these walls."

Rory's hand slammed against her mouth, too late to catch her gasp. The crowd's response was immediate, "Tongue of the beast!"

"Liar!"

Rebecca's voice cut through the chaos, sharp as steel. "Our laws are simple. The girl defended herself against rape and kidnapping. We execute any man who violates a woman inside these walls."

"Who are you to question our faith?" The Messenger's finger twisted like a serpent's head. "You worship a horned beast. In Judah, that alone is death."

The white-robed crowd erupted, but Rebecca stood unmoved. The inverted pentagrams around them weren't worship, they were mockery, rejection of the very faiths that had helped break the world. But explaining that to zealots was like teaching physics to children.

"The girl may carry a child," the Messenger continued, voice dripping with false concern. "The ritual has been performed. By our laws, she belongs to Judah now."

Rebecca spat, the gesture ancient as hate itself. "They ravaged her womb with your barbaric ritual. You had no right to her."

Something flickered across the Messenger's painted features, surprise, maybe even fear. "Our ritual has never sterilized before. She's eighteen, healthy. Your science holds no power. Did it save us when SHC came?"

"Where would your precious Judah be without science?" Rebecca's voice rose, carrying across the crowd. "Our medicine delivered your son, saved your bleeding mother, and removed your bullets. Without science, they'd be dead."

"You would risk our treaty for this girl?" The Tribe of Judah erupted in biblical verses, their voices a storm of archaic words.

"Behold, I have given you authority to tread on serpents and scorpions!" A woman's voice rose above the others, hand reaching toward heaven.

Rebecca's fist shot skyward, a signal. Guards materialized like shadows coming alive, weapons trained on the white-robed crowd. "She's under our protection. She will not leave with you. Not today. Not ever."

"Judah! Defend your mother!" The Messenger's howl transformed her followers into a bristling mass of weapons and fury.

The flare split the sky like a prophet's warning, leaving trails of sulfur-scented smoke in its wake. The crowd's collective intake of breath seemed to pull all the oxygen from the world. Then they appeared, more white-robed figures emerging from the brush beyond the walls, moving with military precision. Their weapons weren't the cobbled-together arsenal of survivors. These were professional tools of war.

The compound's warning horns sounded, each blast echoing off the mountains like thunder. One, then another, then a chorus of alarm that sent birds wheeling into the sky. The message was clear, war had finally found them.

The world contracted around Rory. Oxygen turning thin and sharp in her lungs. Like that night on Irwin Street. Reality began to fold in on itself. Her heartbeat became a hammer in her chest. Each beat carrying a different sound. Losing Dante. Watching more death. Failing to save anyone she loved.

Through the chaos, Rory saw them, Dante and James, making their way down the dirt road. Her heart stopped, then exploded into panic. The Messenger of Light's cry confirmed her worst fear, "There's the murderer!"

The world contracted to a single point, Dante, pale and struggling. But determined to sacrifice herself. Rory ran, her voice breaking, "Are you crazy? I told you to stay put!"

Dante's smile was more grimace than comfort. "They'll kill everyone to get what they want. I'm tired of watching people die. Aren't you?"

"So it's okay to watch you die?" Tears burned Rory's cheeks.

"They won't kill me. They need me."

Rory seized Dante's face, forced their eyes to meet. "There are worse things than death. Look what those animals did to you!"

"I can't bear to watch you die again."

The scream that tore through Rory's throat carried years of loss, her mother, Bruce, Grace, everyone SHC had stolen. It was a sound born in darkness, finally finding the light. She kissed Dante, desperate to memorize the feel of her. "Wherever you go, I go. We made a pact. I'd rather die than live without you."

You learn to make your bed in hell or die alone like the rest on earth.

"Take me instead!" The words escaped Rory's mouth before she could stop them. Her knees hit dirt, hands clasped in desperate prayer to a god she wasn't sure existed anymore. "Please. I'm nineteen. I'm healthy."

"Rory!" Dante's horror-struck voice barely penetrated the roaring in her ears.

The Messenger of Light's touch on her face felt like frost creeping across glass. Those blue eyes, set in their mask of white, held something worse than death. They held unimaginable cruelty. "What a brave child," she crooned, her childlike voice carrying across the sudden silence. Then, to her followers, "God provides! We now have two conceivers!"

The Tribe's celebration rose like a wave of white wings and biblical verses. But Rory heard only Dante's broken whisper of her name. Saw only the horror bleeding across Rebecca's face. The High Priestess's grip on her arm would leave bruises, but her words cut deeper, "You foolish girl!"

Those words burned in Rory's throat. She'd done what love demanded. In a world where everything else had been stripped away. Love was the only law left worth following. Even if it led straight into the mouth of hell.

"They are under our protection." Rebecca's voice carried the weight of a commander. Of promises made and kept through darker days than these. She planted herself between the white-robed figures and her charges, despite the pain still etching lines around her clenched lips. "I won't allow it."

The words hung in the dust-filled air like a challenge. Behind her, the compound's guards tightened their grips on weapons. Faces hard with the memory of earlier battles. They'd built these walls with blood and hope, defended them against raiders and zealots and despair itself.

The Messenger's painted lips curved into something between pity and contempt. "Allow?" The word dripped with false sweetness. "Three days to surrender the girls." Her painted face turned toward the sun. "Or we will purify these walls with fire."

But Rebecca stood unmoved. Even wounded, even exhausted from birth and battle, she remained the High Priestess. The one who'd built this sanctuary from the ashes of civilization. "These girls," she said, each word precise. "are not yours to take."

The threat needed no elaboration. Behind her, thirty armed zealots stood ready, with more no doubt hidden in the hills. Their white robes couldn't quite conceal the military gear beneath. These weren't just believers, they were soldiers.

Rebecca's hand pressed against her side where childbirth had left her vulnerable, but her voice carried the strength her body lacked. "And if we refuse?"

The Messenger's smile spread like infection. "Then every soul within these walls will answer to God." Her eyes, bright as madness, found Rory and Dante. "Every last one."

Whispers raced through the compound's gathered people like wind through a wheatfield. Three days. Seventy-two hours to prevent a massacre.

Rory felt Dante's fingers seek hers. Both their hands trembled with different fears. The touch carried memories of other promises, other choices that had led them here.

"We make camp!" The Messenger's voice rose, carrying across the morning air. "Let them see our fires! Let them hear our hymns!" Her white-painted arm swept toward the compound's walls. "Let them count the hours until judgment!"

As her followers began their coordinated withdrawal, the Messenger of Light's final words drifted back like a curse, "Three days, Rebecca. Then God's will be done."

The sun climbed higher, burning away the morning mist, but leaving a chill no warmth could touch.

HALOGEN EYE

THE SECOND MIDNIGHT reached across the land with an ominous glow. The moon hung impossibly bright. A halogen eye watching their final hours tick away. Its light transformed the rain-soaked hills into something alien. Grass gleaming like broken glass. Trees melting into darkness at the horizon. Their branches reach down like wax drips frozen mid-fall. The downpour had stopped as though the sky itself had run dry of tears.

Inside their room, Dante and Rory clung to each other that first night, desperate minds spinning useless strategies. But you can't negotiate with zealots. Can't reason with true believers. They weren't creative enough to find another solution, or maybe there was never one to find. In the end, they did what all trapped humans do, curled together and wept until sleep took them.

The second day killed what little hope remained. The Tribe of Judah's reinforcements emerged from the landscape like a spreading infection. Ten white-robed figures at a time. Each wave makes the previous group seem small. The Messenger hadn't just prepared for resistance, she'd expected war. Her people materialized from every direction until their bonfires dotted the hills like fallen stars, a constellation of coming violence. Turning night into burning day.

Each new fire was a promise written in the flame. There would be no escape. No rescue. No miracle. Just the slow collapse of options until only submission remained.

Rebecca had one last card to play. She sent two scouts on horseback, racing east toward their sister community. Two hundred warriors strong. They'd always traded more than goods with Rebecca's people. They'd traded loyalty for medical knowledge. The scouts could make it in a day. Return with an army in three. Maybe four. After that, the odds turned ugly.

The walls would hold, at least. Too tall to scale before bullets found flesh. They could pick off the zealots one by one from behind the barricades, if it came to that. But the Messenger of Light shattered even this slim hope when she caught the scouts. Had them dragged to the gates, bound and bloodied. Their execution was swift and callous. A message written in blood splashed across dirt and stone.

Dante fought demons in her sleep, incomplete words spilling from her lips like poison she couldn't quite expel. Her body twisted in the sheets, running from horrors Rory couldn't protect her from. The rain hammered the roof like artillery fire, but it was Dante's broken whispers of "no, no, no" that finally drove Rory from their bed.

She stood at the window, watching moonlight wage war with rain. The glass felt cool against her forehead. A mirror of that day at Alcatraz, when she'd pressed her face to Cell One's tiny window. Back then, she'd told Tala how cruel it was, that the view of the bay teased the prisoners. How it made freedom look possible, swimmable, close enough to touch. But the water had been miles of ice and fury that could swallow a man whole.

Just like now. The hills beyond their walls looked gentle, peaceful even. But death waited in every shadow, wearing white robes and carrying scripture like daggers.

The tap at their door came like a woodpecker in the silence. Rebecca stood there, guilt carved into her face, whispering through the crack: "How is she?"

Rory glanced back at Dante's restless form. "Small progress."

"It's not too late. We will fight."

"We can't let you sacrifice yourselves. There has to be one good place left on earth."

Rebecca nodded, pressing two folding knives into Rory's hand. "Tactical. Deadly at close range. The curved blade..." She swallowed hard. "Hide them in your bras. They won't check there."

She hesitated, then said, "You could run. Right now. We'll say you escaped in the night."

Hope drained from Rory's eyes. "She won't make it."

"That's not what I mean."

Understanding hit Rory like a sucker punch. "No." Her voice cracked. "I love her. I would never do that. Never."

Day three arrived like an executioner's blade. They changed Dante's dressings one last time, held each other, talked about nothing that mattered because everything that did was too heavy to voice. Their window of freedom narrowed to a pinpoint, then vanished entirely.

The Messenger waited at the gates, arms spread wide in false welcome. Her ten white-robed elders arranged behind her like chess pieces. They carried robes, paint, brushes, and metal that caught the morning sun like teeth. Two held massive, galvanized buckets. Another wore a priest's alb with a gold-scripted stole. All women. All painted white. All with shaved heads marked in black symbols that seemed to writhe in the light.

The separation happened with surgical violence. Rory screamed as they were torn apart. Dante, fighting through pain, mouthed "I love you" across the growing distance between them.

The stripping came with methodical cruelty. Clothes were torn away until they stood naked before the crowd. Skin prickling in the morning air. The community's rage erupted like a living thing. Women screaming. Guards reaching for weapons. Fury building like a storm. But Rebecca's raised hand held them back, even as she made one final, futile plea.

The clippers roared to life, a wasps' nest of steel and electricity. They took everything—head hair, body hair, dignity. Dante's teeth chattered a morse code of terror while Rory's heart threatened to explode. Around them, horror froze on familiar faces, turning friends to statues. Someone in the crowd found their motion first, hurling a rock that caught an elder between the eyes. The moment teetered on a knife's edge of violence.

When Rory reached for Dante, whimpering her name, the elder's slap left a handprint on her cheek. Blood trickled from her nose.

"You fucking bitch!" Dante's fury died as a rifle materialized, aimed at Rory's head.

Rebecca's voice cut through the chaos, "Kill anyone on our land and you will have your war!"

They submitted then, Rory's eyes fixed on the empty sky, Dante following her lead. No clouds. No birds. Nothing but blue emptiness while hell unfolded below.

Then came the water, cold as death and smelling of river-stone and moss. It hit like electricity surging through the body, drawing gasps that seemed to steal more than just air. They stood trembling. Skin mapped with goosebumps, while the Tribe's hands painted them white with rough, mean strokes. The turpentine stench burned their eyes. That same chemical horror from the camp came back to claim them.

The knife winked at her from the dirt like a secret meant just for her. Dante's mind raced through possibilities, each more desperate than the last. Kill the Messenger? Watch that child-voice drown in red? No—the guards would cut them down before the blade left flesh. Kill herself? Leave Rory alone in this white hell? Never.

But together... Yes, that could work. Quick and clean, before anyone could stop them. One motion for Rory, gentle as she could make it. Then herself. They could fly away together, find whatever waited beyond this broken world. Better the unknown dark than the horror they knew waited in those white rooms.

The Messenger's voice cut through her planning, "Do you accept the God of this holy book?"

Dante's fingers crept toward steel salvation. The message was clear: their bodies were no longer their own. Choice, as written in that holy book, was just another kind of cage. Burn in their lake of fire or burn in this white hell. Die by God's hand or die by man's.

She smiled up at the Messenger, already tasting metal on her tongue. One quick motion. Deep and sure. The good way. The righteous way. Before hell could claim them both.

MORTAL GODS

THE BLADE CLICKED open under Dante's thumb, her sneer still painted white. The horns came first—a single blast from the east that shook the morning air. Then another from the west, deeper, angrier. Before Dante could drive the blade home, the world erupted in sound. Horns everywhere, inside the walls, beyond them, as if the sky itself had turned to brass and fury.

The Messenger never saw it coming. She turned toward the noise, and Dante's decision crystallized in that heart. Not suicide, but revenge. The blade found flesh with surgical precision, and those ice-blue eyes went wide with shock. Blood painted delicate patterns down that white robe, and Dante smiled.

She didn't see the elder behind her. Didn't notice the second blade until Rory's scream shattered her moment of triumph. She lunged toward Dante, arms outstretched, then stopped as if she'd hit an invisible wall. Confusion swept across her face, brows knitting together.

"Rory?"

"Dante..." Her voice came small and scared. A tone Dante knew too well.

"Dante..." Her shaky arms reached out again.

The sound kept building, saturating the world like an armada attacking from all sides. Beyond the gate, where white robes had gathered for their ritual, the Tribe of Judah's chanting turned frantic and fearful. The horns grew louder still, like an oncoming train. Their movement trackable by sound alone, closing in, closing in.

"Rebecca!" A guard's voice cracked with wild hope. "Wolves and Bears and Foxes!"

The words ignited like lightning through the crowd. Wolves, the mercenaries from the eastern settlement. Bears, the mountain dwellers. Foxes, the western tribes. All coming at once.

"Hundreds!" The guard's cry sent Rebecca's fist skyward, and every weapon in the compound swung toward the Tribe of Judah's white-robed masses.

When Rory collapsed into her arms, Dante's world narrowed to a pinpoint. Blood seeped from Rory's mouth, her eyes boring into Dante's with haunting intensity. "Kiss me," Rory whispered, blood painting her teeth crimson.

Dante had imagined their last kiss a thousand ways during sleepless nights. Peaceful. Gentle. Maybe even happy, if they were lucky. Not this. Never this. Both painted white like ghosts. The taste of copper between them, turpentine burning their eyes.

"I will never let you go," Dante promised, knowing it was already a lie. Rory was slipping away like ash through her fingers. And all her love couldn't build a wall big enough to stop it.

The world dissolved into layers of chaos. The immediate, Rory's blood warm on her hands, turpentine burning her nostrils, the metallic taste of their last kiss. The near, Rebecca's commands cutting through smoke, gunfire cracking like broken bones, steel meeting steel. The surrounding storm, hundreds of boots churning dirt, war cries from three armies converging, children wailing in the distance. But Dante lived in layer one, where Rory's heartbeat fought to keep time from, escaping her chest.

Dante's hands found warm wetness. Fingers brushing against a dagger buried in Rory's back. Her scream ripped through the air like it could tear reality apart. "Rory!"

They lay tangled on the ground. The Messenger watched them with devil-blue eyes, blood fountaining between her fingers as she clutched her neck. Her gurgling turned to laughter. The sound of hell itself amused by mortal suffering.

Rory's grip weakened, life seeping out with each labored breath. "Don't leave me," she whispered. Tears cutting clean trails through the white paint. The turpentine smell burned stronger now, as if their bodies were preparing for spontaneous combustion.

This painted creature in her arms, Dante barely recognized, except for those eyes. Everything else had been stripped away, reduced to white nothing. No, this wouldn't be her last memory of Rory. No, she wouldn't let go. No, death couldn't have her. No she would not make her bed in hell. Or die alone in this burning land.

"I will never let you go. Never." The words came out broken, drowning in grief.

Rory laughed, then coughed red. "You have blood on your lips." The metallic taste still flooded Dante's mouth. Rory's blood, their last kiss marred by fuel for the flame.

Around them, war erupted like a force of nature. The Wolves, Bears, and Foxes crashed against the Tribe of Judah like waves breaking on rocks. Gunshots cracked the air. Screams tore through smoke. Steel met steel met flesh. Bodies burned. Children wailed for mothers who couldn't answer. But Dante heard it all as if underwater, her world reduced to Rory's fading heartbeat.

Rebecca's voice cut through the chaos like a blade, "Halt!"

The morning sun turned the battlefield into a canvas. White robes splashed with red. Grass painted in boot prints and blood. Festival streamers from yesterday were still fluttering above the dead. Nature itself seemed to mock their human dramas. Birds continued singing. Clouds drifted by. The wind carried the scent of spring flowers mixed with gunpowder.

Weapons lowered in waves, though pockets of violence sputtered on until fighters realized they were suddenly alone in their fight. Rebecca pointed at the Messenger of Light's corpse, now cooling in a pool of red. "Tribe of Judah, your messenger is no more. Leave these lands and never return. Leave or die where you stand."

The white robes had turned crimson. Elders lay dead in the dirt. Half the Tribe slaughtered. When reality finally sank in, their wails rose like a tide. They collected their prophet's body like mourning children. One elder wandered in circles, blood streaming from her head, while another pointed at Rebecca with a smoker's rasp, "God will punish you, devil witch."

"Take a good look around you," Rebecca answered. "Your God brought punishment to us all."

"Fuck your God!" The cry came from the crowd, followed by a wave of fury, demands for death.

"Rebecca!" Dante's voice finally broke through.

Rebecca surveyed the carnage. Bodies scattered where festival games had been played just days before. Where children had run with corn sticks. Where archers had competed. Where music had filled the air. Her eyes found Dante and Rory, found the dagger and pooling blood.

She knelt beside them, gentle but urgent. "You must let me examine her." Dante clung to Rory tighter. "If you don't, she'll die."

"She's not dead?"

"No," Rebecca said, pressing harder against the wound. "But we have minutes, not hours." She looked up at the infirmary, three buildings away. "And we're going to have to cross the killing field to reach help."

The white paint on their skin still reeked of turpentine. The scent of transformation, of death, of rebirth.

The Tribe of Judah's survivors were regrouping, and this time, they had nothing left to lose.

REQUIEM OF LIFE

Winter crouched over the community like icy fingers. Snow dusted the world in whispers. Rooftops and walkways and earth all transformed into a world bathed in white flesh over frozen bone. The air carried teeth, sharp with ice. Though a sweetness lingered beneath. Burning cedar was their only ghost of warmth. Sunlight filtered through granite clouds, turning the forest into something ancient and alive. Pine trees stood guard, still green and defiant, while their skeletal brothers stretched bare limbs toward heaven. The forest had become see-through and endless. A haunting that stretched as far as sight could reach.

It was deadly outside. Perfect weather for breaking rules.

They lay tangled under a mountain of blankets. Skin against skin. The world reduced to touch and breath and warmth. Sultry air trapped between them, sticky with shared heat. The fireplace spoke to them in pops and crackles, occasionally launching tiny ember-comets across the darkness. No light except what the flames offered, painting their faces in shifting gold.

They studied each other in silence. Stone-faced. Eyes searching. Waiting. Each daring the other to break first. To crack that mask of seriousness. To let laughter win. Dante waited with the patience of someone who knew every micro-expression, every tell. She could see it building in Rory's eyes, that spark that always came just before surrender.

But there was no smugness in her certainty. Only love. Love in knowing Rory's heart better than anyone else ever would. Love knowing that their hearts had somehow become one thing, beating the same rhythm. They belonged together not because the world had turned upside down, but because it had finally righted itself. Everything was good. Simple. Pure.

"Damn it!" Rory spewed.

Dante's laughter filled the room. "I told you. You just can't do it. You never can."

Rory's kiss caught her by surprise. "What's that for? I thought you'd be mad."

Rory rolled her eyes, touched Dante's face with infinite tenderness. "I love you."

Dante went still, expression distant as though she'd checked out completely. Rory nudged her. "Hey."

Nothing.

Another nudge, worry creeping into her voice. "Don't you love me?"

Dante snapped back to presence, fingers finding Rory's short strands. "That's just not a good word anymore."

Rory's body tensed, face turning serious. She didn't need to speak, Dante read the question in her eyes.

"I feel like love is too weak a word to describe the way I feel about you. There should be another word. Love loses meaning over time. Everybody says it. It doesn't capture this."

Rory's smile returned, transformed into something darker, hungrier. Her voice turned high and giddy. "Okay, then what?"

Dante's eyes found the ceiling, suddenly fascinated. "Hey, have you ever noticed that spot up there?"

Another nudge, harder this time. "Um, no you don't. Finish it."

Still staring upward, pride touching her smile, Dante whispered, "Faith. Cherish. Smile. Laugh. Smart."

Rory moved to leave the bed, annoyance painting her movements. "Fine, don't say then."

Dante's arms caught her, pulled her back into their shared warmth.

"I have faith in you. In all that you do. I cherish every second I'm with you."

Their eyes locked, the world falling away. "Every time I see your face, I smile. And when we're apart, I never smile, because you're not there with me. No one can make me laugh like you can. No one. And you're smart because you chose me."

Rory's eyes turned gooey. "Go on."

Dante's kiss held universes. "Love will never be enough to describe all the ways I feel about you."

They melted together, those five little words expanding to fill the room. More than enough. Because love had found them. Because they never gave up hope or stopped fighting for it.

Dante hadn't needed to search Mexico City for love. It had found her when she least expected, even in a world gone dark. Young hearts prevail. Are precious. Reckless even. Yet powerful. Young hearts change the world. Even if one must travel through hell, then dance purgatory for a while, to reach heaven.

Minutes later, thunder shattered their peace.

The knock hit like artillery fire. Dante shot Rory a warning glare. "If we stay quiet, they'll go away."

"They won't stop." Rory squeezed her eyes shut, bracing for impact. "We have to answer."

Another bang rattled the door harder. Iron hinges groaned protest. Dust rained from cracked stucco like snow.

Dante pressed a finger to Rory's lips, but then—

"Rory?" The voice clawed through pine, muffled but unmistakable.

Rory rose from their nest of blankets like she'd seen death itself. Her hand trembled against her mouth, stifling whatever sound tried to escape.

Dante missed the terror etched on her face. She sprang from bed, grabbed her robe, opened the door. "Yes?"

A man's voice, shaky and desperate, spilled into their sanctuary. "I'm sorry to disturb you. I was told Rory lived here."

A girl's voice echoed behind him. "Hi, I'm Rory's sister."

Dante turned to Rory, watching confusion and fear wage war across her face. "Rory?"

Rory clutched the blanket like armor, staggered to the threshold. Her voice cracked the world in half, "Dad?"

"Thank God!" He pulled her into a trembling embrace, clutching her as if she might dissolve into smoke. The scent of road dust and distant places clung to his clothes. Memories of the broken world beyond their sanctuary.

Dante watched the reunion unfold like a scene from someone else's story. The blanket slipped from Rory's shoulders, but she didn't seem to notice the cold. Her father's tears left dark spots on her shirt, each one a question mark about their future.

"We thought," His voice cracked. "After everything went dark, after the broadcasts stopped... We searched every settlement from Colorado to here."

The sister stepped forward, "Mom didn't make it," she said softly. "But she never stopped believing we'd find you."

Rory's legs gave out. Dante caught her before she hit the floor, held her up like she'd done so many times before. Their eyes met in the half-light, a thousand conversations passing between them in seconds.

"You should come in," Dante said, surprising herself. "It's too cold for doorway reunions."

Hours passed like centuries. They talked until the fire needed feeding, then talked more. About the journey. The losses. The hope that kept them searching. Rory's father spoke of cities turned to graveyards, of communities rising from ashes, of humanity's stubborn insistence on surviving.

Dawn crept closer, painting the windows in pearls. Dante watched Rory with her family. The way she gestured like her sister, laughed like her father. Pieces of a puzzle finally finding their fit.

"You saved her," Rory's father said suddenly, turning to Dante. "Didn't you?"

Dante shook her head. "We saved each other."

The truth hung between them, simple and profound. Rory reached for Dante's hand, fingers intertwining without hesitation. The gesture spoke volumes.

Her father nodded slowly, understanding dawning in his eyes. "Love finds a way," he said. "Even through hell."

"Especially through hell," Rory corrected, squeezing Dante's hand.

The sister smiled, a mirror of Rory's own. "Mom would have loved you, Dante."

Outside, the first birds began their morning song. Life, persistent as always, paying no mind to human dramas. The snow had stopped, leaving the world dressed in white like a blank page waiting for new stories.

Dante thought about endings. How they're just beginnings in disguise. How love doesn't follow maps or plans. How sometimes you have to lose everything to find what matters most.

She looked at Rory. At their joined hands. At the family fate that had returned to them. The future stretched out like the forest beyond their window. Vast, unknown, but full of possibility.

Life would never be simple. The world was still broken in so many ways. Here, in this room warmed by love and firelight, they had built something unbreakable.

Rory leaned into her, whispered so only Dante could hear: "You're thinking too loud."

Dante smiled. "Just realizing something."

"What's that?"

"Heaven isn't a place." She pressed her lips to Rory's temple. "It's this. Right here."

The sun finally broke through the clouds, setting the snow-covered world sparkling like broken glass. Like a house baptized by flame, they had been stripped down to their essence. Not reduced to ash but transformed. Despite time's cruel hands, love remained. It's still there, gnarled and beautiful against the backdrop of a broken world made whole again.

The morning whispered,

We are still here.

We were once lost.

But now—

Now we are found.

To be continued...

UNTITLED

Like a house baptized by the flame
    One
    stripped down to the veins.
     Not reduced to ash. But transformed
through molecular calcification. Despite the demonization
of time,   human hands remain.
     The bloody knuckles that sunk each nail,
     framed each door,
window,
     the ancient sweat absorbed by pine,
is there.   Is still there,   gnarled against the backdrop
of a lush meadow. Beyond that,
an empire of granite glares and rises endlessly into the horizon.
     The veins cry,
          We are still here.
We were once
               over there.

— J.S. Nathaniel